about the author

HEATHER MCELHATTON is the author of *Pretty Little Mistakes*. Her radio commentaries have been heard on *This American Life*, *Marketplace*, *Weekend America*, *Sound Money*, and *The Savvy Traveler*. She and her pug, Walter, split their time between Minneapolis and New Zealand.

jennifer johnson is sick of being single

also by heather mcelhatton

Pretty Little Mistakes

jennifer johnson is sick of being single

a novel

heather mcelhatton

HARPER

NEW YORK · LONDON · TORONTO · SYDNEY

HARPER

JENNIFER JOHNSON IS SICK OF BEING SINGLE. Copyright © 2009 by Heather McElhatton. All rights reserved. Printed in the United States of America. No part of this book may be used or reproduced in any manner whatsoever without written permission except in the case of brief quotations embodied in critical articles and reviews. For information address HarperCollins Publishers, 10 East 53rd Street, New York, NY 10022.

HarperCollins books may be purchased for educational, business, or sales promotional use. For information please write: Special Markets Department, HarperCollins Publishers, 10 East 53rd Street, New York, NY 10022.

FIRST EDITION

Designed by Renata Di Biase

Library of Congress Cataloging-in-Publication Data is available upon request.

ISBN 978-0-06-146136-1

09   10   11   12   13   OV/RRD   10   9   8   7   6   5   4   3   2   1

for heather afton thornswood

find him

This is a mistake. I'm not really here. I'm showering naked under a thundering Caribbean waterfall and when I step out my breath is fragrant papaya blooming in a pearl mist. A well-oiled, well-built island man offers me a rum fruity on a bamboo tray. No, wheat grass, no, who am I kidding, rum-fruity. We lock eyes, I drink the fruity like a shot, and I am in his arms, carried back to my thatched hut where his deep and profound love for me cannot be denied. Important island traditions run through his veins, and I am nailed to the bed making love in the island's most taboo sexual position, "The Inverted Wheelbarrow."

Screech! Slam. Car horns and shouting.

No point looking through the window because I already know what happened. It's a freezing Monday morning in January, the roads are slick, and another citizen has been T-boned on their way to work. Exhaust freezes on the street in thin layers, creating a black-ice layer cake. A slaughter cake. Cars hit the bad patches and they can't stop, they slide right into the intersection and crash into each other, crumpling like pop cans.

Sirens are coming. More shouting.

This is Minnesota.

I lean into the hot water and as steam rises off my body I imagine I do not have to go to work today. No marketing-monkey rodeo populated with animated corpses for me. Instead, I decide to let the well-oiled Tahitian man savage me. Then, after we make gentle, yet rough, yet tender, yet slightly dirty love, we'll fall asleep beneath the mosquito netting as waves crash below us on the sugar-sand beach. When we wake, we'll descend the winding marble staircase, which leads not only to the ocean but also to a freshwater lagoon, which is much more pleasant to swim in because you're not salty afterward, where once again, he'll have to have me and we'll make love like angry, passionate dolphins.

I open my eyes and stare at the squidgy green bath mat underneath my grotesque feet, which no pedicure can cure because of my bulb-shaped toes. They look like they belong to an albino tree frog. *Squish squish squish, up the tree frog girl goes!* I hate them almost as much as my thighs. I don't know who's tacking up those miracle-thigh-cream signs near highways, but they're Goddamned liars. Nothing dissolves cellulite. Nothing.

Just breathe. Relax.

I can do this.

It's always hard to go back to work after the holiday break. It's hard for everyone. In fact, I don't know if people should even take vacations, because going back to your little cubicle after sitting on a beach or even sitting in your room is too depressing. It only reminds you there's a world out there and you're not in it.

Just think positive.

Don't think about the impending roundup meeting or my mother or my sister's wedding or any of the things I was going to do and then I didn't. Don't think about the last ten years, which have collapsed in a lightning split-second, and even though I'm not sure what I was doing for ten years, we can be sure I wasn't getting married or having kids or buying a house or working on getting out of Minnesota.

We can be sure of that.

All I have to do right now is breathe and be *here* in this shower.

Joy is all around me if I open my eyes to it. I open my eyes and stare at the grimy vanilla pudding–colored tiles and zinc-crusted fixtures.

Not helping.

I focus on a row of plastic yellow duckies perched on the towel bar. They make me happy. So does the hot water. Absolutely. Some people don't have hot water or even drinking water and their sewer systems are backed up or nonexistent, forcing them to wallow in filth and muck. Although I will say it seems the filth-and-muck people often end up on *Oprah* and get new Cadillacs. Plus the odds of filth-and-muck people dealing with these particular vanilla pudding–colored tiles and zinc-crusted fixtures are actually slim. I may be the only one dealing with this.

I'm careful not to catch the image of my splotchy beef-carcass body in the mirror above the sink. Securing my pink chenille robe, I step onto my daisy scale only to discover I didn't lose a pound yesterday, despite not eating a thing. That seems about typical. I brush my teeth with my Casper the Friendly Ghost toothbrush and rinse with a Hello Kitty kid's cup. I spit. Despite all odds and increasing global infestation, Hello Kitty still cheers me up.

Mrs. Biggles slinks in between my legs, purring. She knows I was going to be a real writer, but there were a lot of things I was going to do and then didn't. I'm lucky to have my job, because I didn't go to school for anything marketable. I studied creative writing because I wanted to travel the world and write deep, poignant novels that illuminated small but significant parts of the human condition that had heretofore not been uncovered or expressed so eloquently or with such graceful power. Right now I'm writing an ad for men's black dress socks.

I keep thinking it's not too late; I can still turn everything around. I could meet a guy any day now who would sweep me off my feet, and he would happen to be a millionaire just like Jane Austen planned for all us cheeky, uppity modern girls. Then I could become a philanthropist's wife. I could busy myself with giving away large chunks of money to charitable organizations like the Children's Cancer Fund or Animal Rescue. I think I'd be good at that. I think I'd be very good at being gracious and giving away large chunks of money. Noble even. People would say I was noble.

After I moved into my husband's mansion (or castle—I've always loved England), I would donate my collection to charity. My collection of course is everything in my cramped, packrat apartment. I've been perfecting it for years. Retro furniture, Chinese paper lanterns, Fiesta Ware plates, collectible Kewpie dolls, broken Lava Lamps, Vargas girl posters, dangerous metal fans, lipstick salt shakers, nude geisha prints. My walls and shelves are cluttered with anything I've ever found funny or stupid or free. The chaise lounges and low lighting insinuate a low-rent bordello, but my love of metal toys and vintage communist militia posters speaks to my admiration of the slightly insane.

Someone asked me once what look I was going for and after some thought I decided to call it "World War II Brothel."

When I frump into my cheerful kitchen, I pull back the handmade cowboy curtains so I can see the thermometer outside.

Two below zero. Lovely.

I let the curtains fall back, careful not to knock over my absolute favorite belonging on earth. It's a hand-painted porcelain figurine, circa 1950, of a young working girl. She's wearing an olive-green suit with a white scarf and matching shoes and defiantly tosses her blond curls back as she carries her briefcase. She's the fifties' epitome of the liberated woman.

Unmarried, unapologetic, and off to work to be sexually harassed by her boss.

I love her.

I make toast in my Hello Kitty toaster, which stamps a Hello Kitty face on every piece of toast, but I think bread must be a different size in Tokyo, because I've never managed to get the whole Hello Kitty face on my toast, just parts, like the bow and part of an eye. I pour coffee into my bright-yellow smiley-face coffee cup, which my sister gave me.

I think she was being ironic.

Maybe she had good intentions, it's hard to say, but I like giving people the benefit of the doubt. Even my sister. I'm reading a book called *Don't Try Harder, Just Give Up* by Dr. Abhijat Gupta. It's this modern Buddhist philosophy that says when you bang your head against a door all you'll get is a headache. It's sort of a now take on Zen and has all these great exercises to help you let go of what you thought you wanted. In the first chapter you draw your ten most coveted goals in physical form. You're supposed to use "signifier icons," like a heart for love, a dollar sign for your career, or a palm tree for a vacation, and so on . . . and then you burn each piece of paper and let the ash blow away in the wind. Well, you're supposed to let it blow away, but unfortunately my ash got caught in sort of a back-draft whirlwind thing out on the deck and mostly got caught in my mouth and hair.

My cell phone rings. It's Hailey.

"What?" I say.

"Nice," she says. "Real freaking charming."

"What do you want? I'm late."

"Did you forget the bridesmaid dress fitting tomorrow night?" she asks. "You know there's a bridesmaid dress fitting tomorrow night."

I don't say anything and she sighs dramatically, as though this is a weight put upon her that she just cannot bear. "So you forgot," she says.

"Maybe you're manifesting that into happening," I say.

"You forgot my kitchen shower," she says, "and I reminded you three times for that."

"I didn't forget, Hailey, I just didn't go. I don't believe in throwing showers for all the individual rooms in your house. Are you having a front hall closet shower? A boiler room shower? An unfinished garage shower? Are you hoping to get a sterling-silver lint trap at your laundry room shower?"

"Well, aren't you Betty Bitter," she says.

"Yeah, okay. I have to go. Some of us have to work."

"Look," she says in her you're-an-idiot-but-I-need-something-from-you voice, "I know the wedding has been hard on you."

"Yes, it's been ever so hard," I say in a high-pitched British accent. "Why, I don't know why I haven't done myself in yet. Slit my wrists with one of your wedding invitations or choked myself with bridesmaid taffeta."

"I know you want a wedding," she says, "and you'll have one . . ." Then she takes a long dramatic pause, like a soap opera heroine, and adds, ". . . one day."

"Really?" I say, all hopeful, "do you really think so? Gosh, I don't even know what I'd do if a boy asked me out!"

"Oh please," she snarls. "You used to throw fake weddings in the backyard all the time when we were little. You married everybody. You married all the neighbor kids. You married the dog."

"I did not marry *all* the neighbor kids."

"You married that one kid all the time. Who was it?"

"That was David."

"Oh. Sorry. Look, just remember to be at Mom's tomorrow night, okay? And bring the salsa."

"Super! Can't wait to try on a kimono. I mean, why wouldn't there be kimonos at a Scandinavian wedding?"

"They're oriental dresses," she sniffs, "not kimonos."

" 'Oriental' is what you call a rug. Pretty sure you're supposed to say Asian."

"Well, they're *Asian* dresses," she says. "Pretty silk ones."

"Like the ones prostitutes wore on *M.A.S.H.*?"

"Shut up. Asian themes are elegant."

"Asia is not a theme," I say sweetly. "It's a continent."

"So?" she says in her defensive/about-to-attack voice.

"So," I explain, "you're a big Swedish girl from Wisconsin and if I was Asian and I saw some sort of a larger-type person stuffed like an oversized Swedish meatball into a dress from my culture, I might be a little offended."

"Just be there tomorrow night," she snaps, "and don't be a super-freak with my friends. They already think you're a transvestite or something."

"You bet, and I won't tell them Mom and Dad bought you with a coupon."

"It wasn't a coupon. It was a church-sponsored adoption fee assistance program!"

"It was a discount printed on paper. That's a coupon."

"If you forget the salsa I will *kill* you."

"I won't forget your precious baby Jesus salsa!" I hang up. Unbelievable.

Hailey's five years younger than me and everyone's always acted like it was such a big deal she was adopted, like she was an orphan from some destitute place like Somalia or Spain or something, when in fact she was born in Wisconsin. That doesn't stop her from acting like an imported miracle, though, a fragile flower that needs extra love and attention. Fragile flower my ass. That girl could tear a phone book in half. She's Swedish. My family is Danish, which, as I like to tell Hailey, is a small but incredibly important difference. Denmark has Vikings and warships. Sweden has meatballs.

I love Hailey. I love her enthusiasm for anything that sparkles, shines, or costs a lot of money. I'm happy she never had to have a real job in her life and now it looks like she never will, because she's somehow bamboozled Lenny, the Ham Man, into marrying her. He's a head foreman at Hormel and he dotes on her, won't let her lift a finger, and why should she? She's precious! He proposed to her last summer on his fishing boat and they decided to get married on Valentine's Day, not that that bothers me, because it doesn't. I mean, someone getting married on Valentine's Day bothers me a lot, because that's breathtakingly stupid.

No. I'm very happy for my sister, even though there's no way that marriage is going to last. She gets bored with any form of schedule or repetition or anything resembling a responsibility. The good news is she'll never be addicted to anything. Not cigarettes or drugs or even a single soap opera, because she doesn't have the stamina or dedication it takes to form a habit in the first place. I can't see her doing all the little things that make a marriage work. I can't, for instance, see her remembering to feed her children. I bet a few months after the novelty of a new baby wears off, she'd probably forget it at Sam's Club.

Her fiancé, Lenny, however, has a lot of habits. When not working with ham, he loves ice fishing and even has his nickname, "The Fishin' Magician!," painted in swirly script on the back of his truck. He avidly attends heavy-metal reunion concerts, spends every Friday night with his minor-league bowling team, and has two flagpoles in his front yard with huge American flags on them, which he lowers anytime a prominent personality or a heavy-metal star dies. Every December he strings hundreds of red, white, and blue Christmas tree lights between the poles and re-creates a glowing American flag. It's the size of a small hockey rink. You can see it from the highway.

Who am I to be critical of him? At least Hailey got someone to propose to her, even if he does read *Hot Rod Magazine* while he's on the toilet. Everyone thought I'd be married by now. My family used to ask me things like, *How's your love life, Champ?* and *Why don't you bring your fella around?* But then as time passed and I kept showing up alone for Christmas dinner, they started to ask things like, *You hanging in there, Champ?* and *You feeling all right?* like I had an incurable disease or a meat cleaver stuck in my eye. Something no one really wanted to look at closely.

My aunt even gave me a book titled *Single but Not Bitter!* "We just want to support your lifestyle," she said with a little pat on the knee and added, "Whatever that is." I didn't want to be the one to tell her this, but being thirty-one, I didn't choose being single, it chose me. Again and again and again.

I stand in front of my closet and think *Whose clothes are these?* I settle on wearing a black pencil skirt, a black twin sweater set, and a string of pearls. This has been my basic uniform for most of my adult life. I grab my purse, keys, and coffee cup as I head out the door. I blow a good-bye kiss to Mrs. Biggles—at least we'll stay together forever, like people did in the old days, because back then, you stayed together no matter what. If your wife tried to poison you or your husband threw you down a flight of stairs, that didn't mean you were getting a divorce. You just silently hated each other for decades. Then you'd occasionally erupt into torrents of abusive swearing when the other person deliberately changed the channel during *Wheel of Fortune.* That's what my grandparents did.

It's freezing outside. I parked alongside a snow bank on the street and overnight it's become like a solid ice bank. I nearly slide under my truck while trying to unlock the door. (I love this car; it's a 1985 safety-orange Scout, and it looks like Steve McQueen would drive it if he was in a 1980s surfer movie.) I end up having to set my coffee cup on the roof in order to force the door open bit by bit, repeatedly *crunch-crunch-crunching* it into the ice bank until I can wedge myself sideways into my seat. My breath blooms into pale clouds. *Please-oh-please-o-please-start*, I pray, and finally the engine rumbles and the radio blares on and ice-cold air blasts from the vent, freeze-gluing my earrings into my ears. I love this truck, I only wish it had heat.

I pop Dr. Abhijat Gupta's *You Are Somebody* in and take a deep breath as he walks us through visualization techniques. He says to imagine a large field covered with flowers. "Any kind you like," he says and so I picture a big field of yellow daisies even though it somewhat reminds me of a douche commercial. "Can you hear the crickets?" Dr. Gupta asks and I can, partly because the sound of crickets is on the recording.

I pull into the Keller's employee parking lot and I'm digging in my purse, reciting my self-created inner-truth mantras when . . . *Thump thump thump!* Someone's banging on my window and my heart jumps up into my throat. "Stop!" I shout. "What are you doing?"

I wipe a little frost away from the glass and peer out at this absolutely enormous man in a red parka and black ski mask.

"What are you doing?"

He says something muffled.

"I can't hear you!"

"Offee up?" he shouts, pointing to the top of my car.

I dig out my cell phone and dial 9-1-1, keeping my thumb

poised over the Send button as I roll the window down a crack. "I'm sorry?" I say in my best I'm-so-sorry-you're-so-stupid-and-even-sorrier-I-have-to-deal-with-you voice.

"Offee up?" he repeats and grabs at something on the top of my car. Next he's holding my snow-encrusted smiley face coffee cup, which has apparently ridden all the way to work on the roof. He mumbles something incomprehensible. Who wears a ski mask downtown?

"Just put it on the ground," I say, "just put it there."

"Mmmph?" he holds out the cup.

"I'm not opening the door," I put my lips up against the crack. "Put the cup down and go kidnap and rape someone else."

I'm being sarcastic, but I'm not. I heard about this girl that got kidnapped by some kid and he kept her in his soundproof tree house. She eventually fell in love with him and they got married when he turned sixteen. She was thirty-five. They had the whole story and a wedding photo spread in *People* magazine.

The doofy parking lot guy blinks once and then sets the coffee cup down on the ground. He turns around and starts walking for the building. "Hey!" I call after him, "can you move it back a little? It's too close to the door!"

He ignores me and keeps walking, his big, red sausage arms pumping back and forth as he marches for the Keller's employee doors.

The nerve of some people.

I re-do my makeup in the rearview mirror even though I'm already late. Keller's has an employee pep rally every Monday in the lobby. Everybody stands around in their heavy winter coats holding complimentary Styrofoam cups of coffee while Ed, the store president, tells us what a great job we're doing and how we could maybe do it a bit better. Then he leads us in prayer because Keller's isn't just a struggling midrange midwestern department store, it's a struggling midrange midwestern department store that loves Jesus.

This doesn't amount to much, except our paychecks have an *IN HIS NAME!* watermark in the background. We have to listen to the occasional pep-rally prayer, and if you have a problem at work, your department leader will sometimes just tell you to pray about it. Oh, and there's a Jesus fish glued to the Xerox machine.

I run for the building, the cold air like quick slaps on my face. Inside I hop from one foot to the other trying to warm up while repeatedly pushing the elevator button, trying to make it hurry. It's okay if I'm a little late for the pep rally. I can usually sneak in without anyone noticing, but when the elevator doors finally open, who's standing inside but the doofy-looking parking lot guy? I catch the door with my elbow and glare at him. "What's wrong with you?"

"Meef?" he says. He still has the damn ski mask on. He looks around bewildered, as though I may be talking to some other idiot in the elevator.

"Don't you know anything?" I ask. "Do you watch the news?"

He shrugs.

"You're a big guy lurking around the parking lot and now you're waiting alone in the elevator with a rapist bank robber ski mask on?"

He just stands there like a big, dumb confused Baby Huey.

The elevator door starts to bang against my elbow. "You should never speak to women in parking lots unless you know them and you should already know that. Why don't you know that?"

He shrugs.

"Women are very nervous in parking lots *and* in elevators. It's hard enough to avoid actual creeps without regular guys acting like creeps. And I'm not saying you're not a creep, because I have no idea, maybe you are."

He pauses. "Welf, I'm not," he says.

"Well, that's not really for you to decide. Is it."

What a moron.

He looks at his watch, which is buried between his glove and sleeve. "I'm vate," he says.

"You're what?"

He taps his watch. "I'm vate."

"You're late? Well, I'd *hate* to make you late." I get on the elevator. "Besides, I have pepper spray." I put my hand menacingly in my purse, grabbing a firm hold of what I think is a small yellow tube of Burt's Bees shimmer lip gloss. I have no idea where my pepper spray is. I think it's at home under the sink.

"Soffy," he says.

"Great. You're sorry. Take the *ski mask* off then. You look like some pervert who likes to watch women buying pantyhose. Now I said 'pantyhose'. My day is ruined. Happy?"

He blinks and then, with great effort, lifts his giant, red sausage arms and pulls his ski mask off. His hair stands on end and he smoothes it down with an open palm. "Already off on the wrong foot," he smiles, looking down.

My eyes fly wide open and I quickly look at the toes of my boots. My cheeks burn with embarrassment.

He's *gorgeous*.

I clear my throat and take another quick peek. He's North Woods, chiseled-jaw, George Clooney–playing–Paul Bunyan stunning.

I swallow hard.

Time becomes animated. Open to suggestion. I have so many mercury-fast feelings, thoughts, memories, and new future plans packed into the next few moments that if I had to guess, even though the standard morning elevator ride is about thirty seconds, I would say that day the three-floor ride took about half an hour.

I remember the sensation of velocity and something shifts inside me, almost uncomfortably, like when you're standing in the middle of a frozen lake and you hear a crack deep below the surface. Your heart jumps because you know you may fall through.

"Yes," I say loudly.

He looks at me. "What?"

"No, sorry," I say. "Nothing. I'm being silly!"

He looks at me.

The doors finally open onto the wide white marble lobby and the smell of roses and perfume pours over us. A prerecorded voice says: "You are now on the main floor."

We both get off the elevator. I want to say something to him, but I feel weird. Faint or feverish or like I just had a shot of Tabasco sauce. My throat is scratchy. He marches forward and I drift alongside him toward the other end of the lobby where the pep rally has already begun. Employees are gathered around the grand marble staircase, listening to our store president, Ed Keller, who stands halfway up the staircase in his smart black suit. Next to him is his wife, the dreaded Mrs. Keller, who is dry and gray as a dead tooth. She hardly ever comes to the store and I vaguely wonder why she's here.

Ed squints over the crowd in my general direction. "I think that's him!" he says and the group all turns around. "He's always late, but never for dinner!"

I have no idea who everybody's looking at.

I stop at the edge of the gathering and am suddenly thwapped in the face by a big, red parka arm because the parking lot guy is taking his coat off.

"Hold this?" the parking lot guy asks and shoves his hot red parka into my arms.

Ed is extending his hand as the parking lot guy makes his way through the crowd. "May I introduce Mr. Bradford Keller!" Ed says, his voice booming across the floor. "My son and future president of Keller's Department Store Incorporated!"

The parking lot guy dashes up the stairs.

Bradford Keller? The parking lot guy is . . . Bradford Keller?

"Hey, guys," he says, waving at all my Keller's co-workers. Ed tells him he has to speak louder. "Hey, guys!" Brad shouts and everyone says "Hey" back. My heart hiccups and sputters, like some ancient rusty machine.

Brad starts awkwardly giving a prepared speech. He says something about being glad he's back in Minnesota and how he's looking forward to blah blah blah. . . . I'm not listening. I'd love to, but I think I'm having an aneurism. There's a buzzing sound in my ears and my arms are cold.

Christopher sidles up to me. He works in visual display, dressing the mannequins and floofing the store windows. He's excellent at what he does and I live in fear that a bigger department store will hire him away. We've known each other since high school and he's probably the only reason they didn't find me hanging from the aluminum bleachers on the football field. The secret to surviving a religious high school, or any war zone for that matter, is to find your people. Even if it's only one people. One is enough. If you can find one person in the crowd who's like you, then you can survive almost anything. I met Christopher in art class when he made a Pop candy-colored painting of Shaun Cassidy, encrusted on the edges with mirror chips. Right then I knew I had found my people.

"What's going on?" he whispers hotly. "Why did you walk in with Brad Keller?"

I stare vacantly.

When I snap out of my fog, Ed is patting Brad on the back and there is a smattering of clapping from the weary audience. Ed reminds us there are free employee flu shots today on the mezzanine level, and then he leads us in a short group prayer. I lower my head and close my eyes.

"A-men!" Ed says.

"A-men!" we all say back, except Christopher who says, "Gay men!"

I look up and Brad is gone, lost in the crowd. Everyone starts shuffling toward the elevators and Christopher sprints off to some meeting.

Mrs. Keller breezes up to me with a saccharine smile and says, "Is that my son's jacket? He always gets some poor girl to take care of his things."

I nod but forget to let go of the coat. She has such a mean face.

Her eyes sharpen as she tugs. "Can I please have it?"

"What? Sorry!" I release my death-grip on Brad's jacket.

"No problem!" she chirps and gives me a painful little grin as she whisks the red parka away. Something in me panics—I may never see it again.

Upstairs I sit at my chair and stare at my blank computer screen. I can't believe I didn't know that was Ed Keller's son. Why would a guy like that want me anyway? He's handsome, rich, and well-connected. What am I? I'm a low-ranking copywriter in the marketing department of his dad's department store and my skills include writing in-store signage like CHECK OUT OUR NEW LOOK! And coming up with fairly compelling reasons to buy cardigans and sofas.

I do have strong points. I, and I alone, am responsible for last year's runaway best-selling boot sale: RE-BOOT! Also, I suggested we change the KIDS department to be the K!DS department, which won me a xeroxed copy of the employee-of-the-month thank-you letter from our store president, Brad's dad, and two Cinnabon coupons.

Ted bounds into my cubicle. "Did I ever tell you that you're the most beautiful woman in the world?" he asks. I ignore him and turn my computer on. Ted's always saying slightly retarded things he thinks are funny. He professes his love for me on a daily basis, which is ridiculous. Ted in love with anyone is ridiculous. He's the nicest, sweetest little guy you'll ever meet and he treats me like a queen bee, but he's short and has crew-cut red hair and basically looks like a maltreated redheaded wood elf.

"Well, you are the most beautiful woman ever," he says and sets a Starbucks on my desk. "Skim latte with nutmeg."

"Thanks." I take a careful sip.

"Get any sleep last night?" he asks.

I scroll over my loaded e-mail in-box. How can I already be behind when I just got to work? "Some," I say, "eventually."

"Good. Lunesta?"

"I took two Benadryl, drank a glass of red wine, and watched the Home Shopping Network until I passed out."

"That would do it."

"I still didn't get to sleep until about two in the morning. I saw an ad for an FLDS dress and I went online and bought one."

"An FLD what?"

"Fundamentalist Mormon dress. You know those weird dresses Mormon women wear? High collars and poofy shoulders? They look like *Little House on the Prairie* dresses, but without buttons."

Ted makes a face. "Why would you want one of those?"

"They sell them to raise money for their compound or whatever."

"But why do you want one?"

"I don't know, I thought maybe I would start talking to the Mormon girl who sold it to me and we would strike up an online friendship that would end up in a high-risk escape plan where I pick her and her sister-wives up on the Utah border or something. Also I can wear it next Halloween."

He stares at me and rests his chin on my vertical filing cabinet.

"You are so sexy," he says. "I think I might die."

"Did you do Supersaver?"

"Yep," he says. "Done."

"Thank God. I hate Supersaver."

"I know." He smiles. "I'm the best! Do you want to sing the Ted song?"

"No, I do not want to sing the Ted song."

"Oh come on! It's easy. I sing a line and then you just sing out *Ted!*"

"I'm aware of the lyric structure."

"Who's your favorite guy?" he sings.

"Ted," I say grimly.

"Who's the funniest one you know?"

"Ted," I sigh.

"Who's the most handsome man who also does extra work on weekends just to make your life a little easier on Monday mornings?"

"Ted. Ted who needs to get out of my cubicle."

He bows, pivots on his foot, and leaves, but keeps singing. I can hear him bellowing the Ted song as he lopes down the hallway. I gotta admit it, he's pretty funny. If only he didn't look like a woodland elf. The idea of having sex with him seems like it would require a small green condom.

I return to the computer and open my daily e-mail from my mother, who likes to send cleaning tips, smug aphorisms, dating advice, prayer requests, and cute photographs of poodles wearing top hats and/or pictures of her only grandniece, Abbygael, who is ten months old and acts like she might have autism, even though everyone swears she doesn't.

"ISN'T SHE AMAZING?" my mother writes.

I stare at Abbygael's bulbous forehead. There is something definitely wrong with that kid. I think my cousins are beginning to suspect a problem, too, because they're starting to dress her in a lot of sunhats, bonnets, and single lace ribbons, which bisect her cranium and look more like a surgeon's cutting line than hip baby fashion.

I e-mail Mom back.

> *She's so cute! I wonder if that tremendous head growth means she's going to be a superstar in math! Wouldn't it be awesome to have a state champion mathlete in the family? Like a girl-scientist who discovers a new way to animate life or something?*

Mother is not amused.

"Your cousin is a child of God," she fires back, "not a Frankenbaby." Then she says I should come to church more often and learn a little humility, which is a good point. If there is in fact a single male deity in charge of this barn dance, and a confirmed bachelor at that, then we really ought to try and get on his good side, especially if we're going to hatch female family members who need to wear safety helmets to butter toast.

I check my online dating account. I'm signed up on ExplodingHearts.com, which is supposed to match you with people better than you could match yourself, because you fill out a quiz that asks if you prefer walks on the beach or cozy candlelit dinners and whether or not you kiss on the first date. When I filled out my profile I briefly considered just saying everything I know guys want to hear, that I'm a size zero and I like to barbecue steaks in a thong and sometimes I have secret lipstick-lesbian fantasies where I get into a pillow fight with my supermodel girlfriend and then we decide to have sex. But instead I opted to tell the truth, just to minimize the disappointment factor, if nothing else. I listed my real age, my real weight, and my real hobbies, which include watching *Golden Girls* reruns while eating Taco Bell. Might as well cop to it now.

Today I have eight new e-mails, indicated by eight little red hearts that sprout wings and vibrate. Once you've opened an e-mail, the wings disappear. I read through these messages and my enthusiasm turns from curiosity to something resembling that feeling you get when you turn on a light and a creature with a billion legs scurries up the wall.

The first message is from a soy farmer in Ohio. I don't know what soy is.

> *Hey Good Lookin!*
> *Whatcha been cookin? No seriously, I've gotten real used to cooking for myself. I don't expect a gal to cook for me or clean or even come home every night! Ha ha ha! That's a joke I used to tell my wife. She's gone. Write me back!*
> *—Harry*

The second message is from a Russian man who lives in Chicago and wants an "efficient woman" to help him run his security business. Plus she should cook.

Privet milaya moya!

I am of to your love. It is of a preposterous thing. Please to meet me in small dress of the sexy and know that I am of a marrying way.

—Vasya
Вася Пупкин

The third and fourth messages seem so similar, I suspect they are the result of an Exploding Hearts "first-e-mail" tutorial. Like fill-in-the-blank Mad Libs for guys too stupid to write something of their own.

Hi there Jen!

Are you tired of the same old boring guys? Do you want a meaningful relationship? Well look no further! That's what I want! I am a successful, educated professional who exactly matches the description of what you're looking for! Please contact me at your earliest convenience, so we can see if our hearts are meant to explode together!

—UNEVERKNOWRITE?

The second one says:

Hi there sexy!

Are you tired of the same old boring guys? Do you want a good time? Well look no further! That's what I want! I am a business student who exactly matches the description of what you're looking for! Please contact me at your earliest convenience, so we can see if our hearts are meant to explode together!

—The14U!

What's the point of telling someone "about yourself" anyway? Nobody tells the truth. Everything means something else. I've learned what a few things really mean the hard way and I've started my own dating profile–to-English translation phrasebook.

- HANDY AROUND THE HOUSE
  He will not call a plumber under any circumstances. Ever.

- GOOD WITH MONEY
  He's a cheap bastard and will make you go Dutch. Forever.

- FAMILY MAN
  He's still married.

- LOVES KIDS
  He has kids and no daycare provider.

- MATURE MAN
  He's at least fifty, and looks at least sixty-five.

- YOUNG AT HEART
  He's trolling for a preteen.

- CASUAL GUY
  He wears dirty sweatpants out to dinner.

- METROSEXUAL
  He's hoping if he dates one more girl, he won't be gay. Doesn't matter. He's gay.

- LOVES MOVIES
  Loves porn.

- GOOD PERSONALITY
  He's fat.

- GREAT SENSE OF HUMOR
  He's fat and desperate. Will laugh at anything you say.

- OUTDOORSY
  He pees in the sink.

- READY TO SETTLE DOWN
  He's just been dumped.

- LIKES TO HAVE A GOOD TIME
  He gets drunk. A lot.

- LOTS OF FUN AT PARTIES
  He makes an ass of himself in public.

- A GREAT DANCER
  He thinks he's a great dancer. He's not.

- NOT OVERLY EMOTIONAL
  He's a sociopath.

- SELDOM DATES
  Seldom gets second dates.

- UNDERSTANDS WOMEN
  He's been married and divorced four times.

I hate online dating. I really do. The odds are so stacked against the possibility that you might like and be attracted to a total stranger, who then also likes and is attracted to you, that they cannot be calculated. I've been on so many uncomfortable, if not painful, dates that I'm starting to go out on blind dates armed with a suicide hotline number in my purse.

I don't think I can handle one more nerve-wracking, mind-numbing date/freak-fest/judge-a-thon where we sit across the table picking each other apart, hoping we aren't being picked apart, but of course we are and so one of us ends up crying in the car. Maybe I should just quit this site, although they never let you go without a fight, so you have to click through three more screens that ask you:

ARE YOU SURE YOU WANT TO CANCEL YOUR ACCOUNT? CANCELING YOUR ACCOUNT IS PERMANENT AND CANNOT BE UNDONE. YOU WILL LOSE YOUR ENTIRE PROFILE INCLUDING YOUR PICTURES. PLEASE LIST YOUR REASONS FOR LEAVING US HERE. REMEMBER YOU ALSO HAVE THE OPTION TO HIDE YOUR ACCOUNT RATHER THAN CANCEL IT. NO ONE WILL BE ABLE TO SEE YOUR ACCOUNT IF YOU HIDE IT AND YOU CAN COME BACK ANYTIME TO REACTIVATE.

What they're really saying is:

ARE YOU SURE YOU WANT TO CANCEL YOUR ACCOUNT? LET'S REVIEW THE SITUATION. YOU WERE DESPERATE ENOUGH TO COME HERE IN THE FIRST PLACE, SO THINGS WERE ALREADY PRETTY BAD, RIGHT? MOST PEOPLE ARE MARRIED BY NOW AND YOU OBVIOUSLY MISSED THAT

BOAT. THAT BOAT, SHALL WE SAY, HAS SAILED. YOU LET THE GOOD ONES GET AWAY. YOU KNOW YOU DID, BECAUSE MATHEMATICALLY SPEAKING THERE HAD TO HAVE BEEN SOME GOOD ONES. SO NOW THIS IS WHAT YOU GET AND, FRANKLY, YOU'RE LUCKY TO GET IT, BECAUSE STATISTI-CALLY SPEAKING, YOU'RE NO SPRING CHICKEN, NO MATTER HOW YOUNG YOU ARE.

For now I'll keep my Exploding Hearts membership. I'm not up to the mental stamina it would take to cancel the account, and besides, who am I to look down on soy farmers or the Russian Mafia?

Big Trish, the cranky art-department assistant, slumps past my cubicle. She's recently divorced and now dating an ex-cop with two daughters from a previous marriage who have turned out to be demanding little brats that make her life hell. The strain of it is stamping purple half-moons under her eyes and cutting a massive vertical worry wrinkle between her eyebrows. Poor thing. She really has put on weight, though. I try not to notice stuff like that, because I fully understand women's body-image issues, but you can't help noticing an ass that big. I think about how horrible it would be to have my ass balloon up like that and how with portion control and healthy eating habits there's no reason for it. Then I have a sudden, irresistible urge for a Cin-nabon. *Cinnabon Cinnabon Cinnabon.*

What do they put in their icing anyway? Probably sweetened condensed milk and animal tranquilizer cream. I have to stop eating them. Somehow. So what if I splurge today? I hate that word. Splurge. Glurge gorge purge. It sounds like the sudden beginning of something, like if I splurge on a Cinnabon I will splurge right out of my skirt and splurge into the shape of Jabba the Hutt and then splurge into the river, where I can float like a splurged barge.

I think I still have one of those free Cinnabon coupons in the back of my desk. I hid it there so I wouldn't be tempted to . . . there it is! The power of positive thinking works! I Google the calorie count in a Cinnabon. 730 calories. A Minibon only has 300, but those are gone in like two bites. Okay, if I get two Minibons, that's less than one big one. I don't know if the coupon is good for Minibons.

Now this is serious. If I plan this exactly right, I can sneak out before the roundup meeting, get my gooey, sticky Cinnabon and cram it into my big mouth and it could be the best moment of the day and possibly the week. If I go now, I can make it back to my desk before Ted returns from the design goons and I can gorge myself in private.

I must plan carefully and leave nothing to chance. . . . I creep down the hallway and when I round the corner of the wall of mailbox cubbyholes there's Christopher furtively removing something from my mailbox.

I ask him what he's doing and he thrusts whatever he's holding behind his back.

"Oh, come on," I say, "What is it? Did everyone get a free Lancôme makeover coupon and you're stealing mine again?"

He shakes his head no and steps backward. "It's just junk," he says, and so I shrug nonchalantly, like I couldn't care less, and turn to walk away. Then I pounce. When his back is to me, I ninja-leap toward him and pluck the thick envelope he's holding from over his shoulder.

"No!" he says, and scrambles after me as I dash to my cubicle.

"What's your problem?" I smile and plunk down in my chair as I tear open the envelope. "I could call store security and have you arrested for tampering with the mail, you know. Besides, what's the big . . . what is this?" My eyes are scanning over the heavy-weight card inside, all swirly script and raised letters. It's an invitation. A wedding invitation.

Christopher shakes his head. "I tried," he says, looking at the floor.

"Who's getting married?" I ask and my voice seems loud.

"*Him.*"

I sense impending disaster.

Christopher nods. "His."

My stomach twists. I try to decipher the elegant script on the cream-colored card I'm holding but it's like my eyes can't focus, can't latch on to any sentence, just words, like stray bullets scattered across the page. *Mr. and Mrs. . . . . request the honor of your . . . to celebrate the marriage of . . . and David Reynolds . . . First Baptist Church of . . . February the fourteenth in the year of our . . .*

"David? David's getting married? My David?"

Christopher covers his face with his hand. "I tried to spare you, sweetie. I really did. There was no reason for you to ever know. Why the bastard would invite you to his wedding defies explanation."

I turn the card over in my hand, as though it was a precious, valuable object.

"I got one, too," he says. "They're getting married on Valentine's Day."

My gerbil-size brain tries to process this. The wheel spins but I still don't understand. "But, who's he marrying?" I ask. Around me is the clang and chaos of the office. The Xerox machine running, co-workers talking, a radio somewhere broadcasting the news. It's hot in here. Incredibly hot.

"I don't know her," Christopher says. "She's some rich girl from Minnetonka. She bought David a vintage Mercedes. Her father just gave them this big bundle of cash for the wedding and they're having the reception at some country club."

My eyes lock with his.

"We won't go," he says quickly. "I think he was strapped to come up with as many friends and family members as she had. I bet he invited everybody who he didn't owe money to."

My pulse is racing and there are these little white pinpricks of light at the edges of my eyes. I'm possibly having a migraine or a grand mal seizure. Maybe both. I try to center on my inner-nothingness, my core of equanimity, where it is always calm.

Screw calm. I don't even want calm.

I want angry.

I want *Slaughterhouse-Five* angry, Xena the Warrior Princess angry. I want to crash through David's living room window on a black horse and decapitate him. Then I want the black horse to pummel him into the consistency of rhubarb pie filling.

I can't do this.

Frantic mental slideshows start of David and our rocky on-again, off-again relationship, which technically, if you think about it, has been going on since the second grade. That's when his family moved in down the street from my parents' house. We went to different high schools and we never really hung out, but I always knew who he was. Years later I ran into him at a friend's Christmas party and it seemed like we'd known each other our entire lives. It seemed obvious, funny even, that we hadn't dated before because, after all, he was literally the boy next door. I felt this hysterical thrill after we made love the first time, because I really thought he was the one.

God. All the fights we had, all the jealousy, all the money I lent him. He was in a horrible indie rock band named Obscure Cold, which he said was influenced by both Soul Asylum and Prince, which I told him was sort of an incongruous concept, but he said I just didn't get it. Plus he'd had a little success at the start when a small label signed the band and they recorded an album that did okay, but not great. Then David got into a fight with his bass player, who quit, and then his drummer, who also quit, and so he rebuilt the band with new musicians, whom he got along with, and who also sucked.

I had to sit through every single Obscure Cold show, spend countless hours smiling vacantly in half-empty bars while sipping a warming Leinenkugel beer and listening to the hard-to-totally-track beat. Afterward, when the bar managers invariably told him they didn't take in enough money to pay the band, I'd have to prop him up emotionally and financially, tell him it rocked and eventually people would get it. I told him I believed in him, which I didn't.

We fought. We made up. We fought again. The relationship wouldn't work but wouldn't end. We were both stuck in a crappy relationship, but we were both too insecure/lazy/bored/unsure to call it off. We actually dated for two years, and even with all the trouble, or maybe because of it, toward the end, I actually believed he was going to propose to me. He broke up with me in a cheap Mexican restaurant instead. This, the man I thought I would marry. Now he's marrying someone else, and I'm invited to watch him pledge his undying love and eternal soul to some gold-plated bitch from the suburbs.

"It's a gorgeous invitation!" I chirp. I can hear the manic quality in my voice. "It looks so expensive!" I say. "Rich and creamy!"

Then I bite the card. Just tear the corner off and start chewing on it.

"What are you doing?" Christopher shrieks and grabs at it. "Stop it! You're ruining stationery!" He wrenches the invitation away from me and I sit there panting. I spit out a little paper bit.

I feel like my left eyeball is going to shoot out and hit my fabric cubicle wall.

"I have a meeting," I say. "I have to get ready."

"Okay," Christopher says, "but no freak-outs, anger-dialing, or unfortunate e-mails, right?"

"Right."

"And no texting him!"

"Okay," I say. "Fine."

After he leaves I want to scream and cry and weep or at least knock over Big Trish's fern, but instead I sneak downstairs to the third floor, my hands cold on the big glass doors that lead to the skyway. I storm out through the maze of people bustling about, wishing I could give each one of them a good hard shove. I finally get to the familiar red Cinnabon counter and my favorite red-hatted Cinnabon girl. "Hello, Satan," I say.

"Hey." she snaps her gum. "The usual?"

I nod. All self-control collapsed under the heavy weight of the sugar-sweet air. Screw the Minibon. Minibons are for losers anyway, for people who aren't totally sure they've given up. Not me. I know where I stand, and that's directly on a quickly moving conveyor belt to a cow pasture. Plus, I made it all the way here, out of the office, across the skyway, and into the greasy heart of the food court. To wimp out now and get a miniature Cinnabon wouldn't make any sense. The Cinnabon girl asks me if I want extra icing and I shoot her a look. She slathers on more icing and hands me the box.

"Thanks for coming to hell," she says, all cheery. "Come again!"

I whisk away my hot, lard-based contraband, guarding it carefully, as though feral dogs might bound out of the storefronts and attack me. I hear someone call my name. "Jen! Jennifer Johnson! Come here!"

It's the lady in Frontier Travel, the little travel agency three stores down from Cinnabon.

"Hey, Susan," I say, frowning at the slender woman behind the desk. "Any cruises to the other side of the earth today?"

She smiles. "How about Australia! You get free salsa lessons and dry-cleaning plus unlimited shrimp bar."

"No thanks." I glower out the window at the snow storming by. "Why go to Australia when we're already in paradise?"

My cell phone rings and I wave good-bye as I step outside to answer it.

"Hello, Miss Johnson," says a familiar voice.

"Mr. Jennings!" I say. "I see you have a new phone number."

"Well, you stopped answering the other number," he says. I start to walk briskly back to the office, where I know the bad reception will cut us off.

"I thought we had decided you were going to send us a payment, Miss Johnson."

I laugh lightly. "Have I ever told you how much I appreciate you calling me 'Miss'?" I ask. "Really, for most of my life I was a 'Miss' and then I don't know what happened, but it was like by group consensus people just started calling me 'Ms.' Not you, though. You always say 'Miss.'"

"Glad you like it, Miss Johnson. Let's talk about that payment."

"Well, Mr. Jennings, it's a funny thing, I did mean to send the payment, but I got a little behind in my—oh, Mr. Jennings? Are you there?" The phone crackles and goes dead. Ha! Mr. Jennings, my credit-card-debt collector, foiled again.

He's actually a nice man.

I smuggle my precious, precious Cinnabon back into the office and am tiptoeing down the quiet row of cubicles on kitty-cat feet, almost at my office, when I hear, "Monkey-bun? Is that you?"

I freeze. *No, no, no.*

I forgot it was today. Ashley's back.

I should have stapled a Post-it note to my forehead last night that said:

CRAZY BACK MONDAY. ENJOY FREEDOMS NOW.

Ashley is my boss, and she makes me nervous. She's a year younger than me and she looks like a TV anchor or one of those women on a pharmaceutical commercial or a young televangelist's wife. She has perfect Aqua Net hair and wears tight brocade vests and sugary pastel shirts. She's alternately sweet as pie and then viper-sting vengeful. You never know which Ashley you're going to get. Every morning I want to ask her, "And who are we today?"

She smiles when I step into her office. And why shouldn't she? Everything about her life seems easy and lucky. Her husband is a successful commercial real estate agent and she has a naturally high metabolism, making her an unbelievable size zero; she's always giving me weight-loss tips. She calls me "cupcake" and "sugar" and "dumplin'," among other choice endearments, to prove what a fun boss she is, and how nice she is to her underlings, especially the fat ones.

She sits skinny as a stir stick behind her faux wood desk and smoothes a lapel of her tapestry suit coat. I think my grandmother had quilted curtains like that. "There you are!" she says. "How's my little plum pudding been? Oh, don't make that face at me, sweetie. They can't Botox your whole face. I told you, plum pudding is a term of *endearment.* I only call my favorite people plum puddings."

Ashley likes to answer questions no one has asked. In this case, I guess she's answering the question, "Why are you calling me a demeaning nickname?" but we'll never know for sure. My co-workers and I have actually just started to study up on the early warning signs of schizophrenia, just in case we can convince HR she's crazy.

"So, Brad Keller?" I ask, struggling for the right words. "He works here now?"

Those were not the right words. Ashley shoots me a look. "Got a crush? Well, get in line, sweetie. He's a very eligible bachelor."

"Right." I study the ceiling as though it were incredibly interesting. "So, how was Cabo?"

"It was inspiring."

"Well, you got color."

She picks up a brochure from her desk. "You have to go. Maybe you could go to one of those Club Med singles resorts. Or a singles cruise! I wonder if they have them for people your age, though. Usually I think it's a younger thing."

"Sounds inspiring," I say.

She eyes the white box I'm holding. "Another cinnamon roll? Do they have a frequent-eater card or something?"

"I wish." I fake-chuckle, which makes her fake-chuckle, and there we are, fake-chuckling at ten in the morning.

"You're wearing all black today," she says. "I think that's a good choice for you. A lot of the magazines, well, all of them really, say all black is a big no-no, but I think for you it's fine."

She takes out a small bottle of lavender hand lotion, removes her rings one by one, and sets them on the desk in front of her. "I wanted to ask you about the women's accessories launch campaign. 'Arm candy'? I'm not sure what that is."

She dollops a bit of lotion on the back of her hand and starts rhythmically massaging her hands. I stare at her desk. "Ted and I thought it was a cute alternative name for the women's accessories department. Arm candy is like saying, Here's something pretty for your arm. Like eye candy, but arm candy. You know?"

"I see," she says. "The thing is, pork chop, I know you're all very creative and sometimes I actually think that's the challenge. Maybe you should refamiliarize yourself with our demographic. Our customers are hardworking folks. Sensible, practical, economical, brand-aware, and bargain-conscious. Women whose core values are commitment and endurance. Things I know are hard for you to understand."

"Got it." I just want to smash a stapler into her eye.

"Okay, pumpkin, go back and give me something I can actually use. Okay?"

"Okay."

"Super. I don't think the store can hold up the entire women's accessories launch because one little writer can't come up with a name for the purse department." Then she stares at the door. I turn around and it's none other than Mr. Ed Keller. Ashley stands up quickly, knocking a sample book onto the floor. "Hello, Mr. Keller!" she says. "How nice to see you!"

"Oh, don't get up," he says. "I just wanted to make sure you were coming to Bradford's welcoming party."

"Oh, of course, Mr. Keller!" she says, her voice all high and feminine. "I'm planning on being there, naturally!"

"Fine, fine," he says, and then to me, "And how are you, Miss Johnson?"

"Oh, I'm very well, Mr. Keller," I say. "Thank you."

"You look so much like my cousin Ada when she was a girl," he says.

"Yes sir."

"She was a smart tennis player!"

"Yes sir. You've told me about Ada."

"Do you play tennis?" he asks.

Ashley clears her throat. Ed not paying attention to her is torture.

"Yes, I do, Mr. Keller. Would you like to play a match sometime? I have a mean forehand, though; it's only fair to warn you."

"Ha-ha!" he laughs and winks as he points at me. "You're a spirited girl! Just like Ada!"

"Mr. Keller?" Ashley says. "I wanted to know if you needed—"

"All right then, ladies!" he says and knocks on the door frame twice. "Back to work!" And he leaves without Ashley getting to finish her sentence.

She makes a face after he's gone. "What is it with him and his cousin Ada?"

"Is that it?" I ask. "I've got to pull stuff for the roundup meeting."

She nods. "That's it," she says. "Oh, and I meant to tell you that you really look nice today. Your earrings are killer and the pencil skirt really slims you down. Really."

"Thanks, Ashley."

"Gets harder to keep it off the older you get," she says and slips each ring back on her fingers. "Okay! Thank you, pumpkin!" She gives me a little wave.

That's Ashley.

She always sweetens any reprimand with paper-thin compliments because she thinks it builds morale, but basically what she just said was, "The layouts are wrong, your fashion choices are consistently hideous, you're fat, and now get out of my office."

Goddamned Ashley. She ate up all the time I was going to use to eat my Cinnabon at my desk. Ted is probably back by now and I just told him last week I was going on a diet and never eating another Cinnabon again.

I duck out into the rarely used stairwell and stand under the buzzing fluorescent lights, where I cram the Cinnabon in my mouth, just wolf-choke the cake down. I can feel the white cream icing glob up at the corners of my mouth and bits of cinnamon bun crumble onto my sweater and into my hair. It's disgusting and anyone looking at me would be repulsed.

Then I turn around, face full of frosting, Brad Keller is huffing up the stairs with two other executives in tow. I freeze. The three of them see me, pause talking for just the most horrible of split-seconds, and then continue their conversation. If I had one wish it would be that a sniper would shoot me right now, right here.

Really. One wish. That would be it.

The men walk right past me without saying a word. Then they're through the door. That's it. Bang. Door shuts, he's gone. I'm alone on the stairwell with a Cinnabon crammed in my mouth, my heart hammering in my rib cage.

I forgot my keycard and I'm locked out on the stairwell. I have to walk down five flights of stairs to the lobby in order to get back in the building again. This day is super.

I'm sitting at my desk and Ted pops his head in my cubicle.

"Is that icing on your forehead?" he asks. I wipe my forehead and little dry crumbly bits of icing come tumbling off.

"Just great. Brad Keller got to see me with Cinnabon smeared across my face."

Ted shrugs. "I heard he's like the black sheep of the family. His parents made him come back because he drinks."

"Who told you that? That sounds made up."

"Well it isn't," he says. "And what's with his eyebrows? One is higher than the other. You'd think with their money he could get that fixed."

"I think he's handsome."

"Handsome? Oh, are you in love now?" Ted says. "Are you going to marry Brad Keller and have little baby Kellers we can sell at a discount in the gourmet meats section?"

"Shut up."

"Oh, you love him!" Ted says. He leans over, eyes closed and makes obnoxious kissing noises. I hit him on the arm.

"Ouch! Quit it! You're so violent. Hitting people is wrong."

"You're stupid," I say, "and it makes me hit you."

"You really are the love of my life," he says.

"Let's go. It's roundup time."

The roundup meeting is a lovely little weekly event where we all sit in a hot, stuffy conference room and pitch our great ideas to Carl, the executive director of marketing. The worst part of the meeting is that it's become a broken-down version of show-and-tell where everyone showboats and pretends they're exhausted from work, because we all know Keller's is downsizing and nobody wants to lose their job, especially me.

I take my seat and Carl starts the meeting. He's Ashley's boss and he has a thinning wispy reddish mustache and wears pants with pleats in them. There's not much more to say, except in my opinion, a man with a thinning mustache probably shouldn't be in charge of marketing to the teen demographic. It was actually Carl who got me started on the "Gross Sex Game." That's where I sit and silently horrify myself with mental snapshots of what it would be like to have sex with any number of really gross men.

It started one afternoon two summers ago, when Carl was presenting something while wearing really tight pants. I don't know why Carl would wear tight pants except maybe he didn't know they were tight or maybe his wife was off counseling Christian Bible campers for the summer and Carl did his own laundry. Who knows.

Anyway, Carl was standing up facing the room and he was yammering on about something or other, when I saw it. It. A little bulge in his crotchal region. It was like a frightened opossum peeking around the corner and I looked away, ashamed and grossed out, and then I couldn't stop thinking about it.

What if, for some reason, I had to sleep with Carl?

What if a meteor hit the planet and killed almost everyone, except for a group of crazy people, like Mormons or something, and they began a military society where women were forced into marriage and had to produce as many offspring as possible? I would have to let the opossum nudge my nether region. I would have to open my legs and let that hairless, sightless mole creature . . .

"Jen?" Carl is looking at me now. Everyone there is looking at me.

"Yes?" I say and cough, which sounds super fake.

"Are you with us?"

"A hundred percent, Carl," I say, keeping my eyes locked above his beltline. He goes on to announce this year's Valentine's Day slogan, which is: FRESH AS A DAISY!

Carl tells us the marketing team wanted to put a "rejuvenation" spin on the most romantic day of the year. He says people have become so conditioned to all the typical Valentine's Day imagery, they don't even see it anymore. Red hearts and red roses just don't "grab" the customer the way they used to. So to be really "fresh and new," we're going to do something "extraordinary," and incorporate yellow daisies into our Valentine's Day marketing campaign.

Extraordinary.

Of course we're also keeping red roses and red hearts, because we want people to know what holiday we're talking about, after all. "I want everybody to brainstorm about ways to advertise *without advertising*," Carl says. "Got it?"

The room stares at him.

"We're looking for some genuine creativity here, people, some new ideas that really work." Nobody says anything. Carl crosses his arms. "I don't think I have to remind anybody that recent sales numbers haven't been what they could be and we're really counting on Valentine's Day to help us through the spring slump, which, as we know, can be expensive."

By "expensive," Carl means, "make me fire people."

The meeting disbands and we all shuffle off to our little cubicles so we can get going on turning the stickiest, syrupy, saccharine, lie-filled holiday of the year, Valentine's Day, into a douche commercial. Ashley rounds the corner as I return to my desk and I smile brightly at her. Fresh as a daisy, kill kill kill.

After work, I'm driving to Scampers Bar and Grill to meet Big-Kev007—I met him online. My cell phone rings.

It's my mother.

There's no point in avoiding her because she has a strict two-call policy. If you don't answer the phone twice, she will call every one of your friends in alphabetical order until she finds you.

"Hello, Mother," I say. "I'm not in a ditch."

"It's your mother," she says.

"Yes. I know."

"Oh, I'm so sorry to annoy you, Miss Snooty, but your sister is all upset and I got your Aunt Joan coming over here in five minutes and I can't be on the phone all day. I don't know why you girls have to be silly."

"Sorry, Mom."

"Did you forget the bridesmaid fitting tomorrow?" she asks.

"Aren't you using that leather FranklinCovey day planner I bought you?"

"FranklinCovey is a cult, Mom. They sell day planners to fund their sex compounds."

"Well," she sniffs, "they're very good organizers."

"You're right, Mom. You got me there. Say what you will, they do seem organized."

"Don't sass. Do you want this lamp?"

"I can't see what you're holding, Mom. We're on the phone. What lamp?"

"There's a ballerina on it."

"Are you talking about the lamp I had in my room when I was six?"

"Yes. Do you want it?"

"No."

"Well, it's a perfectly good lamp."

"Mother, I don't need a ballerina lamp."

"Don't get snooty. I'm trying to clean out the attic for Hailey's wedding presents. They're going straight from the church to the airport, so your aunt and I are putting all their gifts up here. I don't think they need waffle toasters in Hawaii."

"Hawaii?" I say, trying to soup-strain the bitterness out of my voice. "I didn't know they decided on Hawaii."

"So do you want the lamp?" she asks.

"No. You can have it."

"Well, I don't want it, the shade is torn and the skirt is chipped. Why don't you come over later and look at it?"

"I can't. I have a date."

"Dear Lord, it's not one of those online date setup things, is it? You're going to get yourself chopped up and floated down the river. That's how they found that poor girl in Dubuque. She met a man online. They couldn't even find her teeth."

"Mom, she met that guy on some sadomasochism site. Some dungeons-and-slavemaster thing."

"They're all sadomasochism sites," my mother says.

Again, she's got me there.

"Mom?" I say, and hold the phone away from my ear. "Can you hear me?"

"Jennifer?"

"Mom! I can't hear you, Mom! You're breaking up!"

"Jennifer?"

"I'm losing you. I can't hear you!" I hang up. I've been ending more and more conversations this way lately. My mother thinks I have big problems with my cell phone service, but really, I just have big problems.

I've never been to Scampers Bar and Grill, and when I walk in I know why. It's one of those horrible rock-music-themed places with a simulated copy of Led Zeppelin's guitar and half a Corvette anchored to the walls. I look around for a minute, trying to get my bearings and see if I recognize Kevin from his photo. Sometimes I've heard you just recognize your soul mate. You see him and you just know. Right now all I see are fat people.

Paranoia starts up. *Maybe he's stood me up, maybe that's the universe protecting me, maybe he's an axe murderer or owns an iguana, etc. . . .*

Think positive. Assume the two of you will be dating steadily in a month. Visualize it. Oh, who am I kidding? This is just going to be another runaway float in my great dating shame parade. In fact I'll be lucky if it's just shame and not something more damaging, like getting kidnapped and sold into the slave trade, although I don't know how much different that would be than my current life. Plus, I probably wouldn't have to cover the cost of gas for transportation.

I text-message Christopher.

Me: Mtg BigKev007 at Scampers. Nice guy or serial killer?

Christopher: Put spoon in purse. Good 4 digging if he buries U alive.

I look around the restaurant. Where is this guy? Maybe he had to work late. Lawyers work late. My two main reservations about dating a lawyer are that they're impossible to argue with, and that I've broken a few laws in my day. Nothing major, but I wonder if I'll have to disclose that stuff to him. That could get awkward. I wonder if he could represent me in court, or would that be a conflict of interest? It would certainly be handy to know a lawyer, since eating a rum ball can get you a DUI these days.

This place hurts my eyes. Flashing neon signs crowd the walls, along with the random rock-and-roll paraphernalia. Tatty album covers, old drumsticks, and chipped vinyl records are nailed next to yellowing black and white photographs, framed cocktail napkins with signatures on them, and the occasional piece of sequined clothing. There are televisions everywhere and the hostess stand is made out of two sparkly yellow electric guitars welded together.

"Are you Jill?" the hostess yells. She has to yell so I can hear her over the music.

"I'm Jennifer!" I shout back.

She nods and says, "Follow me!"

She leads me through the crowded bar into the noisy dining room, which is filled with big tables and loud groups. Everyone is shouting and laughing, having a good time. I'm about to become one of these people. There's no reason I can't join the thronging masses of hysterically happy people, who get together in big groups and hoot at television sets. I can do that. I, too, am about to have a good time.

We arrive at a table where a squat, ugly, pudgy man is waiting. He looks at me and sniffs. There must be a mistake—this man is wearing a navy snowflake sweater, which is rounded, because of his potbelly. His little potbelly. He looks like he's going to have a little baby.

"Jill?" he asks, looking skeptical.

"Kevin?" I respond, equally skeptical.

He nods doubtfully. "Have a seat?" he asks like it's a question, like it's up for grabs whether I should sit down or not.

I sit down.

He has a nasty deep-set wrinkle on his forehead, which creases when he talks. "Didn't recognize you," he says and I'm not sure what to say to that, but I'm vaguely aware it isn't friendly. The Scampers waitress shows up, a blonde about twenty-two years old wearing a Scampers half T-shirt that exposes her perfectly flat, tan stomach.

"You want something?" he says while staring at her belly. "I mean, I'm not hungry. I just want a beer. I want a Michelob. You don't want to eat, do you? I don't want to eat. Let's not eat."

I tell the waitress I'll have a chardonnay.

She leaves and he watches her butt. Then he remembers I'm sitting at the table. "Jill, Jill, Jill," he says, and does a little drumroll with his fingers. He squints at me again. "How old did you say you were?"

I don't immediately answer. Despite the constant buzz of the background rock, the particular acoustics of the sheltered booths are such that I can hear the conversation at the table behind us. "She asked where her daddy was, and I didn't know what to tell her," a woman is saying. "I just told her he went on a long trip."

BigKev007 clears his throat. "I mean, it's no big deal. It's just, you looked a little, I mean maybe that picture on your profile was from like . . . a while ago?"

"My name is Jennifer and it's from this summer," I say. "Last June."

"Right," he says, nodding, "eight months ago."

"Seven," I say.

The waitress comes with our drinks and sets them down on lime green coasters. BigKev007 stares at her midriff again as she leaves. He sighs and raises his beer. "Here's to being younger," he says, and we clink glasses even though I don't know what it is exactly we're toasting. After he swallows and smacks his lips, he says, "So you're like what, thirty?"

I take a sip of my drink and pray the earth will swallow me whole.

"Over thirty?" he asks and then waves his pudgy hand in the air as if to erase the question. "No," he says, "sorry, you're right, who cares, right? No biggie." He looks at his watch. "My ex-wife used to lie about her age all the time. I don't know why anyone even asks women how old they are. It's not like they're going to tell you the truth."

We stare at the table.

Eventually I say, "I had a bad breakup, too." I have no idea why I'd say that. You're not supposed to mention past relationships on first dates. Not even first dates that are tanking faster than deck chairs on the *Titanic*.

"What?" he asks.

"I said I sort of went through a breakup recently." Why would I tell him that? Why would I pony up that little nibble of information? Why am I so stupid?

He thinks about this for a minute. "I got the dog in the divorce," he says. "Fucking awesome dog. Piper." Then he asks, "You like dogs?"

I shrug.

"Good. Women that don't like dogs are bitches. Did I tell you

I'm a lawyer? Criminal defense. I have this case right now, a guy who was taking pictures of Chinese kids, boys mostly. Like twelve-year-olds. He was giving them money and clothes, like he was their dad. Being all nice. None of those kids have shit. Some don't even have winter coats, so here's this guy who has a camera and he says he just wants to take some snaps. Asks them to take off their shirts or whatever. The kids get all hysterical and get the guy in trouble. Kids are unreliable witnesses, though, but try to tell a jury that."

"Well, I hope you get him," I say. "I hope you lock him up for life."

BigKev007 makes a face. "The guy is my *client*. Why does everyone think I'm trying to prosecute him?"

I drain my wine and wonder if I have any Vicodin in the car. Then, in what will be our most tender moment, he leans over the table and says, "Pedophiles have a story, too, Jill." He shakes his head sadly. "They have a story, too."

I have no idea what to say. I never met a pedophile defender before. I think if I was a pedophile-defending lawyer and on a first date, this is one little piece of information I would not share.

He tells me what I would consider intimate and illegal-to-tell-strangers information about his various court cases. He goes on for some time and I'm just zoned out, staring at his fat, ugly, pudgy face. The more I look at it, the more it looks like knuckles. He doesn't ask me a single question about myself. He tells me he's been sober for thirteen years, but now he can drink a little. Then he says, almost proudly, like he's passed on the family business, that his teenage daughter is an alcoholic, too. "She's in rehab right now," he says. "I guess the apple doesn't fall, stagger, or collapse far from the tree, huh!"

"I'm so sorry."

"It's not your fault," he says. I hate it when people say this. I know it isn't my fault, I'm just trying to be nice. Hasn't he ever heard of manners? "Was she in rehab for Christmas?" I ask. "Did she have to spend the holidays in a hospital?"

"No," BigKev007 says, "she was out of rehab by then, but I don't know where she was on Christmas."

I tilt my head because I think I misheard him. "You don't?"

"I went to Jamaica with this real piece-of-work redhead who turned out to be a complete bitch. I had to fly in another one because she was just crazy."

The blond waitress comes back and asks if we want another drink.

"No," he says while staring at her stomach, "just the check."

"I'm sorry," I ask him. "You had to fly in another . . ."

"Girl," he says. "I had to fly in another girl."

"But . . . was the first one still there?"

"Yeah, but she got her own room. I had a pretty good time. I did yoga on the beach. You do yoga? I just started."

"So wait," I say. "Your daughter was just out of rehab and you left her alone on Christmas to go to Jamaica with a woman who you ditched for another woman? And then you did yoga?"

He looks at me blankly. "I dunno," he says. "My daughter went to her mother's house, I think, but that's another sob story."

There's a moment of silence as I stare at my drink coaster.

"Can I ask you something?" he says.

The waitress sets a little green plastic tray with the bill between us.

"Sure." This idiot better at least pick up the tab.

BigKev007 leans in and lowers his voice, like he's about to admit he was in fact peeing in his pants when we first met, or some other slightly embarrassing admission.

"I was just curious," he says. "Have you ever thought about losing a little weight?"

White light. Shock. Disbelief. I am stunned silent. He's still talking, but I can't focus in on what he's saying. Something about a cruise he knows about and a friend who went on it and lost all this weight. "Because you have a really pretty face," I hear him say. And then something about carbohydrates and how living in the Midwest distorts one's concept of portions. He finally adjusts his glasses and looks at the bill. "Normally I'd get this," he says, tossing it over to me, "but let's go Dutch, okay?"

Speechless, I nod while thinking, *Lose a little weight, Lose a little weight.*

I come out of my daze and get out a five-dollar bill.

"We need a little more for tip," he says.

I fish out another dollar.

I drive home carefully on the icy streets. I stand at the sink with my coat still on as I gulp down an entire glass of tap water. I call Christopher, but he's not picking up. It's moments like these when I'm not sure if I should tell my friends what horrible thing just happened to me, or if I should just keep it to myself. If I tell Christopher, I'll get to vent and he'll tell me how beautiful I am and what a jackass BigKev is and that I shouldn't let anyone make me feel bad about myself. He'll pack aphorisms and platitudes around my bruised heart like ice chips until I feel better and we agree no one can know the mystery of the universe or fully understand the beauty of the broken world, and so on . . . which frankly sounds exhausting because, let's face it, we've recited this particular script a lot.

On the other hand, if I bury the events of this evening deep, I can pretend it never happened. I can rewind the tape, cut the scene out, and burn it. I can reassign the event to something I saw on TV. Something that happened to somebody else. A story I could even relate to others like, "This one time this one girl went on an online date with some bastard and you won't believe what he said to her." Then I can hear all the *I don't believe it!*'s and *what an asshole!*'s without the humiliating story being attributed to me, already the keeper of so many humiliating stories.

I decide to bury it.

I pour myself a big glass of wine and go to the living room, where I sit cross-legged in front of my small white wooden dollhouse that has green shutters and loads of perfect tiny furniture. I've had it since I was little and I've always messed around with it when I'm stressed out. Miniature things soothe me. So does wreaking havoc on the small Tinkertoy family that lives inside. Right now the scenario is rather spicy. While the kids are asleep in their tiny respective rooms and the little wife is in the kitchen standing mutely at the refrigerator, the little husband is lying down stiffly on the living room couch with a big, nude splayed-leg Barbie on top of him.

I sip my wine and move the family around, giving them new

emergencies to handle. A plastic dinosaur peering in through an upstairs window, a miniature space alien walking through the front door with his laser gun drawn, a Christmas ornament Bambi grazing on the small AstroTurf lawn outside the window. It's a form of art therapy.

I finally get bored and retrieve my sacrosanct bottle of Lunesta. Thirty little blue pills in a prescription bottle to be used only in the case of emergency, because they cost about twenty dollars each. The bottle sternly advises that you take only one pill and you don't drink alcohol, because this intensifies the effect. If only they hadn't told me.

I get in my comfy blue flannel nightgown, the one I wear when there's absolutely no chance of a man being around, and I pop two Lunestas and drink wine while sitting in bed and staring out the deep blue window at the flurry of snow driving past, asking myself:

How the hell did I end up stuck here?

I eventually pass out on my pillow and the day dissolves under my eyelids. I slip into a comalike sleep sponsored by the lovely chemists at Lunesta, and it's all over. No emergency here. It's like the whole night never happened.

At work the next morning I sit in the parking lot and try to pull myself together before I go inside, while the painful echo of BigKev saying *lose a little weight* is playing on a continuous loop in my head. I have this piercing dehydration/humiliation headache and I look like I've been in a small fistfight. I used an antipuff serum and calming facial wash, along with three different kinds of cover-up, but what I really need is some spackle and a trowel.

I can't stop thinking about David. I know he was a bastard, but besides that, he was perfect for me. Tall, creative, musical.

He loved bad bars and strong drinks, but he wasn't anywhere close to being an alcoholic. He was funny. He had such a perfect sense of humor. The only problem with David was he didn't feel the same way about me. He said he did, but he was constantly standing me up and treating me like shit, but if I'm going to be honest, there was something about that that seemed right.

David was very forceful. Sex with him was like being bumped with a shopping cart. Then he was done and snoring next to you.

I linger in my car and re-do my makeup, hoping maybe Brad Keller might show up again. This time I could be charming and funny instead of paranoid and enraged. Maybe he likes angry, complaining women. Some men do, especially if their mothers were that way. Maybe Brad has had his share of women who are people pleasers and sycophants; maybe he's still single because he hasn't found that sassy firecracker he's been looking for. I wait in my car as long as I possibly can, my windows fogging over with my breath until I'm late for the plus-size prom dress shoot.

I get up to my cubicle and wrestle off my hundred-pound Eddie Bauer parka. The thing is double-insulated, double-quilted, and double-stuffed, and will keep you warm in an ice storm, but it makes me look huge and it's freaking heavy. When I wear it I feel like I'm giving a seventh-grader a piggyback ride. "Good God!" I say, dumping it onto the floor. "Why the hell do we live in Minnesota?"

"I don't know." Ted shrugs. "Nice people and lots of parking."

"More like nice apathy and lots of depression."

"Ooh," he says, "those would make good mascots. We could take two Minnesota loons and name them Depression Loon and Apathy Loon. Depression Loon would ask Apathy Loon to peck him to death but Apathy Loon wouldn't care." He looks at his watch. "Aren't you late for the shoot?"

I'm even later than I thought. I try to pull everything together and Ted hands me his copy of the shot list when I can't find mine. I snap it up and scamper down the hall. God. I have to remember to never say "scamper" again.

By the time I get to the studio—a boxy, hot room located conveniently in the Keller's basement by the boilers—they've already set up the lights for the set, which is a series of large white pillars and a wooden gazebo with a barbecue grill in the background. Very midwestern belle epoque Southern plantation hot dish. My eyes adjust slowly, and I make my way over to the coffee table, which I'm hoping will also have aspirin or perhaps prescription-strength pain killers.

I hear someone shout, "The list? Is it here *now?*" and I hurry toward the brilliantly lit set, where Alan, the catalogue director says, "Oh, *thank you*. I hope it wasn't too much trouble to keep us all waiting."

Then Brad blooms into view.

"Mr. Keller here is watching the shoot today," Alan snaps. "He's the new boss. We do anything he says, got it? Ed Keller's direct orders. Straight from the top. The people who have been here for years are not the boss now, the new guy, who just got here, he's the boss."

"Okay," I say and Brad raises an eyebrow at me.

I smile.

"You're going to double-check the shot list, Jen," Alan says. "Since the photo department got bitched at last time, someone from marketing is going to keep track this time. That way if there are any problems, you can all just bitch at yourselves."

I smile and nod, as though he's just paid me a great compliment.

"Sit here," Alan says and kicks an overturned bucket next to the camera. He expects me to sit on a bucket. Lovely. How elegant. I want to slap him right across the face but instead I sit down. Alan storms off to the dressing rooms where he starts shouting at someone else and I try to look pretty, perky, and nonchalant as Brad talks to our new photographer, who's actually a nice guy.

Our staff photographers in the past have tended to be dickheads. We had one who looked like a fiddle-with-the-girls gym teacher, and another who used dental floss on set in between takes. *Flick! Flick! Flick!* The last staff photographer looked like a little boiled midget, a Napoleon-size red-faced guy who was always screaming. He actually dropped dead during last year's Easter shoot. He was yelling at the kids on set, who were all perched on top of Styrofoam Easter eggs and having trouble keeping their balance when all of a sudden he stopped shouting and dropped to the floor. Total renal failure. All the little kids freaked out and started screaming and a boy wearing a powder-blue tuxedo actually peed in his pants.

Alan leads the plus-size models out along with Nell, the chubby wardrobe assistant. God, she's really gotten chunky. She's got a very sweet, perky personality, and she's always good for a smile or a quick joke, but then again she has to be. She's chubby. David once said I was chubby, "in a lovable way," and I cried for two days.

Sitting there, frozen in a pert expression, I smell something strange. Wait. I smell my armpits. How is this possible? How could I have forgotten *deodorant?* I managed to put a top coat of clear gloss on my toenails, but I forgot deodorant? I look around like maybe people are already talking about it and keep my arms firmly clamped to my sides. I text-message Christopher and tell him we have an odor emergency. I can do this. I can accept disgusting body odors are for some reason a natural part of the human condition. I just won't raise my arms. Ever.

The models get in position and Nell shuffles over to me. She squats down and I tighten my arms to my sides. Why does she have to sit so close? "I tried to put her in the Beverly Hills blue dress," she sighs, "but it was too big for her. The plus-size girls get smaller every year."

"Thanks," I say and cross Blue Beverly off the shot list without moving my arms.

"Sometimes I wonder if the dressmakers are secretly trying to make fun of these girls," Nell says. "I mean, why would you name a plus-size prom dress the Clara? That's just mean. That just makes me think of Clarabell the Clown, or Clarence the Cow."

"Yep," I say, wishing she'd pick up on my lack of eye contact or comment and go away.

"And the Queenie?" she snorts. "I mean, come on. Queen-size! Someone somewhere is laughing their ass off."

"I bet they are," I say. Brad walks past us and I hope Nell doesn't notice me stiffen.

"I heard Brad Keller took one of the cosmetics girls out on a date," she whispers.

"What?"

"No, thank you!" she says. "That family is crazy. I would never go out with him."

Well it's not like you're going to have to worry about that, I think, and then by the look on her face, I realize I said it out loud.

She sniffs and leaves. Crap. Now I have another mortal enemy. It's so easy to collect them when you work with so many women.

I study the models as the camera sets up. It's true, these girls look like *maybe* they're size ten. The brunette looks like an eight. I sag. That would mean—no, wait, I try to push the thought out but it comes charging back. *I am bigger than a plus-size model.* I was hanging onto size ten this summer, hanging on for dear life, but this fall I lost my grip and tumbled into a size twelve. And here I was considering the possibility of going on a date with Brad Keller?

Me? The jumbo loser girl?

I sit and think every vile thought I can about myself. I beat myself up. While the lights are flashing I am tearing through an inner dialogue that would make Mommie Dearest frightened. I am stupid, fat, lazy, ugly, unlucky, bad at card games, bad at math, a terrible driver, a worse tennis player, I snore, I get gas when I eat ice cream, I'm utterly tone deaf. I'm stuck in this job in this city in this life and nothing will ever be different because I will never be different. I will always be the same flaky, undependable, untalented, overlooked girl.

Brad turns around and smiles at me. A hard jolt of electricity flashes down my right arm and I almost fall off my bucket. I smile and blush without meaning or wanting to. I have my arms clamped so hard to my sides it hurts. I take out my phone and surreptitiously text-message Christopher, begging him to bring me deodorant.

The strobes keep flashing and the girls strike different poses. In a way, it's easier to shoot plus-size models; it goes more quickly because there are fewer pose options. There's no jumping in the air or squatting for these girls. There's no hugging each other or crossing their arms, nothing that squishes arm fat. There are no serious expressions. No staring in the distance or pursing their lips. Big girls are happy girls, period. They can smile, put one hand on their hip, or pivot. That's about it.

I shouldn't be so mean. I don't mean to be mean—after all, a lot of these girls are just like me. They'll go to prom with their girlfriends, telling each other it doesn't matter that they don't have dates, that they have each other, which is all a girl really needs. And they'll all laugh and sneak a bottle of champagne into the rented limo and they'll all be very careful not to look too deeply into each other's eyes, because behind the fun and festivity, the smiles and the laughing, is a growing pool of panic. If they don't have dates now, will they ever? If they haven't found the man they're going to marry, will they ever?

And if I was there with them, so many years older and wiser, what could I tell them? If I told them the truth, I would say something I never dreamt of believing back then. I would tell them to grab a nice guy and make it work no matter what. I'd tell them to consider arranged marriages, that their parents will be able to pick a better mate than they will. I would tell them no one is perfect and no Prince Charming is coming. I would tell them there aren't any white horses or knights in shining armor to save them. They have to save themselves. I would tell them they have every reason to feel panic, and to hurry.

The shoot finally, mercifully ends and the lights are shut off one by one, cooling the room by degrees. Just as people start leaving, Christopher finally appears.

"Great timing," I hiss. "I've been sitting under these hot lights for hours, smelling like blue cheese, with Brad Keller standing two feet away from me and now that it's over, you show up. What the hell is that?"

"All I could find was baking soda." Christopher hands me the little yellow box.

"Are you kidding me? What am I supposed to do with this?"

"Just put some under your armpits. Baking soda soaks up any smell."

"Where did you get it?"

"Employee break room."

"Great. That's where that guy keeps his diabetes syringes."

I stomp off to the bathroom, which has two people in it already, so I lock myself in a stall and try to put baking soda under my arms. I end up doing this half-swami double helix thing with one foot on the toilet and *poof!* up goes a mushroom cloud of baking soda, right into my eyes and mouth, making me cough and choke. "Are you all right in there?" someone asks, and I say yes and quickly go to flush the toilet, like that's going to explain anything, when *kerplunk!* my foot goes right in the water. I return squishing across the studio floor, slightly limping. Brad is nowhere in sight.

"What the hell happened to you?" Christopher asks. "You look like an angry powdered sugar doughnut."

I spin around right into—who else?—Brad Keller, who's walking back from the snack table. I try to say something but my heart speeds up and my mouth goes dry. I twist my hands together. He's holding a muffin. For some reason I focus on this. "Got a muffin there?" I ask him. Is this the stupidest thing anyone ever said to anyone else in the history of the human language? Why yes, I believe it is. *Got a muffin there?*

"Um, yep," Brad says, looking at the muffin in his hand.

Then, rather than drop the subject and/or excuse myself and/or cease being utterly retarded I say, "Poppy seed?"

Brad looks at the muffin. "I believe it is," he says. "Do you want it?"

I stare at him and Christopher clears his throat.

He holds the muffin out. "It isn't poisoned or anything."

I remain mute.

"Are you *afraid* of the muffin?" he asks. "Did someone torture you once with a muffin or something?"

"Yes, they did!" I blurt. "I did two years' hard time with the Keebler elves, and let me tell you, the shower scene was not pretty."

"Oh, dear Lord," Christopher says behind me.

Brad hands me the muffin. "Let's start again," he says. "Hi! I'm Bradford Keller. You can call me Brad."

"Nice to meet you," I croak. "I'm Jennifer Johnson. You can call me Jen."

We shake hands and I think I might be trembling as our palms touch. I feel like I just got plugged into an electrical outlet. "Sorry about the parking lot thing," I whisper.

"Don't worry about it." He shrugs. "I sort of like women who yell."

Somebody shouts Brad's name.

"Okay, then," Brad says, "see you later."

Everything in the room seems set to slow motion. Like we're all moving through a clear, viscous tar. My face is burning, my mouth dry. He gives me a funny look and walks away, leaving me there holding his muffin. I turn around slowly to face Christopher.

"I don't even want to know what that was about," he says, covering his face with his hand. "I really don't."

Back in the office I promise myself I will not visualize what it would be like to be married to Brad Keller.

I will not.

It'll only make me miserable, because I bet his wife would be the happiest girl in the world. I bet she'd have titanium-gold-zinc credit cards and they'd live in a huge house on a lake, even though I don't need a huge house on a lake; a huge house anywhere would be fine, because I'd probably be out doing my charitable works and giving speeches at junior high schools to young girls who are considering their career opportunities, and I would tell them to always stay true to themselves no matter what, and afterward one or two of the girls would probably even write me letters saying I changed their lives, which I would show Brad and he'd kiss my forehead and say I was the most amazing woman he'd ever met, and then he would show me the two tickets he bought for us to Tahiti.

But I'm not going to visualize all that.

After work, I drive to my mother's with Brad's untouched lemon poppy-seed muffin on my dashboard. I stare at it at stoplights. That muffin represents everything I cannot have. A life of ease and luxury, of prestige and quality bakery items. Who knew there was a son to the Keller dynasty that was my age? Listen to me, "dynasty." That's why I don't have a dynasty, because I use words like "dynasty." That and because the Cinnabon counter girl knows my name.

I take my time getting to the house, which is a sweet and tidy brick Tudor with wooden crossbeams and a steep slate roof. In summer, the automatic sprinklers come on every evening at five, just in time for Mr. Anderson, the cranky neighbor, to come home from work and yell about his car getting wet. My mother reset the timer after he cut down a crabapple tree that was partially on their property. My mother loved that tree. She arranged pink blossom bouquets in the spring and made crabapple centerpieces in the fall. Ever since he claimed it was in the way of his satellite dish and thwacked it with a chainsaw, my mother has passive-aggressively tortured him with ill-timed sprinkler systems, early morning broadcasts of the Royal Danish Orchestra, and convincing his wife every home ought to have copper gutters.

My mother opens the door frowning.

"What?" I ask.

"Just don't start," she says.

This is a typical greeting.

I go inside. My mother's house is very comfortable, warm, and cheerful and perfectly decorated like a Pottery Barn catalogue. I've always wanted my house to look like this, but it's hard to get a crappy apartment to look like anything but a crappy apartment.

I shout hello to my father, who's watching the news in his den, and he grunts hello back. He probably won't come out all night and I don't blame him. The estrogen level in this house is reaching all-time-high levels and the best thing to do is strap yourself down and hang on. I, of course, have to dive into the disaster and I really don't know if there's enough liquor in the world to get me through this.

I hear girl-cackle in the kitchen.

"Did you bring the salsa?" Hailey snaps.

I close my eyes. Super. I forgot the freaking salsa.

"Mom!" she whines. "Jen forgot the salsa!"

"Don't make a fuss," my mother says, opening the pantry door. "I bought some just in case."

"Why do you even need salsa?" I ask. "Look at this spread! Mom, did you do all this?"

She shoots me a look. Of course she did all this.

I turn my attention to the herd of sturdy Norwegian girls flanking Hailey, who have all been her BFFs since high school. They all look like inbred cousins, they're so similar, with their wheat-blond hair and ice blue eyes. They're like Children of the Corn or something, and I've always suspected that if they were smarter, they might actually have some super power, but things standing as they are, I don't foresee any trouble.

"Hi, Lexi!" I say. "Hey, did you lose weight?"

"Me?" Lexi screeches. "No! I'm like a cow."

"Really? Dairy or beef? Beef probably, huh?"

She's confused.

"Is this champagne?" I pick up a glass.

"Have a date for your sister's wedding yet?" someone asks me. They don't mean any harm by this, they're just trying to be nice, and since every single tan, tawny one of them is already married, they don't know the question is like salt in my eyeball.

"Well, I met Ed Keller's son today," I tell them. "Brad."

"Really?" my mom brightens. "He sounds nice."

"Oh yeah, *as if*," Hailey says, rolling her eyes.

My eyes narrow and I take a sip of pink champagne. "Hey, Mom, where's the pickle dish?"

"What pickle dish?"

"The pickle dish. Your heirloom pickle dish."

"Where it always is, I guess. The sideboard."

I study the little bubbles in my drink and say, "I don't think so."

Hailey glares at me.

My mother stops reloading chips into the ceramic Mexican hat bowl.

Nobody says anything and you can hear the stove fan whirring.

My mother rushes into the dining room, and when she comes back into the kitchen she has a bright red face, but very calmly, like Clint Eastwood, she asks, "Girls, where is my pickle dish?"

Silence.

I examine a fingernail. "Ask Hailey, Mom."

"Hailey"—she turns around—"where is my pickle dish?"

"Mom, I was going to tell you."

"Tell me what?"

"Lenny sort of bumped into the table at Christmas."

"Bumped it?"

"He just bumped the table and the pickle dish fell. It broke."

My mother closes her eyes and slowly puts one hand on her forehead and the other one over her heart, and the yellow duck stitched on her sweater, as though she's just been told one of us has cancer. "Leonard broke the pickle dish?" Before Hailey can answer, Mom reaches for the counter as if for support, as if she might fall down. "HAROLD!" she yells. "Harold, your daughter broke the pickle dish!"

"No, I didn't," Hailey whines. "Lenny did!"

Ha. She's already turning him in. Some marriage.

"What now?" My father comes into the kitchen holding his newspaper.

"Leonard broke the pickle dish," my mother says.

"You got any ham sandwiches?" he asks.

"Harold, the pickle dish your mother came across the Atlantic Ocean with is *gone*."

"That's the one!" I chirp. "Smashed."

"That thing?" he says. "Who needs a pickle dish? You want a pickle you get a pickle. Use a jar like everybody else." Then he leaves. I love my dad.

Hailey explodes at me. "You just want Mom to hate Lenny! Well, guess what? Mom *loves* Lenny! I love Lenny! Everybody loves Lenny! The guys at the factory love Lenny so much they gave him a freaking world's-best-boss lifesaver ring for his fishing boat!"

"Well, Hailey," I say calmly, "I don't think Mom's pickle dish loves Lenny."

Hailey throws her special edition of *Cape Cod Weddings* on the floor.

"Enough!" my mother says. "Your grandmother managed to cross an ocean with that pickle dish and yet now it is broken." She nods grimly. "You girls have to learn."

You girls?

"And you knew about this, Jennifer Anne?" she asks.

Crap. Crap. Crap. The barrel of the gun has repositioned. When middle names are used, punishments are imminent. This is what always freaking happens. No matter who does what, it will be my fault. If Hailey roasted my mother's Wedgwood figurines on the propane grill, my mother would ask me what I did to upset my sister. I employ evasive tactics. "Didn't you say Grandma saved that pickle dish from the Nazis?" I ask, knowing full well Grandma Hannah saved the pickle dish from the Nazis by hiding it in her very ample bosom.

"Yes," she says. "Your grandma left Denmark during the war. She got on one of the last boats leaving Copenhagen when Hitler invaded and all she brought was a few things, and one of them was that pickle dish."

"I loved Grandma," I say. "I miss her."

"Faker!" Hailey shouts.

"Well," my mother says, "that's a loss for the whole family. An irreplaceable heirloom lost to carelessness." Everyone in the kitchen is silent. "All right," she sighs, "let's try on the dresses. I'll visit Grandma's grave tomorrow to explain."

We all wash our hands before trundling out to the sun porch where our dresses are hanging. I find the white garment bag that says JENNIFER and unzip it. There it is. The infamous kimono. I hate this dress. I actually *did* drive all the way to the mall to try it on, but I wouldn't let the seamstress take it out or fix the hem or even look at me, for that matter. I never came out of the little fitting room. It was hideous and I told her to just send an extra-large and I was done with it.

I take the dress to the upstairs bathroom so I can change in private. I have to lose weight. It's not funny anymore. It's no longer just a few pounds. I can't take this off in two weeks. I look in the mirror. Oh my God. I am not wearing this dress in public. The backs of my legs look like tree stumps. How could the breasts be too high and the waist too low? It puckers. It puckers everywhere.

"Jennifer?" I hear my mother call up the stairs. "Come down! We want to see everyone together!"

No way. Not going down. No. Those girls will laugh at me. Not to my face, but behind my back. They've always done that. They don't know what it's like to be called Jenny Jelly Belly or Jen-Jen Messy Pigpen. David said I should lose weight. Every man I ever dated probably thought it, even if he didn't say it out loud. I wish I'd never been born. Not if I had to be a fat, metabolism-challenged failure my entire life.

I hear someone knocking on the door and I panic. I can already see this play out. It doesn't matter what I say about the dress. It doesn't matter if I tell them I'm too uncomfortable and self-conscious to wear it in the ceremony, they'll tell me I look fine and they'll make me wear it. The knocking gets louder.

"Jennifer, for goodness' sake, come out already." It's my mother. "I don't know why you're changing in there anyway. There's antibacterial soap and Windex in there. They could ruin your dress. Jennifer!" My eyes snap to the sink and I make a dash for the cabinet. I'm not really even thinking now, I'm panicking, wild like an animal that's caught in a snare. I will do anything to free myself.

The next thing I know, I hear, "What have you done?!" and my mother is standing over me with her hands on her head. The bridesmaids in their perfect powder-blue dresses crowd around behind her. Hailey pushes past them and stares at me with her mouth open.

"You didn't!" she whispers.

"I didn't what?" I look down and there it is, an open bottle of Drano on my lap, clear viscous gel pooling on the shiny light-blue silk.

"What are you doing?" my mother cries and that's when I

snap out of my fog. I can't exactly explain what happened but it's amazing how fast Drano bleaches fabric.

Faster than bleach.

In the morning I rush to the Panty Jubilee meeting. Panty Jubilee is part of the targeted inventory that goes on sale before Valentine's Day. All ladies' hosiery (underwear) and men's accessories (underwear) is discounted, along with select jewelry and chocolates, and sometimes we put stuffed animals on sale, too, but we've never figured out how to comfortably market Valentine's Day in the children's section without looking like pedophiles.

Ted and I hate the name Panty Jubilee. "I'd rather try to market the Taliban Jubilee," he says, "or the Gyne-Lotrimin Jubilee."

We've tried to explain to Carl that the words "panty" and "jubilee" just don't go together, but he's not having it. "We've called it Panty Jubilee since before any of you worked here," he barks, "and we'll be calling it that after you're all gone." So Panty Jubilee it is. It's a jubilee of panties. Hearken to the drummers and let loose the doves, all underwear in the store is twenty-five percent off.

Last year there was also a hullabaloo over whether we should spell panty with a *y* or *ie*. Carl wanted "pantie," because the plural of "pantie" is "panties." He also liked that both "pantie" and "jubilee" end in *e*. He felt there was a "certain symmetry to it that shouldn't be overlooked." Ashley led the panty-with-a-*y* camp, offering the simple and solid fact that "panty" is spelled with a *y* in the dictionary. Carl won, as usual, and so all our marketing copy and in-store signage said PANTIE JUBILEE! I jog to the conference room where Ashley and the rest of the marketing department are already gathered.

"Ladies and gentlemen," Ashley says, "I am quite happy to inform you, this year we will be going with panty-with-a-*y*."

Everyone groans. This means all our signage from last year has to be changed.

"We only had a two-percent increase in underwear sales last year," Ashley says, "and so this year we'll be trying panty-with-a-y."

"Brilliant," Ted whispers, "that'll change everything."

I giggle.

"Jennifer?" Ashley asks. "Something to share?"

My cheeks flush and I shake my head no. She goes on to tell us we have an additional "challenge" this year because Keller's got the wrong shipment of women's accessories from Brazil and now we have two thousand extra units of plus-size underwear to sell.

"Two *thousand*?" someone asks.

Ashley nods. God, she looks perfect today. She told me her husband proposed to her the day after they both graduated from college. He took her out on Lake Calhoun in a rowboat and he brought champagne and chocolate-dipped strawberries, which was the only "kooky" part of the proposal. Ashley said after he proposed and she said yes and flung her pipe-cleaner-size arms around him, his knee accidentally bumped into the little plate of chocolate-covered strawberries and he got chocolate on his khakis. Please. If that had been me in the rowboat I would've bumped the chocolate, which I would try to frantically wipe off right before I capsized the boat, sending my engagement ring and fiancé into the lake. Of course if David had proposed to me, it wouldn't have been on a beautiful lake at sunset, it would've been in a dive bar at closing time. He probably would have used a beer pull-tab for a ring. "Big panties are hot," Ted whispers. "Granny panties are hot."

"The brand name is also a challenge," Ashley says. "They're called 'Guanos.'"

"Isn't guano bird shit?" somebody asks.

"No," I say, "bat shit."

"Language!" Ashley snaps.

"Maybe it makes sense in Brazilian," Ted says. "Maybe 'Guanos' is like *suenos* and means 'dream weavers' or something."

"People in Brazil speak Portuguese," I say, "not Brazilian. We live in America. Do we speak American?"

"I speak American," Ted says. "What's rizzle in da hizzle phoshizzle?"

"All right," Ashley says, "enough."

"Shoot," Ted says to her, "don't hate a pimp!"

Ashley writes the slogan down. "'Dream weavers' is a start," she says. "Sleeping, dreaming. Good. Is there any way to make them more appealing to young people? To the hip crowd?" This is why I hate Ashley, because she says "young people" and "hip crowd." She's always trying to be so cool and it's like when church groups have hip-hop bands.

Just painful.

That's one thing, anyway; David might have been an unemployed musician, but he never said stupid bullshit like Ashley and he never wore pleated khakis like Carl.

Never.

He also never played golf or went to country clubs or talked about weird corporate bullshit. He was real. I mean, he was a real jerk, but he never subscribed to anyone's idea of success. He hated my job. He said marketing was just "putting a shine on shit." I stood up for myself at the time, but as I look around the table at fifteen grown adults trying to think of a new name for jumbo underwear, I see his point.

Now the table grumbles and the PR girls say something

about throwing a granny panty party and someone else says we should give senior citizens an added discount. Ashley flips her legal pad. "What about something like, 'Dreams come true in your dream weavers'?"

"Or Disney it up," Ted says. "Call them Bunchies."

"Bunchies?"

"You know, underwear that bunches up. Put the right spin on it, and people think it's sexy to have hot granny panties riding up their butt apples."

"Bunchies," Ashley says, ignoring the fact Ted said "butt apples." "That's kind of cute."

"Why can't we just be honest?" I blurt. "Why can't we just say, 'You're huge and we finally found underpants that fit you'?"

The table stares at me.

Ted points his pen. "Or, we could shorten it and say, 'Underpants that finally fit!' We don't normally say 'underpants' though. We'd have to clear that with legal."

"Okay!" Ashley says in her sing song voice. "Some nice fresh ideas and a good start. I want a sales idea fleshed out by the end of the day."

Back at our desks I throw a sleepwear catalogue at Ted. "'We'd have to clear that with legal'? What's wrong with you?"

He rubs his leg where I hit him. "What?"

"Oh my God, you had your nose so far up Ashley's ass I bet you could taste what she had for lunch."

"I was just helping."

"I don't even know who you are anymore."

"I thought I might as well save us some time, you know, not wander down the Jymnastics path?"

I groan. Jymnastics were these horrible cheap gym shoes for teenagers that had rhinestones stuck all over them. We bought them in Ethiopia or something and we worked all month and came up with the slogan GET NASTY JYM-NASTIES! to which Ashley said, "We don't use the word 'nasty.' *Ever*. We also don't rename brand products." She made us stay late for days and rework the slogan and refused to pay us overtime, because we "were idiots."

After work I have another online date. This time with a guy named AndyMN, who's a Xerox salesman and plays acoustic guitar. I'm not ready. I haven't done my hair or nails or anything. I'm still trying to get my head on straight. I mean, so what about David? So what if I've failed in the past? What has that got to do with the future? This guy will be different. He has to be different, just by the ratio of odds. People are different, right? There's no reason in the world to think he'll be anything like BigKev007 or Hungry_Joe or TigerGuy or OutdoorsyTom or Sixpakabs or LoveOnly4U or BoredofDating or HeyLadeez5.

I have decided he will be different.

Still, in case he's an axe murderer, I text-message Christopher and tell him where we'll be. I tell him if I end up dead he can have my antique vibrator collection. He's the only one I know who would know what to do with it.

I get to the restaurant, La Belle Vie, which AndyMN picked, and I'm intimidated by how nice it is. The long drapes and the crystal chandeliers make me nervous, which isn't good. Sometimes I have a little problem lying when I'm this nervous. *Mea culpa. Mea maxima culpa.* The weird thing is I don't lie in order to make myself look good, I lie in order to adapt to a situation, or make someone feel better, or fill an awkward silence, which often results in me looking quite idiotic. Like I have some unstudied version of social Tourette's syndrome.

For instance, once at a party where I didn't know anyone

and I was feeling particularly chubby and alone, I managed to join a conversation and the topic of allergies came up. Somebody said, "I'm trying acupuncture for my eczema," and there was an awkward pause, so I blurted out, "I have eczema, too." This led to my new eczema-buddy and I talking about eczema and eczema treatment options for the rest of the night, and by "us" I mean the eczema-buddy talked because after my initial cursory comment about my imaginary skin condition—"I soak in milk and oatmeal baths when it gets bad"—I had nothing else to say. Why would I? I only knew about the milk/oatmeal treatment from an oatmeal Lourdes of London bath powder I use, which says "good for irritated skin!" on the back.

Then there was the time I was on a church-sponsored field trip to Montreal, and totally embarrassed by my churchy American companions. They were so lame compared to the chic French-speaking Quebecois around us. I refused to speak English and adopted the single French phrase I overheard a little girl say in front of a doll shop. "*Que très jolie marionette!*" which I was told meant, "What a pretty doll!" I would say this and only this if I thought a Canadian was in earshot. I just repeated over and over, "*Quelle très jolie marionette!*" They must have thought I was insane.

Then I met some stylish, sexy Brazilian students who had high-tech cameras, really cool backpacks, and spoke English. They were way cooler than my youth group, so I ditched my church friends and ran around the city with them all day, taking pictures and horsing around. We were having a great time, at least I was, and when the sun started to go down and I felt their interest in me was waning, I said, "I know where the best bar in Montreal is."

I was sixteen at the time.

Why I would say this I have no idea, because not only was I too young to get into a bar, but the Brazilians naturally decided we should go there. I should have just admitted to my lie right then, but instead I chose to dive deeper and take them on a circuitous, serpentine tour through the city. I thought for sure we would happen across a great place and I could simply say, "See? Here it is!" But around ten o'clock, one of them thought to ask what the name of the bar was and I said, "Cirque du Monde," which I think loosely means, "Circus of the World."

I knew at this point, statistically speaking, I was screwed. Because we were now not only walking around a dicey residential neighborhood looking for the best bar in Montreal, we were walking around a dicey residential neighborhood looking for the best bar in Montreal called Cirque du Monde. But I didn't give up. I didn't say a word. I don't know what I was thinking, I was becoming hypoglycemic and tired and confused. They, too, were starting to figure out I was full of moose poop and finally one of them stopped in the street and said, "There is no Cirque du Monde, is there?"

I told them, no, there wasn't.

They hailed a taxi right there on the spot, climbed in, and left me behind. I couldn't find another cab for hours and it was three in the morning before I made my way back to the dormitory where my church group was staying and I got yelled at for wandering off without telling anybody, and the next night I was not allowed to go to the hockey game.

AndyMN the Xerox salesman spots me right away and waves. He seems like a genuinely nice guy and not in a bad way. He's not mousy or submissive, he's just friendly and secure. Plus, he actually looks like his photograph: thick sandy-blond hair and sweet brown eyes.

Andy offers to check my jacket, but for some reason I say,

"No thanks!" and stuff it under the table instead. I'm sure he noticed this, but he didn't say anything. Everyone notices everything on a first date, actually, in the first five minutes of the first date. All critical observations, interests, and judgments will be made then. Andy, however, is gentleman enough to pretend to ignore my odd behavior. Another point for him.

Everything starts pleasantly enough. We chat about the icy roads and the terrible driving conditions. Things are going good. Andy is attentive and interested and reminds me we're having dinner, not just drinks, if that's okay with me. I tell him that's okay with me. Definitely. The waiter brings us a nice bottle of Chianti and after perusing the menu, I order the duck.

He orders the succotash crepes.

It's only after the waiter leaves, Andy tells me he's a vegetarian. At first I think he's kidding, and then he assures me he's not. Great, now he's going to think I'm a heartless monster who enjoys ripping the face off something before I gobble it up. I think I might like him, so in an attempt to show him I, too, am an animal lover, I say, "You know, I love ducks. We used to have a pet duck."

We both stare at each other.

I can think of about a thousand things wrong with what I just said, including but not limited to the fact I never had a pet duck. Eventually Andy picks up his wineglass and says, "A duck?"

"Yes. We used to have a pet duck."

He frowns. "A duck," he repeats.

This is not good, because as any seasoned liar will tell you, when people repeat your lie, nothing is going to make them believe it. I try to remember which way people look when they're lying. I think it's to the left. So I look deliberately to the right and say again, "Yes. A pet duck."

Andy raises an eyebrow. Another bad sign. "What was his name?"

Now, I realize here I have an out. A chance to right the wrong, to stop and say, "I'm kidding! Who would have a pet duck?" and we would both laugh and go on about our superfun dinner, but I don't do that. Instead I choose to go deeper into the lie and say, "His name was Quackers."

"Quackers," Andy repeats.

I only have one option now. Elaborate. It's the only way out of a lie. Make it so detailed it has to be true. I begin to describe Quackers. I talk about his cute black feet and his bright orange bill. I say he slept in the house and he'd follow me from room to room. Cute Quackers! I say we had one neighbor who liked him and one neighbor who complained. Andy listens to me dig myself deeper and deeper, answering questions no one is asking. "No, he wasn't really housetrained," I say, "but we did get him to crap on cardboard."

Andy blinks.

"Yeah, when I think back on all the animals I've loved," I say, "I mean, you know, not biblically! Just as pets—I think Quackers was my favorite."

Andy sips his wine.

"It was so tragic when he died. He got caught in the swinging door. Tore his beak right off. We buried him in the backyard."

Andy looks at his watch.

Then the waiter comes and sets down my plate of duck. We both stare at it. I have been describing a beloved pet duck and now I am about to eat a duck.

Brilliant.

I try to redirect the conversation but it's already over. I can see it in Andy's body language. He's listing to the left, he's looking at the door, and he's fidgeting. I pick at my pet duck dinner.

He eats quickly, he hails the waiter over to take his plate, he hardly talks, which makes me chatter like a macaque.

Andy is true to his word. We eat dinner and he pays for it, all seventy-two dollars, even though I put up a really good fight for the bill. He does not want coffee or dessert, which I also offer to buy. Really, I'd buy him anything at this point, including a helper monkey or a set of radial tires, if only they would set things straight. But of course, they will not.

At the door of the restaurant he shakes my hand good-bye, which we all know is just as good as spitting on it. Despite wanting to yell at him for making me feel so awkward, I also want to give him his seventy-two dollars back. I don't even deserve a decent boyfriend.

On the way home I start crying in the car. Not bawling, just a steady weep. I call Christopher and leave a message. "It's not *them*," I say, voice wavering. "It's *me*. I'm the problem. I've been saying guys are jerks and dicks and insensitive and stupid when actually I'm the jerk! I'm the dick! I never act like myself and then I can't keep up the act, or worse, I do act like myself and they get the hell away from me! I am going to be single forever. That's it! No more dates, no more online stalker chats, no more anything! A girl can be happy with just a cat! She can!"

I'm so sick of the wanting and waiting and wondering. Of harboring old wounds and guarding deep secrets and nursing along emotional injury after emotional injury. When does it stop? What did I do to deserve this? I storm into my apartment and hunt down everything that reminds me of David, every photograph of us together, every matchbook from our favorite restaurant, every piece of clothing he bought me: two sweaters, a white nightie, and an unworn string bikini. His tatty old black jean jacket, which I told him I didn't have but did. And I even unearth the dog-eared journal I filled up writing about our painful demise. Then I stack it all in the bathtub.

I should have done this a long time ago. Dr. Gupta recommends creating signifier icons for past relationships, too, and then burning those up, so I get a piece of paper out and draw two pieces of a broken heart on it, along with a guitar that looks like Mr. Peanut and then, because I don't think the pictograms are really doing it for me, I just write DAVID in big block letters and then SUCKS.

I go down to the backyard and dig out the frozen can of lighter fluid from under the ice-encrusted barbecue and carry it back inside, tossing it from hand to hand as my fingers freeze. In the bathroom I set the can down, ceremoniously draw the shower curtain back, and roll up the squidgy bath mat, the backside of which looks like a potato field. Then I stand over my mound of misery memories and squirt every inch down with lighter fluid.

Now for a match.

You'd think I'd have a match, wouldn't you? Possibly plenty of matches? But I look everywhere and I don't. I have to dig out a sodden matchbook from inside the heap. Fine. I think I can make that symbolic somehow. One of our matches is destroying our memories. I think that works. I take my piece of DAVID SUCKS paper and set it on top of the pile and say, "With this fire I release you," and strike the match.

When I light the match, however, I also accidentally light the entire book of matches. My auto-response is to do a little shriek and kick and throw it at the tub. Hard. I miss the memory heap completely and the flaming matchbook lands on the edge of the tub, where it licks at the canvas shower curtain. I use my foot to try and knock the matches down into the tub, but that just shoves them up against the shower curtain, which now catches on fire.

It's not a big fire, it's small, like if you lit the edge of a piece of paper and watched the flame eat its way up, but the very sight of flame sends me into a prewired panic and I run to the kitchen trying to remember everything my parents ever told me about surviving a fire. The first rule, *Stay calm*, is already out.

The second rule, *Get an adult*, is also out.

The last thing I think of, *Get the fire extinguisher*, sends my brain into an epileptic stutter as I try to remember where I put the fire extinguisher my mother gave me. I remember I said to her, "You're such an alarmist," when she handed me the heavy little red tank and she said, "You won't need it until you need it. Just keep it under the sink."

The sink! I clatter through all the cleaning supplies under the sink, rifle through the sticky cleaning products and dirty plungers and mystery aerosol cans until my hand strikes the extinguisher and rips it out, scattering highly flammable aerosol spray cans across the kitchen floor. I sprint back to the bathroom, where the memory pile is ablaze, and I pull every lever, shake the canister hard, squeeze the handle, and nothing. No water or chemical foam or anything comes out. I just throw the fire extinguisher at the fire and run around the house looking for Mrs. Biggles, who I almost catch, but she darts under the bed.

I find my cell phone and dial 9-1-1, hands shaking, unsure if I should be inside or outside making this call. When the operator asks me what my emergency is, I tell her my bathtub is on fire and with the briefest of pauses she says, "Get out of the house, responders are on the way."

I drop the phone and run barefoot down the stairs and outside into the snow, where it takes me two seconds to realize that my feet are in a great amount of pain and I don't have the cat. I charge back upstairs, hoping my bravery is noted in tomorrow's papers, which will chronicle the tragedy. *She wouldn't leave without Mrs. Biggles. That's just the way she was. Selfless to the end.* "Please!" I yell at Mrs. Biggles, who's still hiding under the bed. My voice is trembling. "Please come out!"

I can see my mother's face now when she hears I died trying to save the cat. It's an expression of grim acceptance as she calls the Scandinavian funeral home and requests an all-you-can-eat ham sandwich buffet.

I decide now is not the time for manners and start chucking shoes under the bed until she scrambles out the other side and I chase her to the kitchen and out the back door. Now I only have moments to live and I must decide what I should save of all my earthly belongings. Do I grab my vinyl records? My plaster replica of Princess Diana's wedding cake? My illustrated medical anomalies book? I'd love to get sentimental, but the choice is ultimately easy. I grab my laptop and my prescription bottle of Lunesta. With these items, a new world can be forged.

In the stairwell I remember I also have *neighbors* downstairs. "There might be trouble!" I say/shout loudly while knocking urgently on their back door. Urgently but not too urgently, because, I don't know, it seems rude. There's no answer, which could mean they're not home or sound asleep, about to be consumed in the fire. That I do not want to read about. I can hear the sirens coming, but I know every second counts. I pick up a brick from the loose edging around the dead flower bed and am just about to hurl it through their window when the loud cherry-lit fire trucks of Minneapolis Station 109 scream into our driveway.

The whole backyard lights up with churning red lights, and firefighters charge toward the house. I think it would be beyond sexy to be married to a firefighter. Imagine him storming out into the night to save women and children from disasters and rescue kitty cats from trees. Then there's a stern-faced fireman staring at me, wearing a big black and yellow helmet and clenching his square jaw with a perfect action-adventure amount of five-o'clock shadow.

I smile sheepishly.

"Are there people in there?" he asks.

I shrug and he kicks the neighbor's door down. I'm serious. He just hauls back and with one stomp beneath the brass doorknob he wrenches the door open, splintering bits of the doorjamb and smacking into the refrigerator.

"Get to the truck," he says with a heady blend of concern, protection, and leadership. Then he storms the apartment.

God, I love firemen.

Which is why I really wish I hadn't started the fire.

After two hours of firemen stomping up and down stairs, and me calling my mother to tell her I had a fire, but I was fine, Lt. Herbach comes back to the truck where I wait with a blanket around me, next to Mrs. Biggles in her cat carrier. I am clutching my sassy working-girl figurine. I don't remember when I grabbed her.

"What were you doing up there?" he asks me, all the concern and protection gone and replaced by a single suspiciously arched eyebrow. "Were you burning something?"

I stare at his stubbly jaw. What do I say? Do I tell him that even though I'm a grown woman I have an irrational attachment to emotionally bankrupt men? That I felt burning a jean jacket might alleviate the crushing sense of loneliness and pain in my heart? He's not going to understand that, he's a guy—and what's worse, he's a guy that saves lives for a living. How do you say you think your dharma is out of alignment to someone holding an axe?

You don't.

You shrug and look at your feet, which is what I did.

"Jennifer!" my mother shouts as she rounds the corner in her pink snowflake pajamas and full-length maroon down feather coat. My father trundles along behind her and behind him is Hailey. Good Christ.

"I'm all right," I say, which will do absolutely nothing.

"What happened?" she asks, holding a hand to her forehead. "Were you attacked? Was there a peeper? On the news they said there was a winter peeper, and they usually only peep in summer."

"No, Mom, a fire. See?" I point to the red engine in the driveway. "Fire truck. The peeper truck is mirrored."

"Don't start," she says.

The lieutenant tells my mother they don't know what started the fire, but whatever it was, it was in the bathtub. "The bathtub?" my mother says. "What on earth were you doing in the bathtub?"

"Leave her alone, Mom," Hailey says. "All that matters is she's all right." She looks at me. "Are you all right?"

I nod and feel like throwing my arms around her neck. Sometimes I hate hating my sister, which makes me realize I don't really hate her at all. I just can't stand her sometimes.

Finally the last fireman empties out of the house and walks up to the lieutenant and hands him a plastic doohickey. "Okay"—the lieutenant nods—"we have a positive identification for arson. Suspicion of arson."

"Arson?" my mother says, releasing her coat and taking an aggressive step toward the lieutenant.

"Well, how can you tell that?" my father says, peering at the doohickey.

"This tested positive for lighter fluid," the lieutenant says.

My father grumbles something.

"Who would set the house on fire?" my mother says protectively. "You don't think my daughter would set a house on fire, do you?"

"Unless Miss Johnson has something else to say," he says, showing me the plastic doohickey, as though I knew what it was and could read it as conclusive evidence of my treachery, "we're going to have to call the police."

My mother clutches her coat closed. "The police? Well, you go right ahead, mister. I know my rights. You can't walk in here with your big hoses and point fingers."

"Arlene . . ." my dad says, "please."

"Attempted arson," the lieutenant says and lets the word hang there as though the thought of being convicted of arson would make me feel worse than I already do.

Wrong.

"Were you getting high?" my mother asks me. "Did you do some crack things?"

My father tells her to settle down.

"Oh, she could be in a cult, for all we know!" she says. "One of those ones where they take you to the airport and make you scam the Internet and weave straw baskets!" She bursts into tears. My poor mom. That's it. Game over. When Mom cries, it's time to surrender anything and everything.

"I was burning things," I say. "Things I didn't want anymore."

"Uh-huh," the lieutenant says. "Things?"

"Mementos."

All the firemen stop and listen.

"What's a memento?" the lieutenant asks, and the guy who handed him the plastic doohickey says, "It's like a keep-sake."

Someone else says, "What you put in a scrapbook. Jerry's

wife does scrapbooking. Right, Jerry? Scrapbooking's for mementos, right?"

"And keepsakes," Jerry shouts back.

"It was just stuff my boyfriend gave me. I mean, my ex-boyfriend."

"The *musician*?" my mother says and smacks her forehead. "Him again!"

"Arlene," my dad warns.

"I just wanted to burn it all," I say. "Get rid of it. I thought the tub would be safest. I soaked everything in lighter fluid from the grill. I'm sorry. I'm so sorry."

"I don't understand," my mother says forlornly to my father. "She was such a good baby. A champion ice skater! And she wrote that Mother's Day poem that won the school award. What happened? What did I do wrong?"

"It's okay," Hailey says and sits down. "I would have burnt all that stuff, too. That guy was a jerk."

"Why didn't you just use your grill?" the plastic doohickey guy says. "You can burn anything on a grill."

"If it's far enough away from the house," the lieutenant adds.

"Well, yeah," the doohickey guy says. "I'm just telling her she could use the grill to burn keepsakes if she wanted. Better than the tub."

"Tell her to watch out for glue guns," Jerry says, who's now standing with the group coiling a length of yellow nylon rope. "My wife got that glue gun that got no safety switch. Nearly started the kitchen table on fire."

"When was this?" the lieutenant asks.

Jerry shrugs. "Month ago maybe."

"Well, it would have been nice to know about that," the lieutenant says. "That should have gone in the newsletter."

I put my hands over my face because the tears are coming and there's nothing I can do to stop them. I start to sob. My mother puts her arms around me and kisses me on the head because the crying game goes both ways.

"All right," the lieutenant says, "I guess that's all. We taped up that door downstairs, but you better have your landlord fix it before your neighbors get home."

"Thank you, Officer," my mother says as they load up on the truck. "I'm so sorry. *We're* so sorry about this. She really is a good ice skater."

My family and I go look at my apartment so my mom can make sure there are no peepers, rapists, or ex-boyfriends lying in wait. We stare silently at my charred bathtub and the burned shreds of shower curtain dangling like smoking cobwebs from the curtain rod. My mother goes to the kitchen and reappears with a can of Comet and a green scrubbie sponge.

"All righty, then," she says, "let's get to work."

I sit in a shame stupor on my bed as they all clean the house. Hailey doesn't even get mad when she discovers her old Barbie head on my bookshelf, the one she used to style when she was little until I dyed the hair blue with food coloring and gave it a Mohawk. I just keep saying how sorry I am and how they don't have to help. When I do try to help my mother just tells me to lie down. "Everybody needs to just lie down sometimes," she says.

They work until the ashes and crisp bits of burned shower curtain are gone, and in the end, everything almost looks normal again, but it still smells like smoke. My mother wants me to come home and sleep at the house. "I'll be all right," I tell her and she finally concedes, shaking her head, weary from the world, trying to understand the complicated nature of things.

"First the pickle dish," she says, "and now this."

In the morning I get up super early so I can start my life of utter solitude.

Alone, naturally.

I still smell like smoke. Everything I own still smells like smoke. I do a big load of laundry in the basement. I even run it through twice, but no amount of detergent can wash the smell away. The worst part is it would be cheaper to buy all new clothes than to dry-clean them. I asked my dad if I should call the insurance company, since it was him who made me get renter's insurance, but he said, "Sweetie, renter's insurance is for accidents. Not arson."

So much for renter's insurance. If they won't cover the occasional personal meltdown or anger fire, what's the point in having it?

I drive to work an hour late. I don't even care if I get yelled at. What could be worse than what I just went through? I'm waiting for the elevator, imagining my clothes are smoking and my hair is singed to a crisp when my cell phone rings. It's Hailey.

"Thanks for last night," I say, "for being so nice."

"So, are you going to pay for your replacement dress?" she asks.

"What?"

"Your replacement dress," she says. "We have to pay double because now it's a rush order."

"Can't . . . can't I just wear a dress that's the same color?"

"You can't just try to match the color, Jen. All the dresses are supposed to be identical." She's talking to me like I'm retarded and sounds out each consonant, like "*eye-dent-i-cal.*"

"You wouldn't have to pay for a new dress if you hadn't 'slipped' under the sink," she says. "And I don't think I like you trying to ruin my big day."

"Don't worry," I sigh, "there'll be others."

She hangs up on me. I can't believe her. One minute she's nice to me and the next she's a psychobitch. Why? I punch the elevator button again and consider using the emergency fire stairwell, but before I can decide, Hailey calls back and the elevator doors open. She starts screaming at me about the cost of replacing my dress and accusing me of doing it on purpose.

"No, I didn't," I shout, "that's completely untrue." I step on the elevator. "Well, *I* remember the time you vomited on my sundress at the Valley Fair. Are you telling me you didn't do that on purpose? I know for a fact you did it on purpose. I saw you deliberately eat relish right out of the plastic hot dog condiment thing. Then you turned around and barfed on me and then you cried so Dad would pick you up and put you on his shoulders while I had to walk all day covered in your hot dog vomit. So don't tell me I am the only one that ruins everything, Hailey, because as far as ruining things go, you pretty much took the big ruining cake when they brought you home from the unwanted Swedish baby shelter, all right? Hailey?"

She's gone. The line's dead.

I'm so mad right now I think I'm going to blow an artery. Then someone clears his throat behind me. I whip around and there is Brad Keller.

"Yeah, there's really no way for me to pretend I didn't hear that," he says.

My face gets hot. "I didn't know anyone was . . . was here."

He smiles. "It's cool. Sometimes I hate my sister too. Once she shaved my eyebrows off."

"Oh! I don't hate my sister . . ." I stammer. "I just . . ."

He shakes his head. "Took three months to grow back. Totally bald face. The kids called me testicle head. She still thinks it's the funniest story she's ever heard."

He snickers and I feel this light, free-flowing breeze around me, like someone just opened a window to Tahiti.

The doors open and he steps off.

"Coming?" he asks and I follow him.

We're standing on the fourth floor in the home furnishings department, surrounded by living room displays and mahogany dining room tables. It's relatively empty up here. I immediately imagine these aren't just displays in a department store, they're real rooms. Our rooms. Brad and I are having martinis on the leather Millstone three-piece couch set, and then I'm serving him dinner at the Brownville high-gloss black dining room table, which is perfectly set with white Wedgwood china and sterling silver candlesticks with tall tapered white candles. Then, after proposing to me, Brad knocks the candlesticks off the table and takes me right there on it.

"I hope this isn't weird or whatever," he says, looking a little nervous, "but do you want to get a drink sometime or something?"

I make a face. I don't think I heard right. "What?"

He smiles. I think maybe he's talking about finding a water fountain, and I'm about to direct him to the customer service comfort station when he says, "You know, like a date?"

"A date?" I repeat. A lone saleswoman wheels around the corner carrying an armload of upholstery samples and stops dead in her tracks when she sees us.

"Sure," I say.

"Great. How about this Friday?"

I blink.

"Is that a yes?" he asks. "You've got this sort of . . . unique way of communicating."

The sample woman has her eyebrow arched so high it threatens to join her hairline. "Sure," I say, keeping an eye on her, "you bet."

"Okay, so Friday then," he says, backing away slowly. "You're not going to cancel or not show up or something, are you?"

I shake my head no.

"Okay, good, and you'll get whatever anger management help you need by then."

I smile.

"Good," he says, "good. We need that, because I didn't want to have to call ahead and have them clear out any sign of hot dog relish." I cover my face with one hand. He's practically standing right next to the sample woman when he says, "All right then, see you Friday!"

"All right then," I say to his retreating back. The sample lady looks at me and then back at Brad and then back at me. I quickly retreat to the stairwell, where I can panic in private. I try to call Christopher, but he doesn't pick up. I leave a message.

"Something amazing just happened," I tell him, "and I need you to confirm I am not asleep and this is not a dream."

I dash over to the Skyway. I want to shudder and tingle in the presence of my lovely fellow humans. *Hello, thick-ankled secretary! You're beautiful! Hello, fat man! Aren't you jolly!* I walk right past Cinnabon and the counter girl says, "Where do you think you're going?"

"Not today!" I sing out.

"You'll be back," she says grimly.

I stop into Frontier Travel and pick up a bunch of travel brochures and promotional magazines. I have no idea why. "Planning a trip?" Susan asks.

"Possibly!" I say. "You never know!"

"Ever thought of writing for one of those magazines?" she

asks. "I know one of the editors in New York. They pay for your expenses and everything."

"I would love to do that!" I grin. "I'm not going to be a copy-writer forever!"

I practically skip back to the office, where I promise myself I will not visualize what it would be like to be married to Brad Keller.

I will not.

Maybe a little.

hunt him

There's a lot to fix. I need new hair, new clothes, a new face, a new me. Parts of me are sagging, not shining, or need to be cut off, not necessarily in that order. Completely making yourself over is a time-consuming and costly endeavor, plus most of my credit cards are maxed out, but it helps that I work in a department store. "Have no fear," Christopher says, "a little gay bee is here!"

He takes me down to the visual display department where he works. Normally all nonessential employees are strictly forbidden for insurance reasons. They have hammers and tools and glue guns down there, all manner of loose signage, bolts of fabric, chipped disco balls, glass chandeliers, disembodied mannequins, and sheets of colored Lucite stacked everywhere. "It smells like the inside of one of those chemical barrels," I tell him. "One of those ones kids in Guatemala sniff."

"I know!" Christopher says, taking a deep whiff. "Isn't it wonderful? Now come here. This is for you." He leads me around to his work area, where several heaps of clothing are thrown over the back of a chair, and on his desk is a neat swatch of green velvet displaying several sparkly pieces of jewelry.

"Everything was just taken down from the windows," he says, picking up a red wraparound dress. "It all has to be restocked, but not until Monday! You can wear anything you want for your date."

"The shoes, too?"

He nods. "The shoes, too."

Then he rolls out two matching hard-backed suitcases they use for shipping product and helps me pack everything in them. We work quickly, because if anyone saw us, we'd both be instantly fired.

Its amazing how one small event, like the man of your dreams asking you out, can change your whole outlook on life. Everything seems happy and possible. Colors look brighter. Food tastes better. Gravity seems to be turned on lighter, so walking is easier and keeping my chin up seems more natural. Even Ted sees the change.

"What's wrong with you?" he asks.

"Nothing! Can't a girl be happy?"

"I don't like it," he says, crossing his arms. "I don't like it one bit."

I hum at my desk, I ignore my incoming Exploding Hearts e-mail, I even water Big Trish's fern, and when she snaps at me that it's *her* fern, not *mine*, and she knows *perfectly well* when to water it, some of the leaves are *supposed* to be brown, I take the time to use the interpersonal conflict-resolution skills we learned in last month's employee seminar about building a better co-worker habitat and I say, "You know, Trish, I didn't even consider your perspective on this. I see where you're coming from and in the future I'll be sure to consult you before moving ahead on any plant-watering activities."

She scowls at me but I don't care. I'm on cloud twenty-two.

Christopher buys me a shiatsu massage for Thursday night after work so my head will "be in the right place" for my date on Friday. We dash down a freezing five blocks to the Medical Arts building and go up to the seventeenth floor.

"I didn't realize they had a massage parlor in the Medical Arts building," I say.

He nods. "They also have an anal bleaching office."

"A what?"

"We're here!" he says and opens the massage parlor door. "Paradise awaits you."

The whole interior has been outfitted to look like a miniature Chinese temple, with faux-stone walls and a small marble fountain. Even the dropped ceiling panels have been painted a rich red. There is delicate string music playing and a tiny Asian woman behind the desk is wearing what else but a lovely silk kimono. She looks perfect in it, like an Asian confection with little egg noodle arms.

"I don't feel better yet," I say.

The lady has us fill out medical-consent forms and sit in the tiny lobby until someone else comes and takes us back to the locker rooms, which have wooden lockers and bamboo benches. I take off my clothes and put on the robe. I meet up with Christopher back in the hall and the lady takes us to a cedar-lined sauna and it's hot as an oven inside.

"Ten minute," the lady says and disappears.

"Now just relax," Christopher says. "Breathe deep. Do you smell eucalyptus?"

I inhale and exhale slowly. "Do you think I should tell Brad I'm on antidepressants?"

"No," he says.

"But everyone's on antidepressants. They're like aspirins."

"Stigma."

"What?"

"Nothing. Just don't give him the third degree," he says. "Men hate that."

"Doesn't it show him I'm interested in him to ask questions?"

"No," he says, "and don't talk about your family."

"We bonded over hating our sisters."

"This is supposed to be sexy time, not family story hour, and don't talk about sex. Straight guys think girls are slutty if they talk about sex."

"Well, why don't I just not talk at all?" I say. "I'll just be mute. I shall be Mutey McMuterson from Mutington Downs."

"You can talk about needing space," he says. "All guys want to hear that you need space, that you're really independent, that you're not going to bug them every night, that you have your own money and your own friends and that you're not going to cling to them like a barnacle. Men want to know you're not going to be any inconvenience whatsoever, that you won't interrupt their guy's night out or their sports games or their sudden disappearances. They want a lot of space, like an astronaut who only comes in to dock his penis from time to time."

"Nice visual."

"Whatever you do," he says, "*don't* talk about marriage. If you remember only one thing, remember that. DO NOT talk about marriage, getting married, wedding dresses, cakes, anything. Don't even mention your sister's wedding."

"Don't worry," I say.

The Asian lady returns and leads us to a dim room with large palms and six low beds. There is a metal pipe above each bed, and at first I think it's a sprinkler system. She tells us to lie down in beds next to each other. I lie down on my bed and Christopher lies down on his. Two new ladies wearing white shirts and white pants silently come in and start poking us. It's quite unpleasant. This goes on for a while.

I shut my eyes and try to block the poking out. I try to distract myself by reviewing the signs when a guy is NOT into you. If he stays physically far away from you, like more than three feet, odds are he doesn't want to be "close" to you. Second, if a guy focuses anywhere but your eyes, he's deliberately distancing himself from you. Third, if he stands at an oblique angle, that's bad. I don't know what oblique is, but I'm sure I'll recognize it when I see it. Last is speech pattern. If a guy talks to you like you're at the office, then he probably wants to keep the relationship "professional." Also, if a guy likes you, he'll copy your body language. Like, if you lean in, he'll lean in. If you use your hands to emphasize something, so will he. Monkey-see, monkey-do = he's into you.

Crap! I remember I haven't waxed my nether region. Unshaved for weeks. This puts me in a mild panic. I don't want him putting his hand up my skirt and getting it caught in a pussy Afro. Ouch! This "massage" is taking forever. The woman who's been poking me jumps up on the bed and grabs the pole overhead. She then steps on my shoulder blade and presses down until I think my lung is going to pop.

"I just don't want to embarrass myself," I say to Christopher between breaths, which is considerable, because the woman is now crunching her way up and down my spine. "I figure my date with Brad has a one in two chance of landing me in a mental asylum. I can't take one more humiliating scene. I really can't."

"I don't know how you do it," he sighs. "It's like one nightmare after another."

"Thanks."

The lady starts massaging my arm with the ball of her foot. It sort of feels good, except it's painful.

"Sorry," Christopher says. "I just don't get how you keep putting yourself out there."

"There just aren't any good ones," I say.

"I found a good one," Christopher sighs. "Jeremy the pill. Love that boy."

"Well, what do you mean?" I ask, feeling suddenly and acutely irritated.

"Nothing," he says, "I don't know, I just mean. I think there are still good guys out there. You just have to look."

I'm silent for a minute as the lady switches to my other arm. She kneads my flesh with her feet and stands full body weight on my open palm.

"So, good guys are everywhere," I say. "I just lack the skills to find them?"

"I didn't mean that."

"Well, that's what it sounded like."

"Well, that's not what I meant."

"What did you mean?"

"Just that, I don't know, just that maybe you should be more patient or something."

"Are you serious?"

He doesn't say anything. We lie in silence for the rest of the massage, which is about as relaxing as an emergency root canal.

I shower in the locker room and put my clothes on. I'm already aching all over. In the Chinese-temple lobby Christopher pays and asks me if I want to get a drink. I say no thanks. He sighs. "Are you being pissy?" he asks.

"I don't know, are you acting all high and mighty because you've already found the love of your life and you look down on the poor slobs who haven't?"

"I'm going," he says. "I hate it when you're like this."

"Well, I hated that massage!" I tell him. "What was that? I think she dislocated my shoulder!" I am enraged. Just furious.

"I'll tell you why you're alone," he says, pointing a finger in my face. "Because sooner or later, you attack everyone. You're paranoid and insecure and you pick and you analyze everyone and everything until everything is picked and analyzed to death. You get so insecure, so sure someone is going to leave you, you attack them until they finally go. Well, good job, Jen. Here's one more person in your life that's sick of you."

Then he storms out of the office and it feels like I just ended another relationship, but this one feels like the worst ending ever. The worst part of the whole day is I never found out what anal bleaching is.

On my desk Friday morning is a lemon poppy-seed muffin and a note. It's from Christopher and it says, "Let's not break up, okay?"

I call him on his cell phone.

He apologizes.

I apologize.

He says he won't go to David's wedding.

I tell him, don't be ridiculous, go.

He's sorry we fought, I'm sorry we fought.

He says it was his fault, I say it was mine.

He tells me I'm the pretty one and I tell him no, he's the pretty one.

I tell him I wish I were a gay man.

He says it's his greatest sorrow in life that I'm not.

I laugh. He laughs.

We're back.

Friday I leave work early to get ready for my date with Brad. I tell Ashley I have an emergency dental appointment. Another one. She makes a face at me. I feel the white pinpoint pulsing of a headache behind my right eye. "You're pale," she says. "Do you have another cold? Don't tell me you have another cold."

I tell her I'm fine.

"Except for your tooth," she says, tilting her head. "The one that needs another emergency dental visit?"

"Right," I say, "except for that."

I rush over to Christopher and Jeremy's house. They're helping me get ready. One must always incorporate the gay bees for major functions. It's stupid not to. Christopher has talked Jeremy into doing my hair, which is a big deal. He's like a celebrity hair stylist, which in Minnesota means the mayor's wife, the TV weatherman, and Garrison Keillor, I guess. Anyway, he's never done my hair before.

It's a big production when I get to their immaculate apartment. Christopher has chilled champagne and chocolate-dipped strawberries waiting for me, which immediately reminds me of Ashley's perfect proposal. Music is blaring. These guys are trying so hard to make me feel good, it actually makes me feel good. Jeremy ushers me into the bathroom, where I sit backward on a kitchen barstool staring at my face in the mirror.

He goes to work.

"This color is direct from Paris," he says, glooping some brown paste on my head. "You can't get it in America." He parts my hair in careful sections and massages the dye into my hair. It smells like lilacs. Only the French could make hair color smell so good.

Christopher and I try to keep my panic at a minimum by sipping champagne and rehearsing all the first date do's and don't's, which include, but are not limited to:

- Let him open doors for you.
- Turn your cell phone off.
- Be yourself, but not too much.
- Be honest.

- Be engaging.
- Compliment him on his clothes.
- Don't order anything too expensive.
- Don't talk about your ex-boyfriend.
- Don't talk about money problems.
- Don't come on too strong.
- Don't eat too much.
- Don't eat like a bird.
- Don't drink too much.
- Don't not drink.
- Don't ask him too many questions.
- Don't look at other guys.
- Ignore it if he looks at other girls.
- Be confident.
- Be funny.
- Don't talk about sex.
- Don't talk about religion.
- Don't talk about politics.
- Don't challenge him on his views.
- Be interested, even if you aren't.
- Listen attentively.
- Don't complain about anything.
- Say you like the food, no matter how you feel about the food.
- Use positive body language.
- Touch your hair if you want to sleep with him.
- Keep your feet facing him.
- Mimic his body language.
- Watch to see if he's mimicking your body language.
- Make eye contact.
- Don't yell at him if he looks at other girls.
- No matter what, act happy.

- Flirt.
- Say thank you.
- Think like a winner.
- Don't ask him for a second date, let him ask you.
- Don't call him on the way home.
- Don't call him the next day.
- Don't call him, period.
- Wait for him to call you, no matter how long it takes.
- If he doesn't call you, he's just not into you.
- If he waits too long to call you, he's just not into you.
- If he calls you right away after a date he's possibly a stalker.
- If you call him right away, you're possibly a stalker.

We stop when Jeremy says the color has cooked long enough, and they both get out of the bathroom so I can step into their slate-tiled shower and wash my hair. I use their Paul Mitchell products and really try to enjoy the moment, even though I can feel panic creeping up on me like a shadow.

I wrap myself in a thick white towel, and catch my reflection in the mirror. "Jeremy? Is it supposed to be . . . this red?"

The boys come in and the looks on their faces defy description. Horror is involved, but also curiosity and wonder.

"Don't worry," Jeremy says, "it always looks totally different when it's dry." I nod, but I can't help but notice he isn't smiling anymore. He grabs his hair dryer and sets out methodically drying my hair with long, hard strokes of a natural bristle brush. It's partly the noise of the hair dryer and partly the mounting expectation that keeps us all silent as he works.

I watch my hair get dryer and dryer.

And redder and redder.

Jeremy finally turns the hair dryer off and steps away.

My head looks like a maraschino cherry. A bright chemical-red cherry.

The silence of the hair dryer sends for Christopher, who bursts into the bathroom smiling and then claps his hands to the top of his head.

"Oh my God!" he shrieks at Jeremy. "What have you done to her?"

Jeremy is silent. He mumbles something about the product and maybe it was older than he thought, but still, he's never seen anything like *this* before.

"She's hideous!" Christopher cries. "You bastard!"

Christopher goes on telling Jeremy I ruined the best chance I ever had at happiness and he's personally responsible for chasing away the most eligible bachelor I ever managed to land and he's going to leave him for sure now, because Jeremy is always doing horrible, thoughtless things like this and ruining everything.

I just stare at the mirror.

I mechanically pack up my makeup kits and my cosmetic bags. I think I thank them, but I can't be sure. I don't remember the ride home or letting myself into my apartment. I'm on autopilot, it's all done in some sort of emotionally protective blackout.

I do, for some reason, call Hailey.

She wanted to be an aesthetician one summer and took classes at the Aveda Institute, which went pretty well until she realized she'd have to touch strangers.

"Go get Prell," she says.

"I don't have time to get anything."

"Then use dishwashing soap. Wash your hair as many times as you can with the cheapest dishwashing soap you have. Don't dry it in between, just wash it over and over. Use the hottest water you can stand."

I take a deep slug of whiskey from a rarely used bottle above the refrigerator and grab an old bottle of Joy from under the kitchen sink.

Joy. How ironic.

I get in the shower and scrub my hair within an inch of ripping it out. I wash it over and over again, watching ribbons of vile red dye stream out in the water and swirl down the drain. All the while my cell phone is ringing like crazy, undoubtedly Christopher trying to tell me he's breaking up with Jeremy for ruining my hair.

I manage to shampoo my hair twelve times, and I nearly sear my scalp holding the blow-dryer so close to my roots as I'm drying it. When I'm done, I'm breathless, panting, squinting because I half don't even want to look in the mirror, but as I shake my hair out and comb it back, I'm surprised. The dishwashing soap must be able to take the paint off cars. It's not a hundred percent back to normal, but I no longer look like I work at the circus. So what if it'll be dry as a haystack tomorrow? I'm trying to look on the bright side, and I will, as soon as I find it.

My cell phone continues to ring like a four-alarm fire, but I know it's just Christopher calling to check in/apologize/worry/scream/console. I do my makeup lickety-split, all the while keeping one eye on the clock. *Hurry hurry hurry.* Then before I go I have to eat something because I'm *not* eating in front of Brad, so I decide to slam a Hot Pocket while standing up eating over the sink. It's not only not sexy, it's a mistake.

A big mistake.

As my stomach seizes and cramps, it becomes immediately clear the Hot Pocket is not going to be staying with me long. I sit on the toilet and pray for relief. I eat two Tums and two Imodium ADs—I don't know what the AD stands for.

Another Dimension? After Dinner? Absolute Disaster?

I don't know, but I stay on the toilet for a full five minutes, praying the entire time.

Please, God. I know we don't talk often, or ever, but I need to not have diarrhea right now. If you do exist and you are in fact master of the universe, it wouldn't take you any energy at all to seize up my bowels and make this stop, would it? Is it really asking too much to ask you to let me feel good for my date? This is an important date, God. After all, the way I've heard them tell it, you're a big fan of marriage and monogamy and families. Well, I'm trying to freaking work that out, God, so do you think just this once you could suspend my absolutely shit luck and let me stop shitting? Could you? Just once? In return I will stop judging all the women at work and I'll go to church on major holidays. Is that enough?

Apparently it is enough, and Jesus takes pity on my diarrhea or the Tums kicks in, because my stomach slowly starts to ease up. I try to think of Christopher's pep talk and hold that in my mind. I get my purse, my coat, and my car keys and I check myself one last time in the mirror. "Okay, Miss Sassy," I say to the porcelain figurine in my window, "this is it. Don't screw this up."

Against all odds, I get to O'Hooligans a full ten minutes early. Unbelievable. Crossing the parking lot I brace myself against the wind and feel my eyes tearing up against the cold air. Shit. My coat isn't really warm enough, it's my long black dress coat and it looks way better than my poofy down jacket, but it feels like it's made out of felt right now. I can feel the wind cut through it and I break into a jog.

Inside the warmth almost hurts. My cheeks burn and my nose runs as my body tries to readjust to the rapidly changing climate. I sneeze. Sometimes it's easier to stay in pain.

I situate myself at the bar and order a cosmo. I'm trying to take the edge off my nervousness by smiling so hard it hurts. I get friendly with the bartender, who's busy making drinks.

"I'm waiting for a guy," I say over his blender. "It's our first date."

He smiles.

Whrrrrrrrrrrrrrrrrrrrrrrrrrrrrrrrrrrrrrrrrrrrrrrrrrr goes the blender.

He glops out a foaming concoction into a shamrock-shaped mug.

I look around for Brad and check the time on my cell phone. I realize I never even asked him for his cell phone number, and more important, he never asked for mine. What does that mean? Is that bad? That seems kind of bad.

A group of hearty midwestern girls shows up at the bar, each of them flawed in some major way that makes me feel a little more secure. One is chunky around the butt, and another has a tattoo on her ankle of a blurry lavender butterfly, and it shows right through her sheer tights. There's a girl with a horse laugh who has a wide, droopy nose that seems like a kindergartner could have made it out of Play-Doh and pressed it over her real nose. Not to be braggy, but I feel the littlest bit superior, because I'm sure I look better than all these girls, which makes me feel friendly toward them.

"Girls' night out?" I ask.

"Double-date night!" one girl shrills. Then I see a group of men coming in from the cigar bar and they descend upon the girls with a shout, and every man seeks out his individual partner. That's when I realize they're all *married*. Every one of them, even Play-Doh nose. They're all wearing these deliberate, smug wedding bands. "Time for dinner!" the girl says. "Bye!"

"Bye-bye!" I say with forced gaiety. "Have fun!"

Brad is now ten minutes late. Ten minutes. Ten minutes isn't that bad. If I say, "Brad was ten minutes late last night," that doesn't sound bad. Nobody would feel sorry for me over that; even fifteen minutes and possibly twenty minutes are within the realm of okay. Anything could hold a person up for twenty minutes. Traffic, an unexpected phone call, a work situation, even just losing track of time. You could lose track of twenty minutes and not be a bad guy.

It's *twenty-five* minutes that's the real problem. Twenty-five minutes late is not okay. If I say, "Brad was twenty-five minutes late last night," people would definitely be concerned. They would definitely have questions. Brad would have to have a really good excuse to get out of that one, like his toilet exploded or his cat threw up. And at thirty minutes late—I don't even want to think about thirty minutes. I really can't handle that idea right now.

I sip my cosmo, which is fruity and icy and delicious. It hardly tastes like liquor so I order another one. Two drinks before Brad gets here should probably be my limit. Maybe three? No, two. After three drinks, things can get fuzzy, and I don't want to be fuzzy tonight. I want to be here and alive and having fun, like all these other Goddamned people.

Crap.

I look around. Nobody is really watching me or anything, but I act as though they might be. I mean, if I was here on a date and I saw a woman alone at the bar I might say, "Look at that poor woman over there. She's obviously waiting for someone. Let's see if he shows up." Then I would study her like Dian Fossey does in *Gorillas in the Mist*. What is her facial expression? How is she holding her posture? Does she seem agitated? Is she looking over her shoulder a lot, and possibly at the entrance? Is she trying to attract a potential mate? Where is this potential mate?

Is he fictional or just late? I decide I'm not looking over my shoulder anymore. I'm only looking at the bartender, the television, or my drink. I'd rather look like a skanky barfly drinking alone than a woman being stood up.

Now Brad is twenty-five minutes late.

I stare at my cell phone. I really want to call Christopher, but I know what he'll say. He'll tell me to leave and I don't want to leave. As soon as I leave, the potential fairy tale is over. This dream bubble has burst. As long as I'm sitting here, pretending to be oblivious to the time, then everything could possibly work out, right? Plus, if I call someone and whine about my stupid date, I just know Brad will turn up and hear me. *That's what I'll do!* I'll make a fake phone call and it'll be like when you get up to go to the bathroom so the food comes.

I flip my cell open. "Hello?" I say to no one. "Oh, hi!" I pause to let my imaginary friend talk. "Absolutely," I say, "that isn't a problem at all. I was glad to do it."

I smile at a guy who comes up to the bar next to me. He orders a drink.

"Really?" I say into the phone. "I'm flattered—that isn't necessary though. Like I said, I was happy to help." I look back over at the door. I don't know how long I can keep up an imaginary conversation.

Then, as I'm holding my cell to my ear, presumably already on a call, it rings loudly. I almost drop the phone on the floor.

"Hello?"

"Hello, Miss Johnson," Mr. Jennings says. "We need to discuss your account. Wondering when we can expect that payment."

"I can't really talk now," I say. I hate it when he gets through to me. Every time he calls me I store his number and save it as DO NOT ANSWER. I have seven DO NOT ANSWERS in my phone but he's got all these new numbers now. It's like a game and he gets a point every time I pick up. I get a point every time my phone rings and it flashes DO NOT ANSWER.

"We really need to resolve this," he says. "We're going to turn your account over to a collection agency if we don't get a payment from you."

"The thing is, if I had any extra money, I would give it to you. Really. Right now is a bad time."

"We can set up a payment plan."

I glance at the old-timey clock behind the bar that has four-leaf clovers instead of numbers on it. Brad is forty minutes late.

"Can I ask you something, Mr. Jennings?"

"We have many payment options," he says.

"Why do guys stand you up? I mean, in general, why does a guy say he's going to be somewhere and then leave you waiting around in a bar? Why did he even ask me out in the first place?"

"I'm sorry," he says, "we're going to have to settle this . . ."

"No, I mean just as a friend," I say. "What should I do?"

He doesn't say anything. The noise and laughter of the bar close around me.

"Do you have a daughter?" I ask.

"No," he says after a pause, "but I have a younger sister."

"Well, if a guy stood your little sister up, left her alone in a public place, what would you do?"

"I'd bash his face in."

I'm impressed. I may even pay the bill.

"Look," he says, "I can give you two weeks. That's it. Then it's out of my hands. I've been delaying the collection agency as it is."

"Mr. Jennings," I say, smiling, "you have unsuspected depth."

"I'll call you in two weeks," he says and then adds, "but be careful out there."

He hangs up.

I can't believe it. My debt collector turns out to be a nicer guy than my date.

The bartender sets down an enormous ceramic elf in front of me. Seriously, it's the size of one of those garden gnomes, only this one is filled with liquor.

"You sip from the straw in his hat," the bartender says. "There's over twelve different liquors in there, and it's on the house."

I try to tell him I don't want to drink from a lawn decoration, but he sails down to the other end of the bar. I stare at the elf and the elf stares at me. He has a pointy green hat and a big knobby nose. I wait awhile, look around, and finally take a long sip of the fizzy orange liquid. It's not bad. Like a Dreamsicle and rum. I take another sip.

I'm alone at a bar with a pity elf.

I decide I'll wait here until the bar closes. It's simple math. The pain of having Brad stand me up is far greater than the humiliation of having him be late, even five hours late. I'd much rather have him be late than not show at all. I can't even mathematically quantify how much more I want one more than the other.

I suck ferociously on my elf, but I don't know if there's enough liquor in this world to get me through this. I break down and call Christopher. No answer.

Brad is fifty-five minutes late.

Right now I don't care if he ever comes. The hearty midwestern girls reappear. They're going outside for a smoke.

"You're still here?" one asks. "You want to come join us?"

I tell them no thank you, and point to my elf and say I'm not really alone. They all laugh and I just want to die. I wonder if it's quicker to kill myself by ramming the elf hat repeatedly into my eye or electrocuting myself with the margarita blender.

Then I hear Brad's voice. "Why are you French kissing a leprechaun?"

He looks confused. "How long have you been here?"

I shrug.

"Didn't we say nine?" he asks. "I changed it and . . . my secretary was supposed to tell you.

I shrug. All I'm thinking is *Thank God I didn't leave*.

"So why were you making out with this leprechaun?" he asks again.

"It's an *elf*."

"That's a leprechaun. He's holding a shillelagh."

"It's an elf."

"Well, whatever you were doing to him," Brad says, "it looked like it belonged on some kind of porn blooper reel."

"Then that's what we'll call him—Blooper the Elf." Brad laughs and I feel fantastic and sick all at the same time.

"Are you okay?" he asks.

"No, this is nerve-wracking. I just want it to be over."

Brad smiles. "You really say the worst things to me."

"It's true."

"Well, I love it," he says and helps me up. He asks me where I want to go.

"For real, for real?" I ask, feeling a little wobbly.

He nods.

"I want to get chilidogs," I say, "really cheap, greasy chilidogs and eat them by the river."

His eyes widen the slightest bit and then he throws his arms up. "Then that's what we're going to do," he says. "Let's go."

We march outside to the valet stand and get inside his car (a dark blue BMW 5 series, not that I noticed), and we drive to Dairy Queen, where we load up on every type of junk food possible—chilidogs, french fries, cheeseburgers, onion rings, caramel sundaes, Chocolate Xtreme Blizzards, and paper sacks packed with other things too disgusting and wonderful to mention.

I show him where you can get on the old defunct railroad tracks and drive across the river. We park directly over the black swirling waters of the Mississippi River, which is my favorite place in the world to be.

"This is disgusting," he says, shoving a big bite of chilidog in his mouth.

"I know. My mother never let us have junk food, so now it's all I ever want."

"Where are the cheese poppers?"

"Blooper ate them." I hook a thumb at the ceramic elf seat-belted into the backseat. We liberated him from the bar.

After we're done shoving about six thousand calories each in our mouths, we sit back, relaxed, and let that I-just-ate-something-terrible-for-me malaise sweep over us. It's like a coma, but you can still talk.

"Tell me something about yourself no one else knows," Brad says.

I think for a second. I want to tell him something true.

"I wanted to be an old black man when I was in high school," I say, "a blues singer like Muddy Waters. A Delta blues musician."

Brad looks concerned.

I keep going. I don't know why, I've never told anyone else. Not even Christopher. "I wanted to be seventy and wear long-sleeve plaid shirts with suspenders and porkpie hats. I even had a name picked out for myself."

"What was it?"

"Catfish Johnson."

There's a moment of horrible silence in which I feel he must be calculating the immense geekiness of my very sad personage . . . and then he bursts out laughing. A giant belly laugh. He hammers the dashboard and holds his stomach.

This goes on for some time.

"Catfish Johnson?" he says, tears in his eyes. "You're the whitest woman on the face of the earth."

"But I have soul. Even a white woman can have soul."

He wipes the tears away and nods.

"Well, white woman," he says. "Wanna dance?"

I do. I really do want to dance.

We walk to Nye's Polonaise Room across the river and I carry Blooper.

"Why not leave him in the car?" Brad asks.

"I can't believe you'd even ask me that. What if someone stole him?"

"We stole him."

"Not the point," I say and charge onward.

Inside the hot and sweaty bar the band is in full swing. The place is packed to capacity with every type of cold-weather citizen. Old men, art students, housewives, republicans, Union members, steelworkers, Goth kids, retro-junkies all drinking and dancing side by side.

We set Blooper on the bar and order Leinenkugels. Then the band starts playing a fast accordion version of "Funkytown." Brad says he's sorry, but he has to dance. I can tell I've definitely had too much to drink, because I agree to dance, too. I don't care. He's insanely funny, a really crazy dancer with leaps and jumps and weird jerking. I think he's trying to be weird on purpose, which is adorable. For sure no one's looking at my crappy dancing when he's on the floor. I dance so hard I take off my shoes and dance in my stockings. Brad grabs me by the waist and twirls me around, crashing me into the bathroom door. It's the best night of my life.

Brad grabs Blooper and starts to dance with him, which makes everyone laugh. He does this tango thing, and then the people make a circle and Brad pretends to moonwalk while he spins Blooper on the floor.

"Surf him!" someone shouts, "surf him!" and up goes a cheer as Blooper is passed overhead from hand to hand across the bar. He goes full circle around the room, some women stopping to kiss him or take a picture with him, and he comes back to us relatively unharmed.

"He's back!" Brad says. "You filthy elf!"

"You better ground him for staying out so late," I say.

"I had a stern talk with him," Brad says, "and he's gay."

"He's what?"

"He's gay. Our elf is gay."

"Aren't they supposed to be gay?"

Brad smacks himself on the forehead and kisses Blooper on the mouth. We dance for four or five songs more and then I tell him I'm hot. I'm beyond hot. I'm roasting.

Outside the cold air feels fantastic. I don't even put my coat on. I'm so hot I just want to come out here and steam in the chilly night air. I lean up against the building and put the hot palm of my hand on the cold bricks. Even though I feel tipsy and the world seems a little blurry, that cold brick seems more real to me than anything I've ever felt before. It feels solid and sure and safe. There is something so different about this moment. It's like I'm suspended above the scene, floating and looking down on everything. It's because, for the first time I can remember, I'm happy. I'm not watching happy people on TV or in the real world walking past me, I'm actually one of them. I'm a happy person and I really don't know what to do about it.

"There you are!" Brad says, handing me my beer. "You're not cold?"

"I got so hot dancing," I say. "Look, I'm steaming." I hold my hand out for him to see the slight vapor drifting off my skin.

"Come here," he says and puts his hand on the back of my neck. He pulls my face close to his. We kiss. We're the couple kissing outside the bar. That's us. *Oh, Brad? He loves kissing me on the street. I don't know what it is, some Casablanca complex or something but if we're outdoors, I can't keep his hands off me.*

I pull back. "I like you," I say, trying not to slur my words.

He brushes a strand of hair off my face. "I like you, too." He kisses me on the cheek.

"It's not easy to find guys you like," I say, "guys who eat disgusting chilidogs and take good care of your elf."

"I thought guys were a dime a dozen," he says.

"Water, water everywhere," I sigh, "but not a drop to drink."

"Is that right?"

"I don't want any guy. I want the right guy."

"And who is the right guy?"

"Oh, I don't know." I kiss him.

Brad, Blooper, and I head out into the cold night and I'm stalling because I don't know if I should ask Brad back to my house or not. I totally want to; I've been staring at him all night and I'm ready to melt, but Christopher wouldn't shut up about not sleeping with him right away. I think about texting my little gay bee for counsel when Brad turns to me and says, "So, my place or yours?" and I feel like I'm standing in front of the Cinnabon counter. Do you want to be a big slut or a superbig slut? A superbig slut comes with more icing.

"My place," I say.

Now he probably thinks I'm desperate and clingy, which I am.

"Good," he says. I smile but then it hits me—help me, sweet precious baby Jesus, Brad Keller is coming home with me.

We get to my apartment and I set Blooper down next to the sassy working girl figurine. Sorry missy, but he's my new favorite possession.

"This place is something!" Brad says, looking around my kitchen in wonder. "Where'd you get all this stuff?"

"I steal a lot," I say. "You know, from children and toy stores and stuff."

He laughs. "Have anything to drink?"

"Maybe wine?" I look in the fridge.

"Red or white?" he asks and wanders out to my living room.

"Um, box," I say, picking up a Franzia party ball of pink wine. "I think it's pink."

I pour two glasses. *Just stay calm, just stay calm, just stay calm.* I'm so nervous I feel remarkably sober, given how much alcohol I've already had. That's not good. I'm not going to be able to do what it is I think we're about to do unless I am at least buzzed. I peek to see if he's looking and then quickly slam my glass and refill it. No need to show him I'm a hobby alcoholic quite yet.

I walk out into the living room, expecting Brad to be reclining on my rose chaise lounge, hopefully admiring the irony of my oversize orange kidney bean ashtray or the wit of my Zippy the Chimp poster, but he isn't there. "Where'd you go?" I say in a mild panic. There are so many things I wouldn't want him to discover. The dirty underwear on my dresser, the cat turd museum behind the couch, or the Shaun Cassidy poster in my closet, just to name a few.

He's around the corner, gazing into my little office, which is really just a big second closet, and I realize my stupid "manifestation vision board" is propped up on my desk. It's a big corkboard covered with images of everything I want to attract into my life. There's a couple kissing on a rowboat, a big house on a lake, a private jet midflight as it banks and bisects the setting sun. It's a vision board, not a reality board.

"Whoops!" I say and tug him back by the belt loop into the living room. I shut the white folding door. "It's a mess in there," I say. "Usually it's neat as a pin."

"Was that a picture of a baby," he asks, "above your desk?"

"My cousin!"

He frowns. "It looked like it was cut out of a magazine."

"Here's your wine," I say, "straight out of the box!"

He takes the glass and I lead him to the couch. I turn on some music and sit down next to him, our knees almost touching, but not quite. I'm feeling pretty good, and the wine is finally starting to warm me up. "When I was about eight years old," I say, "my dad took me to this indoor amusement park. I don't even remember where it was. It's gone now, but it was like one of those carnivals that's indoors and open all year. My dad always went on rides with me, and this one time he must have gone on a dozen roller-coaster rides, but I really wanted to go on the Octopus. That's the one where you get in a cab and it spins like crazy and tilts up and down."

Brad kisses my neck.

"My dad said his stomach was acting up. He told me I could go by myself, but I'd never been on a ride by myself. He said I could do it. Hailey was too scared. I said I wasn't scared and I took my ticket and got in line, but the longer I stood in line and the closer I got to the ride, the more scared I got. When I finally got up to the front, I thought there was no way I could do it. I was terrified. All those lights and kids yelling. There was a boy in front of me, a little bit older and about a foot taller. He must have seen me worrying or something. He asked me if I was scared and I said yes. I told him I was scared I'd fall out of the car. I'll never forget it, he just looked at me and said, "'Don't worry, if you fall, I'll jump in and catch you.'"

I look down at my wineglass. "It was something about how he said it. I guess in one way or another, I've been looking for that little boy ever since." Brad picks up my hand and kisses the pads of my fingertips.

"What if white knights exist?" he asks.

"I don't know. What if they do?"

"Would you let someone save you?"

"No," I say, "but I'd certainly go for a ride."

"I think I'd like to take you on one," he says, and that's about the time I decided I would make it my life's mission to marry Brad Keller.

I get up and lead him to the bedroom.

The next morning I wake up alone with Mrs. Biggles standing on my stomach, her paws painfully kneading my abdomen. Brad is gone, and I have a monster hangover.

I call Christopher and tell him Brad left before I woke up. "I'm pretty sure we did it," I say, checking for wet spots on the bed. "Oh yeah. We did it. Twice."

"Did he say he was leaving?" Christopher asks. "Did he tell you he couldn't sleep over?"

"I don't know." I struggle to remember. "It's fuzzy. He might have said something about working. I don't know. I might be making it up in my head. That elf nearly killed me."

"What do you remember?"

"Great date," I say, "lots of talking. Chilidogs, polka, sex twice in missionary position."

"God," Christopher says, disgusted. "If that was a gay date, you could charge him with cruel and unusual punishment."

I roll over and look out the window at the empty street.

"What about the unit?" he asks. "How big?"

"Um, good."

"One image," he says, "the first one that pops into your head."

"Okay. Crabapple baby fist."

"Nice. The shaft?"

"Two Snickers bars."

"Two Snickers bars long or thick?"

"Thick."

"Very good. Approve of the manscaping?"

"He's a little bushy. Needs a trim."

"Well, no deal breakers there. Did you at least get his phone number?"

"Yes, and he has mine. I should wait for him to call me, right?"

Silence. "Tell me you already know the answer to that."

"Is that a no?"

"Please, for the love of almighty God. It's like watching a car accident in slow motion. Do not call him. He has a forty-eight-hour window to call you. After that, you don't pick up."

He's right, of course; the next forty-eight hours will be crucial. If Brad calls within this window of time, then this could be the start of a budding relationship. If he calls after forty-eight hours, then he's not sure, but doesn't want to give up quite yet. If he doesn't call, well, then it was a one-night stand. Something I can't even bear to think about. I'm pretty sure it wasn't a one-night stand. I mean, we had such a good conversation at dinner, that's got to mean something, right?

Still, I did have to go and tell him my stupid boy-saves-meat-the-amusement-park story, and I drank enough liquor to fill a kiddie pool, and I think I possibly threw up in a towel in my bathroom, but haven't had the nerve to check yet. So I have no idea if I should be expecting a call or not. Probably not. But what if he did call? Is that so impossible?

I have Green Mill deliver a cheeseburger with fries. Grease and lots of it is my one and only hangover solution. I drink lots of water and watch a snowstorm blow across my living room windows. I sit in my pink chenille robe and watch *Sleepless in Seattle* on the Lifetime Channel and cry. I'm not crying about Brad, that movie always makes me cry.

Every time.

Twenty-four hours pass and no call from Brad.

Forty-eight hours pass and no call from Brad.

Due to my inability to connect with the human race, I am moving to Iceland to become a sheep herder. It's for the best.

Monday morning it seems like everyone in the office is staring at me, like I grew a grotesque second head or something. It's incredibly quiet all around my desk, and I worry people can hear my thoughts, which are basically: *I had sex with Brad Keller! I had sex with Brad Keller!* I sit down at my desk and decide to be professional. We have a big week ahead of us and I should stay on task.

But before that I sneak onto TrueLove.com and take a relationship quiz that will tell me if Brad and I are going to "make it," or have to "fake it." I enter our names and click on our signs. (Him: Scorpio. Me: Gemini.) The questions are stupid and obvious, like *Does he make eye contact with you?* and *Is sex boring or bull's-eye?* and *Does he know your last name?* But I answer each of the twenty-five questions dutifully and hit Enter. Up pops the result. *Jen*, it says, *it looks like you and Brad are going to make it!* That puts a big, dopey, hopeful smile on my face and I send the test results to Christopher.

Ted bombs into my cubicle and skitters a radio spot across my desk. "Whoa," he says, "looks like your Friday night date was awesome. Is that cake batter in your hair?"

"Quit stomping around," I say. "You clomp like a moose."

"Oh, sorry," he says, "does Brad walk perfectly?" He makes little precious kissing noises and prances about. "Does Brad walk like a Japanese gymnast?"

"Shut up," I tell him. "How did you even know we went out?"

"Kathy in accounting saw you at O'Hooligans. She told Barb in men's casual wear and Barb told the cleaning lady."

"So the cleaning lady told you?"

He nods.

"You talk to the cleaning lady?"

"We have a thing. Don't get all possessive. I just need to know if Brad has a big penis."

"At least find me some aspirins," I say, retrieving my empty bottle. "Five hundred aspirins and it's empty. How did I use five hundred aspirins?"

"I don't know," he says. "Five hundred dates with Brad."

"Oh, go away."

"You're right," he says, shaking his head. "It's none of my business."

"Thank you!"

"I'm bigger than him though. In the pants. I'm sure I'm bigger."

"Go away."

"Okay, I'll go, but you just missed out on getting some pretty amazing information about me. Like that I happen to be a millionaire with a solid gold jet ski and I just do department store copywriting because it's my art."

"I'm not telling you anything, not that there's anything to tell."

"Why not?" he says. "Is he deformed or something? Is it like a sensitive subject?"

I throw a catalogue at him. Then Ashley rounds the corner and stops at my desk.

"What is this?" She holds up a piece of paper.

"I was just getting some dating advice off Jen," Ted says.

Ashley hands me the paper. It looks vaguely familiar.

"Is there a reason you're e-mailing the entire company your TrueLove.com test results?" she asks.

I stare at the paper. It's the test I sent Christopher.

"You sent it to the entire art department," Ashley says.

Ted takes the paper. "Wow! Look at this! You scored an eighty out of a hundred with Brad Keller! Maybe it is true love!"

Oh God. This isn't happening.

Ashley's eyes go wide. "You were taking a love test for you and *Brad Keller?*" she says, and she says it in such a low, vicious way, "Yes. We went out on a date." Then I excuse myself and go discreetly to the emergency stairwell, where I can't seem to breathe. I'm not hyperventilating so much as my chest seems to have some crushing weight on it, like a cobra of panic has wound its way around my torso, and I wobble, as though I might pass out.

The heavy metal door opens and Ted sits down next to me on the stairs.

"You okay?" he asks gently. "Sorry I outed you and Brad."

"It's not your fault," I say and my eyes fill up with tears. "You know how there's always one kid in your class who wets his pants in front of everyone? And everyone tells him not to worry, no one will remember this in ten years?"

"Everyone remembers," Ted sighs.

"Everyone!" I say. "And everyone will remember this too!"

Ted nods. "There's only one way to fix a disaster," he says. "Make a bigger disaster." Then he reaches up and pulls the lever on an emergency fire alarm.

A high, piercing wail starts up and instantly we hear the big metal doors banging open on every floor and a multitude of voices filling the stairwell.

I really have to stop getting the fire department involved in my love life.

Without so much as a flinch Ted links his arm in mine and we join the stream of concerned, chatting Keller's employees on their way down to the parking lot.

We spend about an hour outside in the cold, all hopping from one foot to the other. Ted says it's great because for every minute we're out here, more and more junk mail is cluttering up everyone's inboxes, pushing my test-score e-mail farther and farther down the line.

"Also, at least half these people will now come down with the flu," he says cheerfully. "Headaches, chills, using up vacation days. They're not likely to remember your e-mail with a low-grade fever, are they?"

Sometimes I just want to kiss Ted.

That night I'm reorganizing the dollhouse and assembling a new male harem for Little Wife. I line up dozens of green plastic army men and different-size action figures, who are all going to move in and become Little Wife's personal slaves. They will do her bidding, no matter how perverse. Hans Solo lies down in bed, waiting to service her; the Incredible Hulk is in the kitchen wearing an apron and doing dishes, and Chewbacca is giving Little Husband a death-blow karate chop because his affair with Barbie has been discovered.

Then I hear the chipper *new e-mail!* sound on my computer and I knock my knee against the table as I sprint across the room to my desk.

Brad has sent a new message.

He says, "I had a really good time and would love to hang out again."

Oh, really.

How cruel and insensitive.

Why wait for three days to contact me? If he's going to respond, why not respond right away? I consult with Christopher before e-mailing back.

"I don't know," Christopher says. "It's technically ouside the window. I don't like it."

"But he practically made it inside the window," I argue. "Maybe he was just playing it cool."

"And he e-mailed. He didn't call."

"A call counts for an e-mail."

"No, a call counts for a call."

"No, a text message doesn't count for a call," I reason, "but an e-mail does."

"Okay, you deserve whatever happens."

So fine. I wait twenty-four hours before e-mailing Brad back. I write several test e-mails first and I come up with two or three pretty good variations and I practically have to sit on my hands to not send it.

Instead, I focus on the penis-basket debacle.

The penis baskets were supposed to be bath-gift baskets prepackaged for Valentine's Day, but when we got them, the ripe plum-scented bath balls were on either side of the blue organic mini-loofah, which made it look like a big penis with blue balls wrapped in plastic. "But how are we supposed to fix this?" I ask Ashley.

"I don't know," she says. "That's your job, not mine."

She's had a nasty temper lately.

"What I mean is," I try to explain, "how can *copywriters* fix this? Call it our Valentine's Day penis promotion? The new Keller's Blue Ball Basket?"

"I don't know," she says, "just spin it."

"But how?"

"How should I know?" she shouts like a silverback gorilla. "Just fix it!"

There's no fixing it. She knows it and I know it, but now it's my responsibility, so when we're left with three hundred unsold units, I can do the explaining.

I check my cell phone and e-mail just in case Brad sent another message. He hasn't and I'm still waiting to send mine. So what? No big deal. They aren't supposed to call or e-mail twice, not before you respond. I shouldn't even be expecting that and I'm not, only those rules are for people who don't work in the same building. If you work in the same building, you would normally run into each other. Why don't I know what Brad does? How can you spend an entire night with someone and find out so little?

I'm dying.

I try to meditate at my desk, but when I close my eyes, the slow tide of ceaseless co-worker chatter and Xerox machines and elevator bells and high heels clicking and people eating and gossiping and bitching and moaning expands to fill every molecule of space in my brain, like someone stuck one of those air-compressed cans of Fix-a-Flat foam in my ear, and shot my head full of sticky, gross goo. I can't get away from it. I want to stand up and scream at everyone that now I understand what going postal really means.

After lunch I decide to mill around the executive suites upstairs and come up with a reason for running into Brad. After all, I work here, right? I could have a very legitimate reason for being on the top floor, only my mind is blank and I can't think of one single reason, so I grab a clipboard and go upstairs, where I spend a painful forty minutes roaming the halls examining a blank piece of paper. I don't see Brad, or Ed, or any Keller executives. Only their executive secretaries. They're apparently all running the company.

I go home and send the e-mail to Brad. Then I turn my computer off, because I have better things to do than drink wine and stare at my computer screen waiting for him to respond.

Please.

How totally lame.

No, I'm going to drink wine and impose some law and order in the Tinkertoy home. I clear out Little Wife's harem and install a new God. Two new Gods, in fact. I found two plastic smoking monkeys in my drawer, the kind that smoke little paper cigarettes, which you light with a match. I'm going to name them Depression Monkey and Apathy Monkey.

Depression Monkey will threaten the Tinkertoys with an unholy downpour of plagues and pestilence if they don't offer the new Monkey Gods complete devotion and a steady supply of Wellbutrin, but Apathy Monkey will tell them he doesn't care.

The next day at work Brad has still not responded to my e-mail and I'm in a ferocious mood. I accidentally knock someone's coat off the hanger when I'm hanging my parka up in the employee closet and I don't even pick it up. Instead I stare coldly at it on the floor and think, that's right, life's a bitch. You get knocked down and nobody picks you up, you just lie there in the dark, damp and alone.

I get to work on the "Great Do-Over," a promotion we're launching to revitalize stagnant cosmetics sales. Free make-overs, in-house stylists, makeup artists, and color consultants will be provided at no cost to the customer. They just have to drag their hideous carcasses in here so we can patch them up. These campaigns are easy because it's the same old barrel of switch words. *Renew, revive, refresh, revitalize, retrieve, rethink, re-do*. They would be easy anyway, if I wasn't Bitterina Bitterson, as Christopher calls me. I don't really feel like writing about anything that's fresh or new right now.

I feel like writing about the pointlessness of trying.

At noon Ted brings me a sandwich from Cecil's. "Feeling any better?" he asks.

"No, not really."

"Christopher told me to make you eat more. Here, a Reuben with extra sauce. Nobody likes a skinny Santa!"

I glare at him. "It must be nice," I say, "to not care at all how you look."

He shrugs. "Yep. Wanna sit with me during the employee-bonding seminar?"

Employee-bonding seminar? Crap. I forgot about the lousy seminar. A great day gets even better. I trudge downstairs with Ted and all the other Keller drones to the cafeteria for a mandatory employee-bonding seminar. What joy. I absolutely hate these stupid seminars. They used to be offsite and it wasn't so bad, like when we went to the Holiday Inn and everyone stayed and got smashed in the hotel bar. Now, whenever they have all-staff meetings we have to use the cafeteria, because it's the only room big enough for all of us when the store is open.

The bonding-seminar leader guy, who looks like Gene Wilder outfitted from an L. L. Bean catalogue, welcomes us and tells us we're going to get going right away. I casually look around for Brad. The seminar guy says to pick a partner and turn your chairs to face him or her. There's a wave of quiet commotion as everyone in the room starts knocking into everyone else as they scoot chairs around. "Here we go," Ted says and turns his chair toward me.

I hate this cheer-up corporate crap. If they want to cheer us up they should pay us more and let us work less. The seminar guy says we should look directly into our partner's eyes and reveal our biggest dream. Ted automatically starts talking.

"Once, I had a dream of becoming an emergency room doctor," he says. "Did you know the number-one emergency-room visit is for something stuck up the butt?"

I roll my eyes and look away. I know he's just doing this to make me laugh and what's irritating me is that it's working.

"Seriously!" he says. "You wouldn't believe the stories I've heard. My cousin worked in an emergency room in Houston and she says men will shove anything up their butt."

"Right," I say, "especially their heads."

"And flashlights!" Ted says, eyes wide with intrigue. "Some that are still on. She also said they've extracted maple syrup bottles, whole light bulbs, a peanut butter jar, and once, an egg timer."

"And what do they say when asked how an egg timer got in their ass?"

"That's the best part. They say they slipped in the shower or fell down the stairs. One guy showed up with a Barbie doll up his ass and said he fell down the stairs and landed on his daughter's Barbie doll. I mean, how does a Barbie doll accidentally go up your butt? She said they had to tape his ass open and use forceps to get it out."

"So all this is part of your big dream?"

"Sort of. These are the things I need to see one day. My cousin said one woman came in with a Doberman pinscher on top of her. She was having sex with it and the dog got *engorged*."

"Engorged?"

Ted nods. "Sick, right?"

"Don't ever say the word 'engorged' again," I warn him. "Seriously. I'll vomit."

"They had to give the dog sedatives to get it off her. The ambulance drivers were on their knees laughing."

The microphone shrieks with feedback as the seminar guy steps up to the podium. "Okay, people," he says, "now switch it up! Make sure each person has a chance to share their dream!"

I look at the clock on the wall. "Okay, Ted," I say, "I never thought I'd say this, but my dream is for you to keep telling up-the-butt stories. I didn't know it was my biggest dream, but it is."

Ted doesn't miss a beat. He pulls his chair closer and says, "The worst thing she ever saw was a *cement enema*. This guy came in saying something was in his ass, and she says it took half an hour before he admitted he and his boyfriend mixed up some patio grout and poured it through a funnel right into *his ass*."

"Okay, people!" Seminar Guy says again, "now tell each other one thing you could do to get closer to that dream."

Ted thinks for a second. "I know. I could shove something up my ass and go to the emergency room, where I could fill out a doctor job application. It would be a touching, come-full-circle kind of story."

"Any idea what you'd shove up there?"

"The options are endless. I think I'd start with something small though. Like a Q-tip."

"You know what we're learning here?" Seminar Guy asks. "We're learning our co-workers aren't *just* our co-workers, they're people, too. People with dreams that might be a lot like yours. See? A lot of you probably just found out you have something in common with your co-worker that you never knew about before."

A screen lowers from the ceiling and Seminar Guy kicks up a PowerPoint display. His helpers pass out little white wallet-size plastic cards that have acceptable emotions for the workplace listed on them. He tells us that at any given moment in the day, we can locate the emotion we're feeling on the wallet-size emotions card and then we can work up to the ideal emotion, which is apparently "Satisfaction."

"So, if you're feeling angry," Seminar Guy says, "then you look here and find angry on the emotions card and you work up from there. And you know what the absolute most useful emotion there is? The one that can turn everything around? That's right. *Curiosity.* When we become curious about something, even if we're mad about it, then we start to look for answers. Like you might say, 'Hey, I'm mad about this recent pay cut I got, or at least I think I'm mad. I'm curious to know if I'm actually mad or not.' And then you could look at your emotion-investigation-technique card and try any one of the suggested ideas for investigating your curiosity. You could try this one, and ask yourself, is this event life-threatening? Well, no, it's probably not. Sure, there's a pay cut and that's going to count for some quality-of-life points, but those points might be like giving up your daily doughnut! In that case you turn it into Weight Watchers points, right? I'm kidding, but am I right?"

He drones on and on about transforming something into

something and avoiding something so we can all something-something more effectively. About this time my eyes are wandering around the room and I spot the back of Brad's head. I think it's his head. He's sitting in between two blond women; I think they're from cosmetics. Is that Brianna? Why would he be sitting next to women from cosmetics? Everyone knows they're total sluts who give STDs to the tester makeup when they touch it.

"So when something overwhelms you," Seminar Guy says, "you have to *chunk it down*. You guys know what I mean by that? Chunk it down? Of course you don't, that's why I'm here! If you already knew how to chunk it down then I'd be out of a job! Then I'd have my own quality-of-life points to worry about! Then I'll have to give up my daily doughnut!"

He picks up a doughnut and whips it over his shoulder. A special effects *whoa-oh!* sound blares and the doughnut hits a woman standing by the Tastee Freeze machine in the chest. "Chunking it down means you break the task or problem or co-worker into chunks and deal with each chunk *individually*. Like pieces of pie. You guys like pie, don't you?" Everyone nods and mumbles yes. We all like pie. I like pie. I'd like to smash pie in Brad's face. That is totally Brianna he's sitting next to. I think.

A picture of a cherry pie pops up on the screen behind the podium and a piercing prerecorded "Chunk It Down" song comes on over the speakers. "That's the real key to solving your problems," Seminar Guy shouts. "Chunking it down! I can't stress that enough! I can't tell you how important it is. *Chunk it down!* If I can get one thing across to you—it would be that. One thing and everything else will follow! So the next time you're overwhelmed at work," Seminar Guy shouts, "what are you going to do?"

"Chunk it down," the room mumbles.

"What was that?"

"Chunk it down," the room says again, slightly louder. We close the bonding seminar with a "Personal Achievement" pledge and we each get a magnet that says: CHUNK IT!

On the way out I'm wondering if I have any sick days left when someone tugs on my arm. It's Brad. He's standing there flanked by two cosmetics girls.

"Hey," he says to me.

"Oh, hi, Brad!" Ted says loudly. "How *are* you? You are just doing a *super* job!"

I give Ted a little shove and I must have used more force than I thought, because I almost knock him down. "All right, already!" he says, brushing my arm off, and he sulks away.

Brad winks at me. "Wanna have dinner again?" he whispers.

I peer over his shoulder at the two cosmetics girls behind him.

"With me?" I ask.

"Of course with you," he says. "I'll cook you dinner at my place."

"I don't know," I sniff. "I'll have to check my calendar."

"Come on," he says, "I insist. I won't take no for an answer. This weekend. Let me cook you dinner." I look up at him and he's still the most handsome man I've ever seen.

"Sure," I say, smiling like a lamb on her merry way to slaughter. "Of course."

"No, no, no!" Christopher protests. "Why is he cooking for you? At his house? No. Too soon!" I tell him he seems to forget we've already had sex, so Brad couldn't be trying to get me in bed. We've already been there.

"Doesn't matter," he says. "You see a horror movie on a

second date or go feed ducks. Cooking you dinner at his house? That's too personal, too soon."

"One, I hate horror movies. Two, it's January and any ducks still in Minnesota are frozen to death, and three, I think we crossed over into 'too personal' when I was on my knees in front of him. You know?"

Christopher shakes his head. I get irritated with him. He's crapping on my parade. Then when I ask him what I should wear he gets all huffy and says it's my funeral, I can wear what I want to.

Sheesh. Some people just can't be happy for you.

At my desk, I have two new e-mails from my mother. The first one is the latest mind-numbing layout of the seating arrangement for my sister's wedding. You cannot imagine how many times this seating arrangement has been changed and rechanged. Winston Churchill himself would be impressed at the tenacity, intricacy, and strategy these women have put into who should eat chicken Kiev next to whom. I don't know why I get these updates, they have nothing to do with me and they further agitate my barely suppressed anger at how much money my parents are spending on the stupidest day of my sister's life.

By the time Hailey is done with her requests for silver chopsticks and releasing imported butterflies instead of rice, my parents will be broke and whatever chance I had at a decent wedding will be shot. I'll have to win a free wedding on one of those Mississippi gambling paddleboats. Wedding, reception, and honeymoon all in one location. We can get married on deck, tear up some pull-tabs in the minicasino and vomit over the side of the boat when we drink too much complimentary Champale. It will be beautiful.

The second e-mail is a forwarded list of "stress-reducing tips for the office" from *Woman's World*, the magazine for women who love being bath mats.

According to this article, it's easy to "Let go and Let God!" All you have to do is:

1. *Do something you're really good at!*
   They recommend I bake cupcakes for a sick friend or garden in my yard, but having neither an oven nor a rake at work, I settle for knocking over Big Trish's fern.

2. *Look up!*
   I think they mean this as a general piece of advice, a "look on the bright side" or even "straighten your posture" idea, but I choose to actually look directly up at the ceiling and stare at the fluorescent lights and the three pencils stuck in the drop ceiling Peg-Board. I wonder if one will fall out one day and pierce my eyeball and if they have workers' comp for that. Okay, step two done.

3. *Put on some baby powder!*
   They say applying baby powder brings back fond memories of a simpler time, when you were cared for, except one of my mother's favorite stories is about the time she was changing my diaper and the doorbell rang. "I just went and answered the door!" my mother says. "I left baby Jennifer right there on the changing table and when I came back, she was on the floor! She was perfectly all right, not a scratch on her, and she was just smiling down there, looking at me like she enjoyed her trip!"

Right. I enjoyed my trip.

I have no memory of the event, but if it's true I wasn't crying, I was most likely in shock. I don't see why she thinks it's a funny story. It's probably why I could never learn my multiplication tables. So, forget number three.

4. *Water or feed something.*
Oh, what the hell. I'm hungry anyway, so I go to the employee break room to root around in the refrigerator and steal somebody's frozen Weight Watchers dinner. I actually find a baked ziti, the holy grail of the Weight Watchers dinner collection. It's the only one that doesn't taste like moisturized sawdust, and it's hidden in the back of the freezer under a big ice-fuzzy tub of vanilla ice cream. Somebody hid their stash, but not well enough! Baked ziti is only five points. Sure, it's chemically enhanced, reduced, boiled down, and reformed into known foodlike shapes. It's probably all made of soy-based kerosene, but I don't care, it's only five freaking points!

I heat that baby up quick in the microwave before anyone sees the crime, and on my way back to my desk, I chuck a single piece of pasta into the fishbowl on top of the microwave. There, I've completed the last tip, I've fed Ryan Seacrest, the office goldfish, and by the looks of his furious nibbling, he was hungry. Damn. That article might be right. I do feel better after pissing off Big Trish, contemplating the plausibility of workers' comp, and being kind to an animal with a brain the size of a cardamom seed. Go figure.

• • •

Saturday Brad picks me up and tells me I look lovely. I toss my head back and say I only had a few minutes to get ready, even though it was another grueling all-day affair, not to mention I am officially bankrupt now because I scheduled an emergency dermabrasion session.

"Are we going somewhere first?" I ask.

"First? No, straight to my house!" he says. "I didn't tell you over at your place, it's no big deal, but I'm allergic to cats. I had hives for three days after I stayed over."

"You're allergic to cats?"

"Very," he says and my heart sinks a little.

"Have you tried acupuncture?" I ask him. "It's supposed to work."

"Never tried it. I have no idea where an acupuncturist is."

"I'll find one for you. I'll find you the best one."

"All right, I'll give it a try."

We drive out to his house, which his parents gave him. It's all the way out in Excelsior, and it's nothing like I expected. I pictured him living downtown in a big modern loft or something, but his place is actually an adorable little white cottage with yellow shutters right on Lake Minnetonka. It immediately reminds me of my dollhouse and of a house much nicer than my dollhouse.

"There's about a hundred feet of shoreline," he says when we first pull into his driveway. "Kennebunkport cobblestone walkways. Gorgeous in the summer, you could golf on the lawn. Rosebushes all along the south side. I don't do the gardening, of course. My parents' lawn service comes three times a week to do both houses."

My eyes trace the path of his thumb across his driveway, over a pristine row of hedges, over another wide lawn of uninterrupted white snow, and up to the massive white pillars of the house next door. It looks like the white house, except bigger, like a square four-story wedding cake. "Your parents live there?"

"Figures they'd want me next door, right?" he says, opening the door. "Actually, this is just the guest cottage for the main house. Mom redid the landscaping with the hedges or whatever to make it look like its own property."

I step inside and find myself standing on the glossy hardwood floor of a gourmet kitchen. It has green marble counters and brand-new chrome appliances. The refrigerator even has a miniature television in it, right above the ice cube dispenser. I recognize it because it's the exact refrigerator Lenny wouldn't buy for Hailey because it was too freaking expensive.

"This is a guest cottage?"

"Cozy, huh? Come look at the fireplace in the living room. It's made from stones they hauled out of the lake and all the floors are heated."

Heated floors?

Heated floors are out of my league entirely.

We sit down and Brad pours some wine. He's so good at listening, he asks me all about myself. Where I grew up, what I majored in, how long I've worked at Keller's. I've never known any man to ask so many questions. We stay up for hours talking and then we go upstairs where we have sex three times and his sheets end up damp and tangled on the floor.

I sleep over. Of course when I say "sleep" I mean after we have sex he sleeps and I stare at him. He snores in the most adorable way. I watch the light changing on the curtains and imagine what the room would look like painted a different color. Then around dawn I sneak out of bed and reapply my makeup to look fresh and light, like I have no makeup on at all. This look takes quite awhile to achieve.

When Brad finally wakes up, he stretches and asks me how I

slept. I of course am fake-sleeping next to him, poised in an angelic position, one wrist thrown over my head as though I were a heroine in a silent movie who had briefly, charmingly, fainted. I make my eyes flutter slightly at the sound of his voice and then I smile at him with no spittle or eye crust to worry about. I look fresh as a daisy, just like people do in the movies.

I half expect him to be cranky or dismissive, and maybe that sounds weird, but staying over the whole night, that was something that took David a long time to do. He always got jumpy around three in the morning and said he had to sleep in his bed or he'd be exhausted the next day. But Brad just acts like it's the most normal thing he's ever done.

"Morning, gorgeous!" he says and asks if I want to grab breakfast. Thank God. It's only after I hear the word "breakfast" that I realize how hungry I am. Last night we got so engrossed in talking, we didn't even eat dinner. We get up, get dressed, and go to the Eggery for breakfast. He orders eggs Benedict and a skim latte, extra foam. I order the same. I try to hang on to this information and store it away in my memory banks. Brad likes skim latte, extra foam! Brad likes skim latte, extra foam!

Brad says he has to go to his nephew's birthday party later. "He's the only kid in our family. Man, is he spoiled. My sister spoils him rotten. My dad, though, he's the worst. He bought Trevor a pony, an actual live pony they board at a stable down the road, and the kid's only six."

It's weird to hear someone call Ed Keller Dad, and I try not to make a face. He tells me all about his parents and his sister. About the Keller cabin up north and how living up to the Keller family name is about as fun as it sounds. "My mom had a fit when I moved to L.A.," he says. "They all assumed I would come home to Minnesota and work at the store after I graduated."

"What made you come back?"

He shrugs. "Family, I guess. Hey, you sure look beautiful in the morning." I smile as I wolf down my eggs Benedict. I never really liked eggs Benedict, but this morning they taste amazing.

After breakfast, Brad drives me home. I'm illuminated and floaty, the world full of possibility. It's almost hard to be this happy. Right here, right now, this suddenly. It's almost painful, like after years of darkness, the light hurts your eyes.

When I walk into my apartment, it seems like a cheap card trick. All the junk on my walls and shelves looks tacky and garish compared to Brad's piece of chic lakeside paradise. I notice little things I hadn't before, like how dusty everything is and how there isn't a clean, unbroken line anywhere, just chaotic colors shouting. I want to take bed sheets and cover everything but I settle for climbing in the tub and staring at the vanilla pudding tiles. I definitely don't think I belong here, I think I belong somewhere . . . else.

Monday, I'm sitting at my desk looking up images of Jackie Onassis. I need new wardrobe ideas along with new lifestyle ideas, because, let's face it, I'm not exactly executive wife material. Not yet, anyway. I use my last functioning credit card and order a very expensive peach suit, a Chanel knockoff, but a good one. If I can copy Jackie O, and I mean not just her clothing but her classic style, inimitable grace, and endless poise, then maybe I have a shot.

Now how do I order those online?

Big Trish stomps into my cubicle and tosses a sympathy card at me. "Ryan Seacrest is dead," she says.

"Who?"

"Ryan Seacrest, the goldfish."

"The one that lives on top of the microwave?"

She nods. The card has a sunset on it and says, "Sorry to see you go." I have a bad feeling about this. "He's really dead?" I ask. "He seemed fine."

She arches an eyebrow. "When did he seem fine?"

"I don't know, before."

"Well, he was bloated up to the size of an orange testicle this morning."

We stare at each other.

I'm really hoping I didn't kill Ryan Seacrest with baked ziti. That would be some very bad karma.

"Are you going to sign the card or not?" she asks.

I sign the card. There are already more signatures for Ryan Seacrest than there were for Helen in accounting, whose husband died of a brain tumor last spring. "I'm sorry," I say and hand the card back. She arches the other eyebrow. "Why should you be sorry?"

God, she's a pain. I'm trying not to blame her, what with her having evil stepkid issues and everything. I think a woman being forced to watch over another woman's children is unnatural. On a primal level, shouldn't a female want to kill off a rival mate's offspring? I mean, I know I'm not supposed to say that, I'm supposed to quote some Mother Teresa crap about one world, one love, but frankly, I think getting saddled with bratty twin stepdaughters is biologically grotesque. If I had them they'd end up in the trunk of my car.

I'm being too harsh, I know. Dr. Gupta believes in reincarnation and karma and paying for past actions, which means in my next life I will be something very small and insignificant that perishes at the hands of a very large and careless overlord. Like I might be a butterfly that gets stepped on by a cow. I study Jackie Onassis's face and consider this. I definitely still think it's a step up from the life I have now.

After work I have to pick up the table presents for Hailey. Three-hundred stainless steel chopsticks in green satin boxes. She actually wanted silver chopsticks or at least silver-plated, but they were too expensive. The stainless steel chopsticks were the only ones that fit in the budget and my mother convinced her they looked modern.

The stationery store lady has packed all three hundred boxes in two big Tupperware crates with snap-shut lids, and they're like a million pounds each. I nearly kill myself loading them into the Scout when I slip and almost shoot into the street and under the delivery truck roaring past. The lady inside didn't even offer to help me. Not that I blame her: I think your God-given right when you get old is to be difficult. I myself can't wait to be eighty and never have to help anyone again.

I have to drop them off at my mother's house and when I pull up out front, I see Lenny's gold pickup truck parked in the driveway, so I have to park on the opposite side of the street. Stupid Ham Man.

"We're in the kitchen!" my mom shouts as I struggle through the front door, trying not to drop the precious railroad spikes. I stagger to the kitchen with the heavy boxes. I've been in the house for twenty seconds and I already have a headache.

"Hello," my mother says. "We thought you were coming for dinner."

I huff the stack of boxes up on the counter.

"Oh my God, are those the chopsticks? Don't drop those!" Hailey springs up from her chair to see if I've damaged her table gifts.

"They're heavy," I tell her. "I could have used some help."

"Heya, Jen!" Lenny says and stands to give me his patented good-guy handshake-hug-thump-on-the-back howdy-do.

"Hello, Leonard," I say, taking off my coat and folding it over the back of a chair. "Nice truck. Don't see gold fleck much these days."

"Matches the boat!" he says. "You gotta come fishing with us this summer. I got the walleye spot!" Then he says something to my father about using hot dogs for bait.

"Do I smell squash? Like, burning squash?"

"No, it's the candles." Mom points to the centerpiece—three thick rust-colored candles resting in a nest of spray-painted pine cones. "Aunt Joan made them. These are pumpkin pie. Spiced pumpkin pie."

"Ruin any irreplaceable dresses today?" Hailey asks me, her face all screwed up.

"None of that," my mother says. "Jennifer, have hotdish."

"Shoot," I say, "no thanks. I just had hot cheese."

Mom cuts me a hearty wedge anyway. Her version of seven-layer hotdish goes like this: Take a casserole dish, spoon in a layer of browned hamburger, then a layer of mashed potatoes, then strained carrots, then frozen peas. Repeat. Sprinkle a heavy blanket of grated cheddar cheese on top and then pour a can of Progresso Cream of Mushroom soup over the whole shebang. Bake until it's solid enough to use as an anchor for a Carnival cruise ship.

Hailey sits down and tells me I'm lucky the chopsticks aren't ruined and I tell her if I'd wanted to ruin them, I would've taken them to the Minneapolis College of Art and Design and hired a first-year art student to weld them together into decorative fruit baskets. Not that I'd thought about it.

I tell Mom her casserole tastes great.

"She used extra cheese," Lenny says. "Wisconsin Amish cheddar. Them Amish might not spring for beer, but they know how to make fuckin' cheese!"

Hailey smacks his arm.

"Sorry," he says, "freaking cheese."

I make a face and put my fork down. "Cheese from Wisconsin? Mother, you whore."

Her eyes fly open. "Jennifer!"

My dad chuckles and Abbygael toddles in sucking her thumb and trailing a purple blanket behind her. I'm amazed she can walk upright with that pumpkin head.

"Hi, sweetie!" my mom says. "Did you finish your cartoons? Come here."

Abbygael stares at me.

"There is seriously something wrong with that kid," I say.

"Jennifer!" My mother covers Abbygael's ears.

"What? She can't hear me. I don't think she even knows people are here."

"We have Abbygael all weekend," she says, smooching her on the forehead. "Aunt Joan couldn't watch her—she's at a craft fair. She's selling those candles all over now. Did she tell you?"

"Yeah, and she's giving us free candles for the wedding," Hailey says. "White cake ones."

"White cake what?"

"White cake–scented candles."

Great. This adds yet another unpleasant dynamic to their wedding. Now the entire place will reek of whatever my aunt thinks white cake smells like. Probably burned apple jelly or Spam. Hailey asks me if I heard about David's wedding. "He's marrying the daughter of that car dealership guy," she says. "That guy, what does he call himself? The Pick-Up King."

"Yes," I say, "I heard."

"That's her ex-boyfriend," she explains to Lenny, who never knows what anyone is talking about. I swear, she's like his hired-for-the-handicapped world interpreter. "You should get his new wife to give you a car!" she says. "Oh my God, Lenny, you should see that orange thing she drives around. It's like what hunters drive when they go kill deer."

"Deer season isn't for months," Lenny says.

I ignore them. "Well, I don't really care. I've been dating somebody."

"Really?" Mom asks. "Who's this now? Is he coming to the wedding? The caterer's order is already in. Do you think he'd want the chicken or the beef? I hope he doesn't want the beef. We're already short on the beef."

"Shoulda let me bring ham," Lenny says and shakes his head.

Hailey smacks him. "Nobody eats ham at weddings, Lenny."

"He's a vegetarian," I say, "so forget it."

Brad is not a vegetarian.

My mother looks perplexed. "A vegetarian? Well, I don't know what that means. I don't think you should bring a vegetarian to the wedding," she says. "That doesn't sound right."

"Oh, she's not bringing anyone." Hailey rolls her eyes. "Just wait and see. She'll hire a date like in that one movie. That one where that one girl hires a date and then they fall in love."

"You could have ham at a wedding," Lenny says. "Why not?"

"Shut up, Lenny," Hailey says. "No one's talking about ham anymore."

Brad calls me and asks me if I know of a dry cleaner that only uses hypoallergenic products. I don't, but I Google every dry cleaner in the state until I do. Then I find him an acupuncturist who makes house calls, a masseuse who will come to the office, and a tailor who can turn a suit around in two days.

I order his groceries for him online and even attempt to cook dinner for him because he's useless in the kitchen, which frankly is fine by me, because there's nothing worse than a man who's a better cook than you. Not that that's hard with me as a standard. I've made him fried chicken the consistency of a leather shoe, meatloaf that looked more like stew, and wild rice soup that clung to the spoon like glue.

Brad and I have been dating for two weeks. I ask Christopher if that means we're exclusive. "Two weeks for the gay bees is considered married." He sighs. "In Straight Land I have no idea. Shouldn't you be asking him?"

True, but I don't know if I can bring it up with Brad or not. I mean, I assume if we're sleeping together we're connected and exclusive, but Christopher says it only means we're sleeping together at that *particular* moment, and at any other particular moment, he may or may not be connected to any other wharf whore.

"Wharf whore?" I ask. "What's a wharf whore?"

"It's an expression."

"No, I don't think it is."

"Just ask him!"

"As if!" I say, smacking him.

I am not asking Brad anything about anything. Instead, I focus on making our dates superincredible while making it look like it's Brad who's making them superincredible. For instance, when he said he wanted to try out the new restaurant on Hennepin called Duplex, I called ahead and reserved the corner table. I actually told the girl who answered the phone exactly what I was doing. I reserved a table for eight o'clock and said, "I'll be wearing a dark blue dress and he'll be in a suit. I'll pretend we don't have a reservation. I'll just tell you his name, Brad Keller, and you act like you know who that is. Look surprised or something, like it's a big deal, and then give us a good table. It'll put him in a really good mood."

"I heard that," she says. "They all love a little ego fluff."

"Exactly," I say, and then I tell her something Christopher told me to use if I ever go to New York City and can't get a table or need special treatment. I say, "I promise I'll take care of you *in the right way.*" He told me the wording is very specific. It leaves the reward open to the imagination and the maître d' curious. They don't know what it means exactly, but they fill in the blanks themselves. In this case I slipped the girl a ten-dollar bill and a coupon to Cinnabon. Bet she didn't see that coming.

But all my work is worth it. He never suspects I've been two steps ahead of him smoothing things out. He just feels lucky when we're together. Well, almost every time. I don't think he felt very special the night we tried a new Indian restaurant and he discovered a hair that looked very much like it came from the pubic region in his extramild masala. Mostly, though, we get good tables, great treatment, and lots of smiles. We get let into the VIP room at First Avenue and "free" tickets to opening night for *A View from the Bridge* at the Guthrie Theater. (Christopher's mom works in the box office, thank God. Those tickets would have been a fortune.)

It spreads like a Girl Scout fire through the woods that I'm dating Brad Keller. Everyone at Keller's knows. I can tell they know by how they straighten up when I'm around, lean in to each other, and whisper. They look at me with their chins slightly elevated, their noses turned up, eyeing me up and down as if to say, *Why her?*

I thought dating a Keller executive might make my current position a little easier, but no. If anything, the opposite is true. I hear whispers and snickering when I walk by. Women who used to be nice to me aren't anymore, and one morning in my mailbox is an interoffice envelope with a xeroxed article inside.

"Why Affairs in the Workplace Are Inappropriate" is the title. The sender is marked out with a black pen.

Ashley calls me into her office and tosses the couch-sale script on her desk. "What's this?" she asks. I never know how to answer these rhetorical questions; I never even know if they're rhetorical, so I usually play dumb.

"That's the couch-sale script," I say.

"I *know* it's the couch-sale script," she snaps. "I just don't get it."

I try to explain. "Well, it's an announcer, a *Twilight Zone* 'Rod Serling' character, and he—"

"I can *read* the script," she says. "I know what it says. I can read, you know."

"Yes"—I nod—"you can read."

"You're not the only smart cookie around here, Miss Cinnabon."

I stare at her awards on the wall. Every one of them is from Keller's.

She tells me to sit down and I sit on the very edge of her couch. "Jen, I'm worried we have a problem," she says.

"We do?"

"Yes. You haven't been around lately. You've taken several half-days and you leave early a lot. People notice."

I don't say anything.

"And your work," she says, standing up, "I don't know. There seems to be something missing. The quality is different, like part of you isn't here. A big part."

I don't say anything.

"Is something bothering you?" She perches on the corner of her desk. "Something at home maybe?"

"No," I say, "nothing like that."

"Dating trouble?" She crosses her arms.

I raise my eyebrows the slightest degree. So this is what she's after; she wants to know about my relationship with Brad, which I'm very careful not to talk about in the office. Nobody asks me about it either. It's the elephant in the room that we ignore. Looking at Ashley's awards, I feel an odd sensation I don't immediately recognize. It's not happiness, or kindness—it's something like power.

My inner analyzer goes to work and I feel even a little stronger. This is one place I have everyone beat. A lot of people can beat me at a lot of things, but *no one* can beat me at finding potential disasters. Ashley has probably only heard rumblings about Brad and me, and she doesn't know where we stand. She probably wants to fire me and is checking to see if she can. These are simple eighth-grade social skills. Right now she's trying to figure out whether to distance herself from me, or become my best friend.

"I am negotiating a personal challenge," I confess.

"Really?"

"I'm learning how to balance work and a relationship at the same time."

She pauses. "Relationship?"

"You're so good at these things," I say, standing up, "juggling your family and your career. I don't know how you do it. We really should have a girls' coffee sometime and you should give me some pointers, because frankly"—I put my hand on her arm—"I think this is the one."

I have to borrow money from my parents. Well, from my dad actually, because no way was I going to ask my mom. It's his money, anyway; he's worked at the insurance agency his entire life. How did Mom get such a good deal going? Where are men like my dad now? The ones who are breadwinners and come home from work and put on their slippers and smoke a pipe silently while reading the paper? All you had to do was make them a Manhattan and serve a hot casserole every night, maybe have a kid every two and a half years and that was that. Your bills were paid.

"I'll pay you back, Dad," I say, standing in his den. "Promise."

"Don't worry about it, sweetie," he says. "My pleasure."

"Really. I will. I just need some money to . . ."

He holds up his hand to stop me. "You're a grown woman," he says. "You do what you want with it."

"I just have some new expenses. That's all."

He looks up at me. "You're all right, though?"

"Yes. It's nothing bad. I don't need a doctor or anything."

"Well, good," he says, going back to his paper. "Your mother would enjoy someone in the family getting a disease too much."

"Thanks, Dad." I kiss him on the head. He smells like tobacco and lime aftershave and love. I wish I could ask him a few things about men, but it isn't really like that between us. I'm just glad he's still here, braving the den.

Of course the money he gives me is gone in an instant. Already spent. My spending has gone way up, which is weird because even though I grease palms and sneak tips, Brad pays for absolutely everything. He has seriously never even let me get near a check. It could be because I've been buying a lot more outfits and more expensive makeup and even more expensive hydrating lotions. I don't care how much a new face lotion costs, I'll try it, because, let's face it, after a certain age, it's all about hydration.

I even got an expensive personalized "love Tarot reading" online for eighty bucks. Stupid, I know, especially since it told me Brad and I are totally wrong for each other. If I could just calm down about him, get comfortable, not feel so jumpy about him leaving me for another girl, maybe I would spend less. But how can I spend less when he may be the last living breadwinner in America? A man who would gladly and easily pay all his wife's bills? When am I going to meet another one of those in Minnesota?

I'm not. That's when.

I just need to balance my expenses more. Cut down on food and gas. Maybe drag the Weber grill into my living room and heat my apartment with a small, ongoing fire. I have to do something, cut back somewhere, but where? I tried to start one of those bill-paying programs that track where your money goes and generate a morbid-looking pie chart so you can see where you can economize, but after I entered all my line items, the pie chart didn't say much of anything. Only that eighty-five percent of my income was going to nonessential items, which is ridiculous.

Christopher is getting really irritated with me. "Are we ever going to hang out again?" he asks, "or has Lard Boy taken over your life?"

"Don't call him that," I say. "He's gained a little weight since we started dating. So what? *Vogue* says it's normal to put on weight if you're in a happy relationship."

"You'd think with all his money he could pay someone to suck it out."

"That's mean."

"He's mean." Christopher sniffs. "He's got you running all over town doing his errands like some errand girl, only he isn't paying you. You're just going broke dressing up for him."

"I like helping him! He just moved here and he's under all this pressure. His whole family is watching him to see how he does. So what if I pick up his dry cleaning from time to time?"

"And you pick up his groceries and his new stereo system and his hemorrhoid cream."

"Just stop! It's normal to help your boyfriend."

"Please. You don't even know if he is your boyfriend."

"I do so. We hang out together all the time."

"Wow," he says, rolling his eyes. "That settles it. You're as good as Matlock."

Of course I have no idea if Brad's my boyfriend. None whatsoever. I mean, I think he is; we spend enough time together that he seems to be. He already gave me keys to his house. I even drive his car sometimes. I know it's only been a few weeks, but doesn't that sound like a girlfriend?

"Did he give you front door keys or back door keys?"

"Back door, but we only use the back door!"

I decide to be brave and ask Brad directly. We're always together, so I can ask him if we're a couple, right? Sure I can. Just play it cool. No big deal. I get my nails and hair done and then buy salmon with dill sauce at the gourmet counter, which I say I cooked for him, as I serve it up by candlelight in the sexiest dress I own.

No big deal at all.

"That was just delicious, babe," he says, tossing his napkin on the table and unbuttoning the top of his pants. "Best yet, light and tasty. Perfect after work. Work was a killer today."

"Was it?"

"Dad has been on me all week. God. The guy's going to retire next year, he's got to let go of some control. You know? He's a control freak."

"Ed's retiring?"

"That's off the record," he says, "but yeah. And if I play my cards right, you're looking at the new store president."

"Very nice," I say. "Want some dessert? Pumpkin pie."

"Let me digest. Damn, that was a good dinner. You spoil me."

"Thanks, sweetie," I say, picking up my wineglass and gently swirling the expensive pinot noir I bought. "I just wanted to know if— God, this is so stupid."

"What?"

"No, I mean it's no big deal either way. I just wanted to know if, you know. About you and me. About us."

He leans back. "Am I in trouble?"

"No! I mean, it's just that I was at dinner at my mom's house and Hailey asked me if you were, you know, if you were my boyfriend."

Brad doesn't say anything. I can feel the deck chairs sliding as the ship begins to tank.

"I mean, I don't care." I say. "No, not that I don't care, just, I didn't know what to tell her, you know?" Brad picks up his wineglass and takes a sip. He seems to be thinking. Thinking of what? Of how to profess his undying love? Of how to politely tell me he's dating thirty girls right now and can't possibly commit to just one?

"I wish you'd say something." I laugh. "You look so serious."

"No," he says, "not serious. Preoccupied I guess. Work and everything."

This is not going the way I planned at all. I get up and clear the dishes. If he had two IQ points to put together in his head he would follow me into the kitchen and tell me I'm his girlfriend. Kiss me at least, but no, nothing.

I shovel out two pieces of pumpkin pie onto hand-painted dessert plates and bring them back to the dining room, where Brad is still staring pensively at his wine.

"Here," I say, dumping a plate in front of him. "I didn't bake it."

"Sorry if I seem out of it," he says, and my heart catches.

"The thing is, the board still has to vote. About the presidency. About my position. It's sort of an all-or-nothing deal."

The presidency? Here I slave all week getting ready for this dinner and he can't even look me in the eye? I take an angry bite of pie and that's when I realize we're sitting at the Brownville high-gloss black dining room table I saw when he first asked me out. I feel sick. I'm not his girlfriend, I'm his cook. His maid. His personal assistant.

"You talk about work too much," I say with whipped cream in my mouth. I'm stabbing at my dessert like I'm checking to see if it's dead.

"Yeah," Brad sighs. "Hannah says that, too."

I swallow. "Who?"

"My ex-girlfriend."

"Your ex-girlfriend? Which ex-girlfriend? You still talk to your ex-girlfriend?"

"Why?" he asks. "Is that bad?"

"You said, 'Hannah says that, too.' Present tense. You still talk to your ex-girlfriend?"

"Well, yeah, we're friends."

"Friends?"

"Don't you talk to your ex-boyfriends?"

"Nope. Can't say that I do, but it's great you talk to yours and you get advice from her even! That's super."

"Jesus, you're mad." He sighs.

"I'm not mad." I'm actually furious. "I think I'll go home now. To my house."

He rolls his eyes.

"You just rolled your eyes!" I point at his face. "Scientists say that is the number-one indicator that a couple will not stay together. The number-one indicator!" I cross my arms and refuse to speak.

We sit there in silence until I can't take it anymore. "So her name is Hannah?" I ask.

"Yes."

"Lovely."

He shuts his eyes. "Jesus."

"It's none of my business, Brad. It's your life. I don't even know if you're my boyfriend. So you talk to whoever you want to."

"Come on. All I said was she agreed with you, that I talk too much about work!"

"You never even mentioned this Hannah person before."

"We only lived together for like six months before she broke up with me. It totally wasn't going to—"

My eyes open wide. "*What!?*"

His eyes open wide. "What?"

"You lived together? She broke up with you?" My head is reeling. "You never told me you lived with anybody. You never told me that!"

"I thought I did."

"No, I would most certainly remember you living with some-one."

"It was four years ago! Before I went to China!"

"Before you went to China? I didn't know you went to China."

"Well, there you go," he says, frustrated. "I went to China. I took a three-month vacation. Sabbatical. Whatever you want to call it."

I think about this for a minute. Something doesn't seem right. Something seems most definitely wrong. "Wait a minute," I say. "Did you go to China because of her? Like to get away from the pain or something?"

He shrugs.

I glare at him. "You lived with someone who broke your heart and you had to go to China to get over her. Nice. I'm glad you enjoyed the salmon."

"Maybe you should go," he says.

I feel tears welling up in my eyes.

"Fine," I say. "I'll go and why don't you go back to China! Go get over your soul mate ex-girlfriend you still talk to."

Then he actually gets up and leaves the room. I stand there, speechless. Humiliated. I open my heart and he leaves? I will never speak to him again as long as I live.

I storm out to my car. He doesn't even come out after me. I just drive away in the night, alone and unloved, and certainly not anybody's girlfriend. I'm just me.

Chubby, boring Jennifer Johnson.

I don't understand what I did wrong. Am I too picky? Is that it? Should I have settled, like every other woman I know? I have sat through more weddings where I knew for a fact the groom had a drinking problem or more than one affair under his belt or even a violent temper from time to time and still every bride was ecstatic. White dress, rosy cheeks, happy parents, successful life story. Brother. Is it that important to land a man?

I should just focus on my life and me, on making my world better. I really need to clean everything. More than just the junk drawers. I need to scrub, boil, and disinfect everything in my entire place. I make a list of things to buy even though I probably shouldn't buy anything right now. I'm not really a "budget" person—in fact I really don't know how much I have in my checking account, I just use my cash card for what I want and hope for the best. I know that's bad, but if I'm overdrawn there's nothing I can do until my next paycheck, and looking at the negative numbers in my bank account is only going to depress me.

By midnight I've left four messages on Brad's phone. The first one was just a sniffle and some weepy noises. The second, I was angry and told him two can play the flirt-with-others game. The third, I apologized for the second. And the last message was about ten minutes long and I don't really remember what I said, but regretted saying it.

Christopher says he's going to come chop my hands off if I don't stop calling Brad. "Just leave Fatty Glumpkin alone!" he says.

"I can't believe I'm such an idiot," I sob into the phone. "I really think he's going to break up with me!"

"Maybe he will and maybe he won't. Maybe you should break up with him for being an emotionally bankrupt asshole."

"I ruined everything."

"If it's meant to be, it'll be," he says. He's already said this three times during this conversation.

"Maybe I should call him again, so he knows I want to talk."

Christopher sighs. "You already called him too many times. It's like when you overwater a plant. All you can really do is wait. You don't keep watering it, right?"

"I guess so."

"That's right," he says. "All you can do is wait."

The next day at work, I check my cell phone and e-mail every thirty seconds to see if Brad has tried to contact me. I don't leave my desk all day, except once, for the Heart Bear fiasco. The Heart Bears were these little stuffed teddy bears that were supposed to be made by deaf kids or epileptic refugees or something, and Keller's was selling them for Valentine's Day. They were red with white hearts on their bellies and they had a small recording device tucked in their butts, so you could record a special Valentine's Day message like, "I love you!" or "Marry me!" or "For the best Grandma ever!" Keller's was giving the bears away with any purchase over twenty dollars or for five dollars apiece, a buck of which went to the deaf kids or the epileptic refugees or whatever they were.

We got a truckload of these red bears and built a special Heart Bear kiosk that had big Lucite walls and a light-up sign that said, GIVE A BEAR TO SOMEONE WHO CARES! And as an added incentive, you could have your Heart Bear mailed anywhere in the lower forty-eight for free. So you could buy a bear, record a message, and then get it shipped to your niece or nephew or the person you were stalking and it really didn't cost very much. People started to buy them in quantity. HR even hired two temps to shovel these bears out to the public, so the regular salespeople wouldn't be hampered by the mad rush. Except that turned out to be the problem. Every bear these two temps sold had gone missing.

Four hundred and eighteen bears. Gone. What's worse, someone leaked it to the *Skyway News*. "Heart to Tell?" it read and noted the missing bears were not made by deaf children or endangered penguins but in fact by factories that use child labor in Mexico. Ed was livid and put Ashley in charge of media spin. Now she wants the marketing team to come up with "Sorry we fucked up and lost your Heart Bear" replacement gift ideas.

As we trudge to the meeting, Ted tells me he's already prepared a list of possible gift ideas for us to pitch. "We could give people a gift certificate for labia piercing," he says, "or toasters. Maybe both! I bet we could find a toaster that also pierces labias. Probably just a small mechanical adjustment, you know?"

"Sure," I say glumly.

"I also thought bereaved Heart Bear owners might enjoy *actual* bears," he says, tapping his notepad with his pen. "There's a game reserve in Alaska looking to relocate a couple hundred older black bears that have stopped hibernating and become 'nuisance bears,' which is another term for 'bears who attack people.'"

I nod as we go into the conference room and check my cell phone one last time to see if Brad called. No. Of course he hasn't. I'm not even listening to Ted anymore, who's going on and on about bear ideas. "We could even get gourmet honey from the imported foods department so each bear would arrive with a jar of honey tied around his neck."

We sit down.

At the head of the table next to Ashley is a Keller's employee I seldom see, Larkin, the head of store security. He's a tall, serious man who wears black horn-rimmed glasses and dark blue suits. He looks like a 1950s CIA agent, or Cary Grant, except meaner. I've never seen him smile, ever. Maybe now that Brad hates me he would be good dating material. I don't intend to smile ever again either.

The meeting begins and he stands. He clears his throat. "As you know we've been looking for a certain unit of Keller's merchandise called Heart Bears," he says, "and after a thorough investigation, we have concluded the merchandise was not stolen." Then he sits down.

No one says anything.

"Well, they had to be stolen," Ashley says. "They're gone."

Larkin looks at his file. "I'm aware they are gone."

She makes a mean face at him. "Shipping never even got them."

"I'm aware that shipping never got them," he says.

"Well, thank you for repeating everything I say! Maybe you could tell me if you checked all the surveillance tapes!"

Larkin nods. "We checked them. Nothing. No one breaking in, no one breaking out, no moving parcels or suspicious activity. Nothing."

"Well, you have to find them," Ashley says.

"I'm in charge of security," he says, "not Lost and Found."

Ashley frowns hard enough to make her Botoxed forehead crease. "Well, what do you suggest we do? How do we find all these lost bears?"

Larkin shrugs. "I don't know, maybe put them on the back of milk cartons?"

This is the closest thing to a joke I have ever heard him say.

Ashley, however, is not amused. "So you're saying the bears got up and walked out the door?"

This doesn't ruffle Larkin in the slightest. He just checks his watch. "Perhaps they did walk out," he says, deadpan. "Perhaps there was a Teddy Bear picnic."

Okay, he's definitely dating material.

Big Trish comes huffing into the room with a red, splotchy face. God, her ass is big. She hands Ashley a file folder, and the room goes quiet. I can hear the overhead fan kick in.

"Well, they found them," Ashley says. "The janitors found them in the incinerator. The geniuses selling them on the floor mixed up the mail chute with the garbage chute and sent all the bears down to the incinerator."

Someone titters. Ashley's eyes fly open.

"Is that funny?" she asks. "Is it? Is it funny that four hundred and eighteen bears got set on fire? That all their recording devices sounded off and when they melted they said disgusting things, which apparently Keller's customers recorded, but which I am too much of a lady to repeat? Is that funny?" When no one answers she picks up the file folder on the table and rips out a sheet of paper, apparently an eyewitness's testimonial. "Bears that were manufactured to convey loving affection," she says, "said things like, "'Put your meat in me'" and "'Teddy wants a blow job'" just before they burned up? Is that funny?" There is a pregnant moment of silence and then the room explodes with laughter.

Ted and I spend the rest of the day mocking up an apology postcard that will go out to all customers who lost Heart Bears. We draft a version, three people have to sign off on it and make notes, we redraft and they check again, and so on. It literally takes us all day to do this.

Dear Valued Keller's Customer,

It is with great regret we write to inform you that the arrival of your Keller's merchandise, HEART BEAR, will be delayed. It was an unavoidable circumstance, we assure you. One of those things that happens once in a lifetime and then hopefully never happens again. The rumors in the press are all untrue, we assure you. If you haven't heard them, don't even bother looking, because it's all under control now.

As you know, we strive to offer the highest standard of customer service, and apologize for this untimely delay. Please call the number below and confirm your order and shipping address and a replacement Heart Bear will arrive at its intended destination promptly.

—Keller's
"The only store you'll ever need"

The next day Brad still hasn't called. I trudge through work and keep my head low and my eyes on my desk. I don't want to look at anyone. They all probably already know anyway, I can just hear them sneering with delight in the break room. "Did you hear Jennifer Johnson actually thought she was Brad Keller's girlfriend? Can you imagine? Poor thing!" Then they'd cackle like black crows. Anytime I hear anyone laughing anywhere in the office, I cringe.

I'm sure they're laughing about me.

Depression wraps around me like a heavy blanket. I screwed everything up. Of course I did. That's what I do. Jennifer Johnson, human wrecking ball. Think something's secure? Can never be torn down? Think again. Give me a shot and I can bring it all tumbling down on my head faster than a union wrecking crew.

After work I pick up some Chinese food and go home, where I eat chicken with peapods right out of the container while sitting at my laptop, bidding online for a set of miniature dollhouse wine bottles. I already have little cans of Michelob in the dollhouse refrigerator and little champagne glasses on the shelf, which I allow my Tinkertoy family to use every New Year's Eve. After waiting for twenty minutes I don't get the wine bottles. I'm outbid by some jackass in Virginia.

I take a bath and read a little bit of Dr. Gupta's book. I note the section where he says when we help other people, we help ourselves. Okay, who can I help? Even if I've destroyed my life, and Brad is going to break up with me, I can still help others. That's what they'll say about me at my funeral: she died a spinster, but she was very helpful.

I dial the number on the Mormon dress Web site. The phone only rings once before it's picked up by a young girl with a sweet voice. Poor thing.

"Hello!" she says. "FLDSdresses dot com!"

"Hi there," I say. "I need to return a dress I bought from your Web site."

"Okay then," she says, "do you have your purchase order number?"

I'm so surprised I got right through to an actual compound person, I'm a little ruffled. I have to handle this right. Very delicately.

"I think I do." I say. "Do you need help?"

"Pardon?" she asks.

"No, I'm sorry," I say, "start again. What's your name?"

"Eliza," she says. If this isn't a creepy sister-wife name, I don't know what is.

"Okay, Eliza, I just wanted to know if you need any outside intervention. I mean, if you want me to come get you, I will."

She pauses. "If I want you to come *get* me?"

"I know it's hard to break out of these situations—well, I don't personally know, I've never been married, let alone to a cousin or whatever."

"I think you have the wrong number," she says and hangs up.

Great. Good going. Another victory.

No, just breathe. Relax.

I can't sink into despair. I have to take action, some kind of action, so I find my TO DO IN THIS LIFETIME list and see what's on it.

- Find true love.
- Travel around the world.
- Write great American novel or something that sells well.
- Have two children.
- Save someone's life.
- Get down to a size six.

Okay, so of everything on here, getting to a size six seems the most probable right now, so on Saturday I drive over to a rapid weight-loss clinic called "Weight for Life!" conveniently located between a Kentucky Fried Chicken and a Mexican bakery, both establishments I'm already familiar with.

I've driven past this clinic more times than I can count. There's a pink neon poster in the window that says, FREE WEIGHT LOSS

PLAN. Beneath that it says, WHAT ARE YOU WEIGHTING FOR? I park in front of the brightly lit Exec-U-Tan just as an enormous lady in a purple coat waddles past. She looks like the big human grape in those Fruit of the Loom commercials. That'll probably be me in a few short years. Huge and alone, wandering down the street like oversize novelty fruit.

I'm being too dramatic. Maybe the clinic won't even take me. Maybe they'll say I'm being absurd. They might shake their heads in disbelief and say, *You thought you needed to lose weight?* Then maybe they'll show me some photographs of truly obese people, like this woman struggling in front of me, and tell me, "If you ever look like this, c'mon back! But for now, you get outta here, silly!"

I crunch down the icy sidewalk in my big winter boots, ignoring the completely unfair and mouth-watering smell of original-recipe chicken and deep-fried cinnamon. I do not read the loud neon posters advertising extra-spicy chicken wings and 99-cent churros. I just march into the front door of the clinic. The small fluorescent-lit lobby has a half dozen folding chairs in it, and three other girls waiting. They are all smaller than me. One actually looks sick. The cramped room smells like warm lemon air freshener and the front desk girl looks bored.

Stay positive, I think, *you can do this.*

"Hi! I'd like a free personalized weight plan."

"Great," she says, and whips out a green sheet of paper with a grid of prices. "Would you like the Iron, Silver, or Platinum program?"

I'm confused. I try to make sense of the tiny numbers on the green sheet. "I just want the free weight-loss plan," I tell her, "like the sign says in the window."

"Every program has a free weight-loss plan," she says. "The

Platinum Program here is our best value." She circles something on the sheet with a red Sharpie. "Not only do you get unlimited Web site points and an upgraded personalized weight-loss plan but you also get a free mineral composition analysis, a year's supply of Vita-gized! energy supplements, and a voucher for half off our patented Weight for Life! water ionizer, as seen on TV."

"How much is all that?"

"If you use the rebate certificate," she says, "it's only a dollar a day."

"I just want one day. Today."

"The Titanium program includes everything on the Platinum program," she says. "Except it's six months of Vita-gized! energy supplements and a voucher for twenty-five percent off our patented Weight for Life! water ionizer, as seen on TV." She's staring off into the parking lot. Then, without even looking at me, she says, "You'll probably want to join our moderate group—it's for people with a little more to lose."

I take out my purse. If I don't get away from this woman I might get a migraine. "How many days do people usually sign up for?" A headache is creeping up behind my right eye, and my boots are getting really hot.

"Our finance package and payment plans all start at six months," she says, "but one year is a much better value."

"Six months? I just want to come today and get my weight-loss plan or whatever."

The doorbell sounds behind me and two women walk in. "Hi, ladies!" she says. "I'll be right with you." Then she shoots me the faintest of dark looks. "We also have financing options."

"Look"—I try to keep any trace of hurt, humiliation, anger, fear, dread, or loathing out of my voice—"I'm not signing up for a year or six months or whatever and I don't need a water ionizer. I just want the weight-loss plan." She takes out a drab, mustard-yellow sheet of paper and slides it across the counter. "Our base-cost plan then," she says.

"And how long is this one for?"

"One class, one weight-loss plan, and a keychain. Seventy bucks." She holds up a plastic keychain in the shape of a daisy that says, DON'T WEIGHT!

I tell her I'll take it.

"You'll need to fill out this questionnaire and this medical consent form," she says. "I'll need an emergency contact and payment in full."

She hands me a stack of papers and pamphlets. I'm not a hundred percent certain my credit card will work, so I write a check for seventy dollars and she hands me the daisy keychain. I feel somewhat, in a minimal way, satisfied. I fill out the questionnaires and sign away all my rights, consents, and medical histories. I only lie a little on my medical evaluation. *No known medical conditions, no history of blood clots, seizures, or depression.* Well, three out of four isn't bad.

She points me down the hall to a dingy low-ceilinged classroom with faux-wood paneling and a semicircle of folding chairs. A handful of women are already there, waiting. I sit in a chair and study the brightly colored inspirational pictures on the wall. There's one poster with a yellow butterfly on it that says, "The achievement of your goal is assured the moment you commit yourself," and as much as I'd like to get onboard with the motivational poster people, I can't help knowing this is patently untrue. I can think of dozens of situations in which someone's commitment did not assure achievement. Every silver medalist in the Olympics, for example, or the people who work at the motivational poster place. Can I think of a job that would suck more? I cannot. What about the people who didn't achieve their goal despite definite planning and commitment, not to mention catchy phrases and theme songs, like the Nazis had? And aren't we glad they didn't achieve their goals? Would we sit Hitler down today and say, "If only you'd wanted it a little more?"

A skinny blonde wearing a pink sweat suit comes in. "HEY, GANG!" she shouts at us. Her face is orangey-brown and she has deep wrinkles around her mouth. She looks like a chemical whipped dessert, something you could buy at a gas station. She says her name is Indra and she welcomes us. "I have an important question for you ladies," she says. "And if the answer is no, you can walk out that door right now."

We all shift nervously in our seats and wait for *the big important question.* Indra smiles and says, "Are you ready to become a better, thinner YOU? The YOU you've always dreamed of being?"

I try to count how many times she just said "you."

"C'mon, people!" she says. "*Are you?*"

"Yes," we say, and I must admit, we sound like a halfhearted group.

"That's the spirit!" Indra bubbles. "Great!"

She hands each of us two index cards and tells us to write something positive about ourselves on them like, "I'm good at tennis," or "I love eating healthy foods."

Okay, Indra, really. Be serious.

If any of us could in all honesty write those down, then we wouldn't be here, would we? I fight the urge to write dark things down like, "I am awesome at destroying any chance I have at happiness," or "I can eat a whole pie." I try to take it seriously and I put, "I like cats" and "I can spit farther than my sister." That's all I can think of.

When we're done, she tells us to keep the cards in our purses and pull them out anytime we're about to snack. Great. That should keep me away from a bucket of original recipe.

She has everyone scoot their folding chairs into mini-circles and we're all supposed to tell each other what's bothering us.

People begin blurting out their weird, bizarre problems. One woman doesn't like her kids, another has not one but three different eating disorders, and yet another cheated on her husband who has cancer.

Oy.

Indra nods reassuringly when people talk, but the subtext look on her face says: *I can't believe I'm stuck here with you losers. How did you get so fucking big? Couldn't you put down the Hershey bar? Really? Don't, don't, I mean whatever you do, don't touch me.* She grins so hard you think she's going to shatter her teeth.

I tell them all I just broke up with my boyfriend.

When we're finally done with personal-problem vomit time, we weigh in on the big digital scale at the head of the classroom. A person steps on and the red digits race up and then blink whatever humiliating weight she happens to be. Indra writes it down and then she steps off. It's like a game show for the unlovable.

When I step onto the scale my cheeks are burning but I refuse to let embarrassment stop me. "Okay," Indra says, "the scale says you're three pounds heavier than what you put on your intake sheet." I'm confused. "That's what I weighed this morning," I say, "and I only filled that form out like half an hour ago."

She turns to the class and winks. "Whoopsie boopsie!" she says.

What is "whoopsie boopsie"? How is that supposed to motivate me? How is "whoopsie boopsie" going to keep me from polishing off a pint of mint chocolate chip ice cream at midnight? This won't work. What I need is a hard-core weight-loss boot camp. A military-style program where the instructors are tough and the consequences are severe. I can imagine a mean German woman in a tight olive green uniform goose-stepping around me after I gained weight.

"Vee see you haf not chosen to participate in zee program," she would say. "Vee see you haf gained two pounds, hafn't you—you leetle piglet!" *Whap!* She cracks her riding crop against her boot.

At this point she could offer up a whole host of horrifying punishments. She could threaten to post a naked picture of me under fluorescent lights online, or she could even threaten to kill a kitten. If I knew that upon any weight gain, no matter how insignificant, a *kitten* would be killed—I would never gain an ounce again. Fear and shame I respond to. "Whoopsie boopsie" I do not.

My Lee, this pretty Hmong girl without an extra pound of fat on her anywhere, gets on the scale. "Well, My Lee," Indra chirps, "congratulations! Once again, you're well within your recommended body weight!"

My Lee looks disappointed. "I didn't lose anything?" she asks. "I was at a hundred and twenty-two last week, and this week I was trying to get to a hundred and twenty-one."

Indra gives her a sympathetic little pat on the back. "That's all right," she says. "You keep trying. Our ideal weight is whatever we want it to be."

"Even if it's medically unsound?" I ask.

All the women shoot looks at me and Indra ignores the comment.

"We can up your dose of ephedrine," she says and makes a note on her chart. "You'll have that pound off in no time. *My Lee* gets to pick My Lee's ideal weight. No one else."

After everyone weighs in, the gold star goes to Babsie, a battery-shaped woman from Kentucky. Babsie is trying to lose eighty pounds, but her mystery allergy to vegetables and the fact that her husband hasn't touched her in three years is slow-ing her down. She bursts into tears when she is declared the "biggest loser" of the day and tell us all that we are her best friends.

"Okay, ladies!" Indra says. "That's all the time we have. You all did great. I'll see you next week and remember our motivation quotation!" Then the whole group answers in unison, "I can be the ideal me. Through change and love and un-i-ty."

I leave early. I think this is a cult and not in a good way.

Sunday afternoon, *four days* after our fight, Brad calls. Why even bother? I'm nearly dead with worry at this point. I've spent my nights drinking red wine, crying, journaling, and doing terrible things to the Tinkertoy family. I gave them an earthquake by briefly rattling the house with both hands, made oversize plastic novelty ants invade their living room, and gave the children drinking problems by scattering miniature beer cans all around their rooms.

My hands are shaking while I'm on the phone, but I try to stay cool. Brad asks me to meet him at some Mexican place tonight so we can talk. I say sure.

I hang up.

He's definitely breaking up with me.

1. *He asked me to meet him there, not drive together.*
2. *He knows I hate Mexican food.*
3. *No one has ever said, "We need to talk" and meant about something good.*

This is all besides the fact that David dumped me in a Mexican restaurant and to this day I can't even see a burrito without feeling sick.

I smell trouble. I smell big, big trouble.

I prepare myself by having a three-hour talk with Christopher, drinking two glasses of wine before I leave the apartment, and popping a Vicodin in the car.

I hold my head high as I walk through the grimy glass doors of the restaurant and into the humid smell of oily taco seasoning and beer. There's a sign at the hostess stand that says, INDIAN TACO AND BINGO NIGHT!

Instant headache.

"Jen!" Brad waves to me from across the crowded room. He's early, which is suspicious action number four. I smile weakly, feeling all my plucky resolve draining out of my feet. This is going to suck. This is going to be up there with my top three bad, regrettable, terrible no-good memories, possibly locking in at number one, depending on how much I drink.

I sit down at the faded red-and-white-checked tablecloth. A lone red candle flickers.

"Hi," I say.

"Hey." He leans over and gives me a quick, awkward kiss on the cheek. He says something about how cold it is outside. Great. We're already talking about the weather. The short, bored waiter arrives and asks us what we'd like. "What's an Indian taco?" I ask.

He doesn't look up as he answers. "Corn," he says. "No beans."

"That's it?"

He shrugs. "Free bingo card too."

"Great, we'll have the Indian tacos," Brad says, obviously already annoyed at how much time this breakup is taking.

The waiter scribbles down our orders. His apron is greasy, and acne pebbles his face, but he has a thick wedding band on his finger. He probably has a happy wife at home and three brilliant kids. He's probably been married since he was eighteen.

"Jen, are you listening?" Brad asks. "Do you want just one margarita or should we get a pitcher?" The waiter is still there tapping his pad with his ballpoint pen.

"Whatever's biggest," I say. "Bathtub, goat bladder, pitcher, whatever. Perfect."

Brad smiles tightly. "Pitcher then."

The waiter leaves and some other guy walks up. "Hi, fucker!" he says to Brad, pounding him on the shoulder.

Brad beams. "Hey, asshole!"

Then the guy leaves. That's it. That's the total of their conversation.

"What was that?" I ask. "Do you hate each other or something?"

"That's just how guys say hi. It's a form of flattery."

"Isn't flattery a form of flattery?" I ask. "And a more direct route?"

"You wouldn't understand it. Girls don't get it."

"Girls don't get it because it's stupid."

Brad rolls his eyes and scoots his chair out farther so he can see the horrible band. Conversation over. Communication done.

Maybe I should just tell him I never want to see him again right now over the oily tortilla chips in the red wicker basket. Maybe I should blurt it out first, so I can be the one who dumped him. So I can say to people, "You know, it just wasn't working out. We weren't right for each other, so I told him it was over." Then I could pretend not to care, and talk about true paths and destiny. I could tell people I'm ready for whatever wonderful plan the universe has in store for me next, even though what I'm fairly certain the universe has in store for me next is another humiliating crack on the jaw.

Brad drums his fingers on the table to the music. So this is what the slaughtering field looks like. Yes, this is definitely a breakup. I list the things I don't like about him in my head to try and make this process easier. *He snores like a Kodiak Bear, he picks his nose without looking to see if anyone is watching, I caught him downloading porn on his laptop, he farts without apologizing, he's selfish, and he expects me to give him oral sex, rarely with any reciprocation.* (Don't get me wrong, I don't mind giving head, but there's a limit. Twenty minutes actually is the limit. If he doesn't cum after twenty minutes of me having my jaw unhinged while fighting my gag reflex, I get up and turn the lights on.)

A pretty girl walks by our table, a tight little blonde, and I study Brad out of the corner of my eye to see if he looks. Of course he looks. Very briefly, but he tries to be all clever by not moving his head, only his eyes. Like I can't see that.

"Is it really *that hard* not to look at other women?"

"What?"

"I asked you if it was that hard not to look at other women."

"I don't think I did."

"Oh, you did, Brad. You definitely did."

"I don't know. Maybe it's a knee-jerk reaction?"

I snort. A knee-jerk reaction? What is he, a feral dog or a domesticated raccoon?

The waiter sets our Indian tacos down.

"I'm glad you finally called," I say casually, poking at my food as though it looked fabulous. "I was starting to think we were never going to speak again." I'm hoping to convey an insouciant ambivalence here and not sheer terror.

"Of course I was going to call," he says, shoveling a forkful in his mouth.

"Could you not talk with your mouth full?" I ask.

He rolls his eyes.

What do I care? It's not like I'm ever going to see him again.

"So if you were going to call me, what did you do for three days?" I ask.

Brad takes a sip of margarita. "I just spent some time with my mom. She wasn't feeling good."

"Nothing serious, I hope."

"No. Migraines. She's all right now."

"Well, thank goodness for that."

We eat in silence. The mariachi band stops and the bingo announcer tells us about all the amazing prizes we might win. Wow. I might go home not only single tonight but with a waffle press and a trip to Grand Casino to see Merle Haggard perform.

The sad part is, I would love that.

The announcer says that the game will begin shortly, so we should all get our cards ready. Before that though, we'll be enjoying the soothing sounds of some acoustic guitar.

Our plates are cleared, we've finished most of the margarita pitcher, and there's still been no mention of breaking up. I start to think maybe I've imagined the whole thing. Maybe Brad isn't about to publicly humiliate me, but then he takes my hand and says, "Jen, we have to talk about us."

"We didn't get bingo cards," I blurt out. "Why didn't he give us bingo cards? He said bingo cards came with Indian tacos. I think if we're going to eat racist food, we should get bingo cards."

"Jen, it doesn't matter."

"Oh really? It doesn't? Why don't you tell that to the Board of Native American Affairs? I don't think they'd care for the name 'Indian tacos.' "

At this point I realize everyone around me is staring at me.

"Oh God," I say and run to the bathroom, where I think I might be sick. I suspect Brad's consulted some kind of "breakup advice" Web site because he seems to be doing this with great caution and very calmly. I myself have read these sites often, so if and when a guy starts to break up with me, I'll know the signs and can beat him to the punch. Brad has already executed the top two breakup tips.

1. *Always break up in public, but never at a bar or restaurant you like, because it'll spoil one of your favorite places.*
2. *Never break up at the beginning of a meal. Wait till after you eat or you'll have a very awkward/hostile meal.*

I urgently text-message Christopher from a bathroom stall.

Me: He's breaking up with me!

Christopher: Good riddance.

Me: No! I don't want to break up!

Christopher: Oh just get it over with. We hate him. Everybody hates him.

Me: Not helping!!

Christopher: Spill a drink on him. He won't break up with you if it looks like he peed his pants.

When I go back to the table a musician is onstage painfully plucking out "La Cucaracha" on his guitar, which will now and forevermore be the soundtrack of the Brad breakup. "The Cockroach." How perfect. The guy is playing horribly, like maybe he isn't a paid musician, but somebody's unemployed cousin who needed a gig.

Brad looks nervous. He's gearing up to say something.

I bump my margarita, hoping to knock it over, and it wobbles momentarily but then infuriatingly rights itself, so I pick the glass up and drink the fizzy, salty drink down whole. If it's not going to help the situation one way, it'll help in another.

Won't be enough, though.

The waiter flashes past and I grab him. I mean I physically lean out and grab his arm with my hand. Waiters hate this more than they hate anything. I know because I waited tables at a pub in college and anytime someone touched me I spit in their beer. I tell him I want a shot of tequila, no two shots. Spit be damned. Spit is the least of my problems right now. There's nothing left to do except let this happen.

Just breathe. Relax.

I can do this.

Brad takes a big sip of his margarita and clears his throat.

"What man drinks margaritas?" I ask suddenly.

"What?"

"Seriously. I've never met a man who drank margaritas. They're too girly."

"Jen, I have to say something."

I want to throw up. The waiter plunks down two shots of tequila in front of me. There's a special place in heaven for this man. He's delivering essential field medicines to the mortally wounded. I slam the tequila. Both shots. My heart is hammering in my chest and "La Cucaracha" tap-dances on my last nerve.

Brad starts to talk but I cut him off.

"No," I say, holding up my hand. "I don't want to do this."

He's perplexed. "Don't want to do what?"

"I don't need a man, I don't want a man, I'm fine without a man, I'm *better* without a man." I stand up and sling my purse over my shoulder.

"Jen?" he says. "Where are you going?"

"Anywhere *that man* isn't playing the guitar," I say, pointing at the stage.

I pause. Again, the music has stopped and the whole room,

including the musician, is staring at me. "Oh, come on!" I say and storm out.

Brad follows me outside, where I pant in the cold air, while trying to remember where I parked my freaking car. A guy in a full-length safety orange snowsuit is leaning against the window smoking a cigarette. I can't help noticing him, because his snowsuit is the exact same color as the Scout. I briefly wonder if he *is* the Scout, in human form.

"Jen," Brad says, "please, let's talk."

I put my finger in his stupid face. The tequila is thrumming deliciously in my head. "I get it," I say, "it's over, but let's spare each other the speeches, okay? *I get it*. You love me but you're not *in* love with me. We've grown apart. You don't feel that spark anymore with me. You met someone else. You need to be alone right now. You're moving across the country. You have a disease. Whatever it is, you want to move on. I don't care."

He tries to say something, but I won't let him. "I know you still care about me and you want to be *friends*, Brad. I get it, but here's what you don't know, I don't want to be friends with *you*."

"But, Jen—"

"I don't want to be your friend because you're a snob and because your penis bends to the left. Because you don't clip your toenails and I know you downloaded porn called 'Grannies Who Chug Cock.'"

The orange snowsuit guy says, "Ouch!"

I go on. "I don't want to be your friend because you won't stop bothering me about anal sex and you never once asked if you could pick up *my* dry cleaning."

I'm really getting going now and his bad habits are popping up in my head like a field of bright yellow daisies. I can hardly pick them all in time. "Because you don't like my toy collection or my cat and because I called you once and told you there was a spider as big as my head in my bathtub and you didn't come over and kill it!"

The orange snowsuit guy shakes his head. "Ya gotta kill the spiders, man," he says. "Ya gotta."

I put my hands on my hips. Maybe it's my nervous exhaustion or my new tequila-sponsored honesty, but I feel a jolt of something I can only describe as angry joy surging through me. "I don't want to be your friend, Bradford, because worse than everything else combined, worse than you being selfish and inconsiderate and always late, you're a *mama's boy*."

There, I said it.

I step back, out of breath. He gulps air like a big, stupid fish.

"But, Jen," he says, "I wanted to apologize."

I don't think I heard him right.

He shakes his head. "I wasn't breaking up with you."

"Uh-oh," the orange snowsuit guy says.

Brad tucks a strand of hair behind my ear. "I was trying to tell you . . . that I want to be your boyfriend."

"You do?"

"Yeah, you nutcase." He wraps his arms around me.

I feel unsteady. Tears ready to roll. "Really?" I whisper.

"Really," he says and kisses the top of my head. "I love you. You're the only woman I want on this whole broken planet."

"I did not see that coming," the orange snowsuit guys says, shaking his head.

"I love you, too!" I say and bury my face in his coat. He smells like heaven. Absolute, perfect heaven. "I wasn't trying to download 'Grannies Who Chug Cock,'" he whispers. "I swear. I clicked the wrong thing."

I laugh, eyes full of tears, and we kiss. It's like no other kiss before. It's deeper, truer, and with more tongue. I'm flooded with relief, like I'd been dying of thirst and now a river of crystal-clear water is washing over me. I look up at him and frown. "Why did you take three whole days to tell me? You should have just told me right then! We wouldn't have had a huge fight."

"Just shut up and be my girlfriend," he says.

"Really?" I ask. "Your girlfriend?"

"Really," he says. "My girlfriend."

God, I love this man.

"Let's go home," he says. "We can talk about all that other stuff you said, um, tomorrow or maybe never." He links his arm in mine and we walk down the sidewalk together.

I hold back the tears for two blocks.

I throw myself into fervent "good girlfriend" research. If there's advice, I want it. If there's a tip, I'll take it. I don't care where it comes from. *Vogue*, *Cosmopolitan*, *Woman's Day*, *Teen Beat*, they all have a *lot* of articles about "capturing" and "luring" and "keeping" men. It's like getting a man to stay with you is the equivalent of hunting for large game. The ultimate goal is to find the tastiest prey, hunt it down, and then nail it to the altar.

Woman's Day says the best way to keep a man is through his stomach. They have recipes *he'll love!* and provide ample ways to incorporate comfort foods with intimate evenings so your guy starts to associate food and sex with you. "Capture a man's appetite, and you capture the man." This of course is pure, unmitigated bullshit. The key to keeping a man is to keep him *wanting* you, and that particular code has as many variables as there are men.

Vogue says men will tell you what they like; you just have to watch for the clues. They've been trained to keep what they really want subtle to invisible for fear of being clocked in the head with a flying stiletto so they recommend paying attention to your guy's "stories." Especially about their friends. Example: He says, "My friend XXX likes anal. Is that weird?"

Brad isn't subtle at all. He wants anal bad, and I won't budge on the matter.

"It hurts," I told him. "It'd be like me trying to stick a rolling pin in your eye socket. Is that sexy? No. So don't ask me anymore. The day I can stick a rolling pin in your eye is the day I let you put your thing back there. That's it."

Elle says the hardest part about capturing a guy's heart is playing it cool. They insist a girl has to act nonchalant even in the most ardent situations. The minute guys think they have you, they lose interest in you. It comes from caveman days, when men hunted for food and chased after creatures that ran away. The minute they caught it the hunt, and therefore the thrill, was over. So you have to keep the hunt going by acting like you don't really care, like you could take off at any moment. If you start acting "caught" or, worse, advance on him, he'll be the one to turn and run.

So great. While I'm cooking scrumptious meals in the kitchen and being a triathlete in the bedroom, I also have to act like I'm bored. And how long am I supposed to keep that up? For life? Am I supposed to be emotionally detached and generally uninterested when we're ninety-two and sitting in rocking chairs next to each other on the porch?

While it's almost impossible to ignore Brad, it's very easy to ignore Ted, who's gotten really moody lately. We hardly talk anymore, but then again I hardly talk to any of my friends. I'm too busy. I'm always scrambling to get my work done, not that it matters because Ashley hates everything I do and has hit a new level of hostile.

"What's this?" she shouts at me in her office, holding up the

Super Saver coupon book. It's just this stupid book of nearly meaningless coupons, like twenty-five percent off men's socks and buy-one-get-one-free pencil cups. We spend about half a day doing the marketing copy, which goes on the front, and in this case says, KELLER'S! COME INTO CLASSY!

"What's wrong with it?"

"What's wrong with it? Are you telling me that I'm showing you this and you do not automatically know what's wrong with it?"

I shrug. Why doesn't she ever call Ted in to yell at him about this stuff? We write all of it together. "I'm sorry, Ashley," I say, "I'm not sure what to look for."

"Why don't you look for the word 'classy,'" she says, "and tell me if we did or did not decide to spell classy with a *k* this year."

"Oh, you wanted it to say, 'come into Klassy' spelled with a *k*?"

"No," she says. "*We* wanted it spelled with a *k*. The entire marketing department. We all agreed and you were at the meeting. No, wait! Maybe you weren't at the meeting. Maybe you were out gallivanting around on one of your extralong lunch breaks or spontaneous pedicure appointments! Or maybe you were there and your brain just doesn't have the capacity to retain a single thought anymore!" I just stand there with the coupon book in my hands.

"I'm sorry, Ashley," I say. "I'll try to do better."

"Super!" she says. "Just grand. You better pull your act together, my little lamb chop, or you will be out of here. Consider this an official warning."

"Seriously? You're writing this up?"

She doesn't say anything.

I ask her again, "Are you serious?"

She holds up a manicured hand and shoos me away.

I sit at my desk and stare at my photograph of Mrs. Biggles. My phone rings. Brad asks me if I want to grab dinner after work and then he asks me what's wrong.

"Nothing," I say. "I just, I got in trouble but I don't know why."

I tell him about Ashley writing me up and what a terrible day I'm having; just like any girl might tell the guy she's dating. That's the whole point, right? Spend time together and talk so you can get to know someone? Share your dreams, your troubles, your stories of psychobosses? He tells me not to worry, everything will be all right, and I tell him I'll be okay. I feel a little bit better after we hang up and I meet Christopher in the cafeteria for lunch.

We both bravely try the chicken cacciatore.

When I come back to my desk, Ashley is standing there with Ed Keller. Ted is sitting in his cubicle across the way with a weird look on his face. No one is speaking.

Am I about to get fired? For all I know this is how it happens. Ed comes down and says, "Get out and remember God loves you," and then a beefy security officer comes down and hustles you past your sneering co-workers and out the door where you stand on the street, probably never to get another job again.

"Hi?" I say, like it's a question. "Are you, are you here to see me?" I'm blinking and wincing as though someone might slap me.

"We are here to see you," Ed says and clears his throat. "Ashley here has something to say to you."

Ashley's eyes are locked on the carpet and they do not leave this position at any time. Her voice is low and steady. "I'm sorry," she says. "I'm sorry that I communicated inappropriately with you earlier and I promise to express myself in a more respectful manner in the future."

Good Christ!

I look at Ted, who seems equally baffled. My mind races through the variety of possibilities that could explain her bizarre behavior, which include a brain tumor and Ashley's sudden religious conversion, but then I think of my phone call with Brad.

Crap.

Ed steps forward and smiles benevolently. "We value you as an employee," he says, "and that goes for all of you!" He raises his voice over the tops of the cubicles for all to hear. Of course he must realize every single person in the office has been at their desks straining to hear this interaction the whole time. "No one here should accept disrespectful behavior at any time!" he says. "Not from their co-workers and not from their managers. We're a company with God at the helm, and we strive to act as he would!"

That Ed, I tell you, he has claws.

He pats me on the shoulder as he leaves. "We expect to see you at the house for supper sometime soon," he says. Then he turns and marches down the corridor, Ashley in tow.

They go into her office and close the door. They're in there together for about five minutes and when he comes out, he shuts the door behind him. It stays shut for the rest of the day.

Brad takes me to his parents' house for dinner, and he promises it's no big deal, just "super casual." Ed is away, so it's just me, Brad, and Mrs. Keller, which is what I'm told to call her, and unless someone corrects me, what I think I'm expected to call her for the rest of my life. I shouldn't worry about her correcting me, though; I don't think that will be a problem.

Mrs. Keller is a tiny woman and yet she walks into a room like a lit furnace. You always know she's there; you can feel her sharp eyes watching you and her sharper mind making mental note of every detail she surveys. Details are her thing. She has a short silver pageboy that she sprays into a perfect helmet. There's never a single hair out of place. She always wears feminine pastel dresses made of highly flammable materials, which flounce and ripple when she walks. There's an almost forced innocence, a living-doll quality about them, as though she was a seventy-year-old little girl.

When I meet her she's wearing a knee-length Pepto-Bismol-colored dress with poofy sleeves and a high neck that doubles over into a wide ruffle so her head looks like a pink Gerber daisy. She tells us to take off our shoes because she's just had the carpets done and I wish to God I'd thought of this possibility before, because there is the smallest hole in the toe of my stockings.

Mrs. Keller has a crippled Pomeranian named Boots, who has her back legs strapped into a doggie wheelchair. Boots rolls along with us as we take a tour, beginning in the immaculate mostly white living room, which looks like a nondenominational church sanctuary. Then we go to the gleaming dining room, which has a table that can seat twelve. We end up in the spotless kitchen, which has every kitchen amenity and appliance invented.

"What's that?" I ask, pointing to a big boxy thing. I think asking questions might make me seem polite. "Why, that's a bread maker!" she says, tapping it with her manicured nail. "Hasn't she ever seen a bread maker before, Bradford?"

I was surprised to learn the Kellers don't have a maid. "But your house is so big!" I say, wondering how on earth she cleans the cathedral windows in the living room, which are two stories tall. "I do all my own housework," she says proudly, "all the cooking and cleaning. I believe it's a good mother's duty. Isn't that right, Bradford?"

"Mom's a great cook. She baked every birthday cake I ever had."

"Bradford loves pecan pie," she says, "but I'm sure you already know that."

I didn't know that. I also had no idea pecan pie was considered a type of birthday cake, or that anyone made it after 1959.

She busies herself with getting dinner ready. "No point in using the dining room," she says, taking a dish out of the oven. "That's for special occasions."

I wish beyond all wishes I could ask for a glass of wine.

"We're having duck casserole," Mrs. Keller says. "Do you like duck, Jennifer?"

"Yes, Ma'am!" I say and she gives me a funny look. She takes the potatoes and carrots out of the oven, which have been roasting in their own special potato and carrot oven-roasting dishes.

"Jennifer," she says, smiling over the steaming vegetables, "would you like to help?"

"Of course!" I say, jumping up and knocking my knee painfully into the table leg.

"Why don't you get the butter," she says. "In the Frigidaire."

I practically sprint to the refrigerator. I think the last time I heard anyone call a refrigerator a Frigidaire was on an episode of the *Honeymooners*.

I'm taken with not only the number of items inside her Frigidaire but also the fact they're all facing labels-out. "See it?" she asks and I say yes, but I don't see it. You keep butter in the door, right? In the little flippy-lid butter compartment? But there is no flippy-lid butter compartment, just rows of short shelves that hold every kind of jam you can imagine and a tall wire rack that neatly holds cans of pop.

"I guess I don't see it," I say, looking over my shoulder, and possibly see her rolling her eyes as she walks over, but I can't be sure. She shows me the heavy crockery pot on the top shelf, where she always keeps butter, like that's where any sane person would keep butter.

After we're all seated, I've already picked up my fork when Mrs. Keller begins to pray. "Dear Jesus," she says, "blessed Father, blessed be this food and this house and all the people in it, including the people who are in our family as well as the people who are not in our family. We ask that you be with us here tonight, Lord, and to guide us in all our thoughts and decisions. Amen."

I open my eyes and half expect Jesus to be sitting there at the fourth place mat. "Is there anything to drink?" I ask meekly, holding my empty water glass.

Mrs. Keller drops her fork loudly and says, "If it's not one thing, it's another," and pushes her chair back. Brad is oblivious, slopping glops of duck casserole on his plate.

"Here you go," Mrs. Keller says, holding an earthenware pitcher and pouring a liquid that looks like rust water into my glass. I take a sip, and it burns.

It turns out Mrs. Keller makes her own apple cider. The strongest, spiciest cider you ever tasted that doesn't have a drop of alcohol in it. My eyes water and I nearly choke when I take a sip. "Isn't it good?" Brad asks, taking a big gulp.

"Is there pepper in it?" I ask, dabbing at my eyes with my napkin.

"Family secret!" Mrs. Keller says, eyes glowing.

Boots stares at me from the floor.

Mrs. Keller starts asking me questions. She asks me about everything from where I went to school, to whom I've dated, to what my father does for work, to my religious beliefs, to whom I voted for in the last election, to which kind of lettuce I prefer.

"Romaine?" I say, thinking it's the most biblical-looking lettuce of all the lettuces. I can't picture iceberg lettuce at the Last Supper.

I keep looking at Brad to help me, but he seems as curious as she does. I do my best to answer her questions the way I think she wants me to answer them.

I lie.

It's not hard to know what she wants to hear. Not really. You know you're on the wrong track if she starts zipping that gold cross around her neck back and forth on its chain. By the time she serves us two pieces of strawberry shortcake with big dollops of whipped cream on them, I am exhausted, utterly drained, and I've given her every impression I'm a highly religious, politically conservative virgin who wants Brad to join my Bible study.

I still don't think I did it right.

"My husband said you look just like his cousin Ada," she says, looking me over, "but I don't see the resemblance at all."

I go to the bathroom and press my face against the cool peach walls. I flush the toilet and run the water, even though I wouldn't dare actually use either for their original intention. When I go back, they're already almost done clearing the dishes and Mrs. Keller says not to worry, I can do all the washing up next time. *Next time*. Dear Lord in heaven, there might be a next time.

When Mrs. Keller is off getting some article on sailing she cut out for Bradford, he tells me he thinks the night was a great success and his mother really likes me. He thinks we should make meals together a regular habit since they're so close and everything.

After a round of small hugs and polite kisses, Mrs. Keller tells me how good it was to meet me and how she does hope I can come back soon. "And, Bradford, buy the girl some new stockings!" she says, shaking her head at the hole in my toe. "Goodness. She looks like an orphan from *Tobacco Road*."

We finally escape down Mrs. Keller's perfectly appointed walk. Then we cross the driveway and follow the short Kennebunkport cobblestone path up to Brad's back door. It takes about thirty seconds total.

"Isn't that nice?" he says. "We don't even need to get in the car to visit. They're always right next door."

Hailey wants to "really go wild" for her bachelorette party. I'm not sure why I said I'd go. The idea of dancing to remixed eighties house music and slamming girly alcopop like the Buttery Nipple (butterscotch schnapps mixed with Irish Cream), the Kickin' Chicken (whiskey and Tabasco sauce), and Liquid Cocaine (peppermint schnapps, Jägermeister, and 151-proof rum) gives me a girly alcopop headache.

Maybe I said I'd go because disasters are entertaining. Ten girls, a rented limo, and my sister in a Life Savers–covered "suck-a-buck" T-shirt? True disaster and whatever happens I want my mother to have an eyewitness account.

I'm not jealous. How could I be? All the prepackaged "significant moments," it's all just built-in disappointment, like Christmas or your birthday. Birthdays are such a big deal when you're little. Everything is so amazing. You plan for months beforehand and you invite everybody. Every present thrills you; it hardly takes anything to make you happy. Clowns are great, balloon animals are great, grocery-store sheet cake is great, and dollar plastic prizes you get after you smash a piñata to pieces are great. You get so hysterical and crazy running around playing with your friends that eventually you have to be separated from the group.

Then when you get older your birthday sucks no matter what

you do. If you saw a balloon animal or a piñata or a rented clown on your birthday now, you'd just cry and cry and cry. Sheet cake is still cool, but nothing can really completely bring back that feeling you had when you were little of being utterly thrilled, of feeling like you were literally the luckiest person in the world and this is the best day of your life. When's the last time you felt like that?

Maybe that's why falling in love becomes so important. The hope of it. Because it's the last standing pillar in the temple of thrill. When you fall in love with someone, it's your birthday and you are nine. It's sunny and your parents love you and there are clowns and they don't creep you out or make you wonder what they did in life to end up a clown; they just thrill you through and through with this radiant green joy that feels like maybe it's going to last forever.

I guess I'm jealous after all. Hailey is experiencing her ninth birthday all over again, and here I am trying to poop on it every chance I get. That makes me feel awful. It really does. God help me. The nice side of me is in hell, the dark side is in heaven.

"We said we would pick you up at six," Hailey snaps. "Where are you?"

"You said seven! You did! I was just stopping to get you some champagne!" I hold up the wrapped bottle with a blue ribbon on it, as though it was proof, over the phone.

"Well, we're here," Hailey says, "sitting like idiots in a white stretch limo in front of your ugly house. God, this is a shithole."

"Did you get the limo with strobe lights? Because those actually can give you seizures."

"Well, if it doesn't have strobe lights," she says, "we'll go get one that does."

"I swear you said seven. I have the text message you sent. You did."

"You suck," she says.

"I suck? Who goes out at six p.m.? Are you seventy? Where are we going, Old Country Buffet?"

"If you don't get here, we're leaving."

"I'm just pulling around the corner. Seriously. Can you see me?"

"No, I can't," she says, "and we're only waiting one more minute, Jen. Seriously. You so suck." One of the girls behind her shrieks, "You suck, Jen!"

"You suck," Hailey says, "everyone thinks you suck." She holds the phone away from her ear. "Okay, group vote!" she shouts. "Should we leave my stupid sister behind or should we wait for her?"

"Is she bringing any guys?"

"Shut up, Lexi! It's my bachelorette party. She's not bringing any guys."

"Then leave her!"

Up goes a chorus of "Leave her! Leave her!"

"All right, shut up, you guys! Shut up! Okay, Jen, we're waiting five more minutes and if you're not here, you're queer. We're leaving."

"You do know the bar you're going to is gay, right?"

"Excalibur is not a gay bar. It's an alternative bar."

"I don't think you know what alternative means."

"Yes, I do, it means they're funky but they're poor."

"You're an idiot." I hang up and speed through two more lights and turn the corner to my apartment just as my cell phone starts vibrating so my spasmodic sister can tell me she and the titty-studded booze crew are leaving.

"I'm here, I'm here!" I park alongside an ice bank, praying there won't be a snow emergency and the Scout won't get towed. I dash out of my car and take a single sharp breath of cold air only to duck back into the hot, perfume-heavy, neon-blue-lit limousine that's waiting for me.

"Hi, guys!" I say. "Wow, Hailey, nice shirt."

My sister is wearing a white-sequined miniskirt and a white tank top covered with unwrapped Jolly Ranchers.

"We couldn't get the Life Savers to stick," Lexi explains, "but if you lick a Jolly Rancher and press it hard enough, it sticks really good!"

They're all drinking prebottled Pink Squirrels and blasting old Blondie songs. Lexi tells Hailey about a book called *Penis Pokey*, which has a hole on every page in the book that's big enough for a guy to slide his penis through, so his dick looks like anything from an elephant trunk to a fire hose to an old man's nose. Before I know what's happening, they decide they want to go find this book and the white limousine pulls up in front of the Barnes and Noble in Calhoun Village. All the wild, screaming girls pile into the store, fanning out through the aisles looking for *Penis Pokey*.

I stand at the counter, where an employee asks if I need help. Her name badge says KELLEY. "Hi, Kelley," I say, "I'm looking for *Chicken Soup for the Suicidal Soul*. Do you have that book? Because that's the one I need."

She blinks and says maybe the crafting aisle.

Then Christopher calls. He's broken down on Highway 12 and there's a two-hour wait for a tow. "I'm just afraid someone will stop and it won't turn out like the porno I imagined, but look more like the Matthew Shepard story."

"Where's Jeremy?"

"Cooking class," he sniffs. "I can't even get a cab to look for me, because I can't tell them where I am. All I know is I'm on highway twelve about a quarter mile past that hotel where we had a three-way with that bingo guy."

"The bingo guy?" I say. "I know right where you are! The Fairfield Inn, right off the Ridgedale exit. You've told me that story a thousand times! I'll be right there."

"I have to go," I tell Hailey. "I'll be right back. Christopher broke down. Just go have dinner and I'll see you at Excalibur."

She pouts and calls me the Ruiner.

I have a cab take me to my place and I get my car. I think that's better than paying a taxi to cruise highways looking for my little wandering parakeet.

I drive down Highway 12 as slowly as I legally can, which is forty-five miles an hour. Have you ever actually driven forty-five miles an hour on the freeway? You might as well get out and crawl. Cars pile up behind me and honk, drivers shout expletives and give me the finger as they zoom past.

Christopher turns out to be exactly where he said he'd be, precariously huddled in the center of the highway against the median about a quarter mile past the Fairfield Inn. I pull the Scout off onto the narrow shoulder and honk twice. He's actually got the hood up on his car and is peering into the engine, like he has any idea what he's looking for.

"What are you doing?" I holler over the cars speeding past us. "Get in!"

"I think I've got it!" he says, and motions me to come look. I pull the emergency brake—I guess because this is an emergency—and make my way alongside the cement divider to the front of his car. "I think this is it!" he says and pulls whatever totally retarded, wrong thing he's got ahold of and suddenly sticky green fluid explodes everywhere.

"Oh my God!" I scream. "Is it acid?"

A truck roars past and hoses us down with a huge sheet of slushy ice water. We both do this weird "it's-all-over-me-get-it-off-of-me" Riverdance thing as we run to the car. Inside, out of breath and panting, Christopher makes a face.

"It smells like damp hamster bedding in here," he says.

"I'm sorry, would you prefer to wait outside?"

"We could have stayed out there." He licks his lips, tasting a smear of green on the corner of his mouth. "I think it's antifreeze."

I rummage around the backseat to find my gym bag under the crumpled nest of Taco John's wrappers. I dig out a pair of pink sweatpants and a torn Replacements T-shirt for him, and a zip-up lime green terrycloth cover-up for me.

Christopher raises an eyebrow.

"It's for poolside," I say.

"Is the pool in a rent-controlled Palm Beach retirement community?"

"Well, my fundamentalist Mormon dress is back there, would you like me to wear that?"

Christopher's eyes light up and he dives into the backseat where he thrashes around until he finds the opened FedEx box. "It's hideous!" he squeals, pulling the thick powder-blue dress from the cardboard box. "I love it! The high collar! The pleated shoulders! It's so Polygamist Couture! So Porn on the Prairie!"

"I have to return it, it's huge. I mean, I know they're supposed to be roomy, but this looks like a tea cozy for a refrigerator."

"Is that how it came?" he asks. "Packed in straw? Using hay is so Ralph Lauren 1988. They should get Gaultier to redo their packaging. Maybe he could redesign the dresses."

I look in the rearview mirror and try to fix my makeup. "Yeah, I'm sure Warren Jeffs wants his next child-bride to wear haute couture."

Christopher sits back down in his seat and wipes his hands off. "Well, I don't know. You should see what Gaultier did with a burka for the spring collection. Amazing."

"God, even fourteen-year-olds in Utah can find husbands. That's depressing."

"Why don't they just airlift Queen Latifah into one of those nasty little fundamentalist towns? She'd sort it out by sundown. Can you imagine Queen Latifah at a sister-wife prayer meeting?" He claps his hands. "Why don't they do that!"

"God," I sigh, "I don't want to be around a big group of insane women right now. I don't want to go to Excalibur."

"Hailey's bachelorette party is at Excalibur? That's right! Let's go!"

I tell him it's for girls only.

"Please," he says, "I'm better at being a girl than your sister will ever be."

"Can you go to a gay bar in sweatpants? Isn't there a law?"

"No," he sniffs. "Track suits are like the unofficial uniform for gay bees. Plus, my natural charm overcomes any outfit. Um, I don't think it could overcome yours though."

I put my head on the steering wheel.

POP!

I lift my head and Christopher is holding a foaming bottle of champagne.

"That's for Hailey!" I shout. "Where did you get that?"

"I don't know." He shrugs, holding the bottle as it foams. "Under the seat?"

"What do you mean, you don't know? You don't know where you just got this?" I snatch it away from him. "That's how your mother raised you? You find a bottle of gift-wrapped champagne in someone else's car and you open it?"

Christopher pats the little blue ribbon on his head like a tiny blue crown.

"Yes," he says.

I glare at him and then I start laughing. I can't help it.

I take a swig and pass the bottle back. "Fine. Let's go to a bridal shower."

I step on the gas and as we go charging into traffic, Christopher holds the champagne bottle out the window and says, "To evil!" and then adds, "I'm hungry. Do you have anything to eat in here?"

We hit the drive-through at Wendy's and order a triple cheeseburgers, and extra-large fries, and two Sprites, which we mix with champagne. Christopher calls them Drunkdrivetinis. We eat as we drive and I don't look in the rearview mirror once, because I can feel mayonnaise and ketchup glooping on the corners of my mouth, and why should I look at something I don't want to see?

We're a little inebriated by the time we arrive at Excalibur. I valet the car. Normally I might be ashamed that I look like a slutty senior citizen in my lime green coverall or that my car is festering with junk-food wrappers, but tonight I don't care. I drop the keys in the valet's hand and step over the empty Taco John's cup that rolls out with me. "Look, Buddy," I tell him, giving him a twenty, "I'm about to have a really bad night. Can you just keep it out in front for like twenty minutes?" The guy looks so happy, like I gave him a hundred dollars or something.

"Yes, Ma'am," he says, "you bet I can!"

Inside the bar it's dark. The walls are red leather, it's humid and warm, and I feel slightly grossed out, like I've stepped inside someone's mouth. I can smell sweat and stale cigarettes, even though smoking hasn't been allowed in here in years. The music is so loud and the bass vibrations so strong I can feel my heart straining to readjust to the beat. The stage on the far side of the room has a line of half nude men dancing on it, and several patrons leaning far across the brass rail to try and stuff money in their G-strings and cowboy boots.

Christopher leads me through the crowd. There's the main bar downstairs with the strippers, and then upstairs there are a series of connected rooms with different themes. One room looks like an English pub with a billiards table and darts, and another room is like a funky Mexican siesta room with a margarita bar and young boys wearing sombreros lounging around. "They're at the Damsel in Distress table," I shout over the deafening music. Standing on the open highway seems peaceful compared to this.

"That's in the drag emporium," he shouts, "up here and left!"

We weave our way up another set of stairs through the thick crowds and into another large vaulted room, where a drag show is under way. There's a woman onstage singing "Somewhere over the Rainbow," and her hair is in an enormous set of red braids. She's wearing a blue gingham dress and ruby-sequined slippers—which she clicks together—and a painted rainbow drops down onstage behind her followed by a multicolored disco ball. The music changes to a house beat and she rips off the gingham dress to reveal a blue-sequined thong and red pasties with long tassels, which she starts to twirl.

"I think that's the Damsel in Distress table over there under the portrait of Phyllis Diller," Christopher says, "but I don't see them."

Then I feel someone tapping me on the shoulder and it's Lexi, who promptly spills half her cherry-strawberry-bumbleberry-whatever-it-is drink on my leg.

"You have to come!" she says. "Hailey got the gays mad! *Come, come, come!*"

Christopher corrects her. "Don't say 'the gays,' sweetie,"

"What should I say?"

"Just say gays. Nothing good happens when a straight person says 'the gays.'"

"Okay."

Lexi hurries us to the other side of the room and out into the service hallway, which is littered with service carts and dirty drink trays. Hailey is there, arms akimbo, and she seems a little tipsy. Her tank top is conspicuously devoid of Jolly Ranchers, and they've each left a little rectangular-colored candy shadow on her shirt. She's squaring off with a giant man in a Las Vegas showgirl outfit, whose giant peach and yellow plumes fan out from his sequined headdress and gyrate when he wags his finger.

"I don't think so, missy," he says, "but nice try."

"You let the table go," Hailey says. "You should comp us!"

"What's all this about?" I ask.

"We were here like ten minutes late and they let the Damsel in Distress table go to another party," Lexi says. "They gave us a different table."

"Which one?" Christopher asks.

"The Clamshell."

"Then they were already mad at you, honey."

Lexi frowns. "When the bill came, Hailey said the Clamshell table sucked. It was way in the back and had a blocked view so she didn't want to pay. They told us we had to talk to Janet Reno."

"Who?"

"Her." She points to the magnificent drag queen, who stands at least two feet taller than my sister. "I don't care what they told you on the phone," she's saying to Hailey, "we hold the table for *five minutes* and then we give it to people who are *actually here*. If you hadn't noticed, it's sort of a popular place."

"We *were* here!" Hailey shouts. "Do you see us here? We're

here! You can't take a reservation and then just cancel it. Don't you have any idea how to run a club?"

This apparently was the wrong thing to say, because Janet Reno seems to grow ten feet taller. "Listen, sister," she says right in Hailey's face, "don't bring your bitching and your big old bleeding vagina in here and tell me how to run my place!"

Hailey takes a step closer and I'm impressed she's not backing down. I would have run like hell by now. "Well, why don't I take my *big bleeding vagina* to the police and tell them you're scamming people up in here!" she says.

"Go ahead," Janet Reno says. "You're banned."

"Banned?"

"From this club," she says, "for life."

Hailey throws her hands up. "Oh, how terrible! Banned from a mediocre gay club that sells seven-dollar mineral water? Oh heavens, where else shall we go?"

"Try Applebee's," Janet Reno says and summons her security team—men waiting in the wings wearing tight police uniforms with shorty-shorts.

"You can't ban me!" Hailey shouts. "You have stubble on your tits!"

"All your little breeder friends are banned, too," Janet Reno says. "Now pay your bill or Monty here will help you open your little Louis Vuitton knockoff."

My sister gasps and grips her purse. My sister loves her purse and, yes, it's a fake, but only I knew that. This is why she loves it, because it cost ten dollars and all her girlfriends think her fiancé bought her a real one.

"That's right, honey," Janet Reno says, "when the Home Shopping Network told you it looked just like the real thing, they were lying. We can all tell it's fake. Everybody can tell."

Now, I know Hailey is a pain, but that was a little mean. Calling her a bleeding-vagina breeder is one thing, but insulting the integrity of her purse is something else.

Before I can say anything, though, the security guys swarm in and start hustling everyone toward the stairwell. "Wait a minute!" I yell and the security guys stop.

"Let me see the bill," I say, and Janet Reno rolls her eyes, but she swishes up her skirts and hands me the check. I look at it and say, "Hailey, this is fine. I'll just get it. Okay? You guys wait outside; I'll take care of this."

Hailey looks at me with total disgust. She mutters something inaudible and then says, "Fine. Come on, you guys, let's go. Let her pay if she wants to."

They all head downstairs and Christopher approaches Janet Reno with me. I smile when I apologize for my sister's behavior. "She got involved with this real douchebag," I say, rummaging around in my bag, "and she's been a real pain ever since." Janet Reno smirks and the security guys seem disappointed there won't be a scene. They glumly disperse into the club and look for other sources of trouble.

"The problem is," I say, taking out a wad of cash, "you can't tell which guys are dreamboats and which guys are douchebags, you know?" I wink at Christopher and he winks back, but looks confused. "A real douchebag can look like anyone," I say, counting out the money, "even when they're wearing a tacky dress that looks like it belongs on a dinner theater stage in Branson."

Janet Reno's eyes, deeply hooded with fake spidery lashes, narrow slightly.

"I don't like it when people disrespect my sister," I say, dropping the cash on the floor, "so don't ever do it again." Janet Reno looks down and I slap her right across the face. It's a good, solid, old-fashioned slap, like when women in the 1950s would slap men in bars if they got fresh. Christopher gasps.

Janet Reno steps back, aghast, her ruby-red lips slightly parted. I can feel the dry, powdery pancake makeup on my fingertips. I hoist my purse up on my shoulder and spin on my heel. Christopher nods at Janet Reno. "See you, Janet," he says.

"See you, Christopher," she whispers.

Brad invites me to the Keller cabin, which is a big freaking deal. He told me the Kellers are like the Kennedys—they don't invite strangers to their vacation compounds. They're for family only. Family. Only.

I almost think it's a trick because I haven't been dating Brad for that long and I'm pretty sure Mrs. Keller doesn't like me. I don't think she likes any girls near Brad. The only reason I can think she'd let me come is that she's possibly luring me out of the city to a secluded area so she can kill me with a Jesus fish.

Christopher and I consult on my North-Woods wardrobe, as there are so many pitfalls to consider. First, it's important to pack light so no one associates you with heavy luggage, but the problem is it's winter and so I need bulky stuff. We want to go with a Hemingway Hunt Club look—you know, cable-knit sweaters and jodhpurs—but I also have to consider evening wear. This is a nightmare.

He comes up with a wardrobe color system for me, where every piece I'm packing works with every other piece. Everything on his list says "ecru," "cream," or "khaki."

"Can't you just say black, white, or beige like a normal person?" I ask him.

"No, I can't," he snaps, "because you look hideous in those colors."

I tell Ashley I need Friday afternoon off because Brad wants to go to the family cabin and she gives me this tight, pained expression that might have been a smile, or severe constipation, or both. "Everything all right?" I ask.

"Just perfect!" she says.

"Do you not want me to leave early Friday? I was asking for your permission. If you need me, I'll be here."

She smiles. "Whatever you want. You just do whatever you want."

She's never uttered the phrase "do whatever you want" to me before, and it's freaking me out. I know she can't fire me, Ed's already made that clear, but she still finds ways to belittle me in front of co-workers and make my life a general hell, so goading her like this is bad news. I guess I'll deal with her and whatever she has in store for me when I come back.

That should be fun.

Brad and I drive five hours north up Highway 35W, which turns into Highway 61 after Duluth. I've never been this far north before. It's already ten degrees cooler outside and the pine trees pierce the blue sky like tall green church spires. We stop at the Naniboujou Lodge, an old campy 1930s resort that still has its grand totem-pole dining room. We catch a light supper, breaded walleye and chicken pot pie, and midway through dinner I get a sinking feeling and excuse myself to the bathroom.

I have my period. Of course, because why wouldn't I have my period? We're up north with his whole family and in the vicinity of bears, aren't we? It's the most unsexy thing that could happen, isn't it? Perfect. Luckily the lodge has a complimentary cup of medium-flow Tampax in the ladies' room and I scoop up a big handful. Thank God for small cardboard-wrapped favors.

We head back out on the road and Brad says we're really close now. All my exhaustion and road-weariness solidifies into nervousness and fear. Why on freaking earth did I say I'd come here? I'm never going to match up with whatever kind of girl the Kellers hope their son brings home. Never.

About fifteen miles later, we take a sharp right onto a gravel road and follow it around until it dead-ends beside an imposing structure that looks more like a hotel than a cabin. It's only ten o'clock when we drag our suitcases through the doors, but everyone is already in bed. We find a note on the kitchen counter from Brad's mother telling us she's disappointed we missed dinner, but of course with me having to work, we probably left the city late. She tells us Brad's bedroom is on the main floor, overlooking the lake, and my bedroom is upstairs in the loft.

"No way!" I whisper. "Separate bedrooms? For real?"

"You bet," he says. "No sleeping together unless you're married."

Fabulous.

Brad points to a staircase by the far wall that's so steep it's actually more of a ladder. "There's a bathroom up there, too," he says and kisses me goodnight.

I lug my bag up the staircase and try to see in the dark, but it's nearly pitch black. I feel my way to a little lamp on the nightstand, which winks on and dimly lights the room. It's more of a crawl space than a proper room and I think it's where the kids usually sleep. The narrow beds have big, ominous clown faces painted on them, the kind they used to put in kids' rooms to make them seem cheerful, only to find out years later all the kids had nightmares and developed deep-seated phobias of the circus. There's a tiny rocking chair by the window and a big teddy bear sitting on a wooden toy box painted with interlocking pink hearts. Mrs. Keller has stuck me in the kids' room.

Just freaking typical.

What's worse, the "bathroom" is just a tiny child-size sink anchored to the wall next to an equally tiny toilet. It might actually be a bidet. They're both right next to the wooden banister overlooking the main room of the cabin, so if you were standing on the far side of the living room, you could easily see a person doing their business. I wonder if all the rooms have pervert toilets like these.

I try to make myself comfortable, which basically means putting on my flannel nightie, then brushing my teeth and splashing cold water on my face at the children's sink. I do all this slightly hunched over, because the sloped wall doesn't give you room enough to stand up. I skip peeing because *no way* am I peeing in a kids' crapper. I'll just wait till tomorrow and try to find a normal bathroom downstairs.

The next morning, I wake up with a splitting headache to the clatter of pans and water running. People talking. I can tell by the light coming through the small window that it's late in the morning and I hit my head on the slanted ceiling when I sit up.

My bladder seizes. Holy hell, I have to pee bad. Like burst-a-pipe bad. I can't possibly make it downstairs. I briefly consider the empty Glacéau Vitamin Water bottle on my nightstand, but the mouth is too small. Maybe the toy box? How often does anyone actually look inside it?

There's a toilet in the alcove.

I peer over the banister to make sure the living room is empty. It is. The voices I hear are coming from the kitchen, so if I pee discreetly and quickly, I just may pull this off. I hike up my nightgown, squat over the little toilet, and pee. I pee and I pee and I pee. I'm pretty sure this is not how sexy girls pee. They piddle at best, some dainty golden droplets that are fresh as spring rain. This sounds more like someone pouring barrels of ammonia off the back of a loading dock. I vow to never pee in front of Brad, one of the many things I vow never to do in front of him, including passing gas, belching, vomiting, and scratching myself. That's getting to be one hell of a long list.

"Hello up there, sleepyhead!" Ed shouts. He's suddenly directly beneath me in the living room, and Brad's standing next to him, smiling. Luckily, from this vantage point they can only see my grinning head, not my body. I wad up a fistful of toilet paper from the roll next to me and hold it in the bowl, under *the stream*, so it cushions the sound of my peeing.

"Hey!" I say, trying to muster the most normal voice I can while peeing into my own hand. "Hi there! What's the . . . ah . . . plan for today?"

Ed has a newspaper in one hand and a cup of coffee in the other. He holds his arms out wide and says, "The world's our oyster! Whatever we like!"

"Whatcha doin', hon?" Brad asks, sipping his coffee. "You stuck or something?"

Just then Mrs. Keller rounds the far corner of the living room, drying her hands on a dishtowel. From her vantage point, unfortunately, she can see everything.

"She's hung up on the kiddie potty!" Mrs. Keller snaps the dishtowel over her shoulder. "Jennifer, why on earth are you using the kiddie potty?"

She storms across the room and starts to come up the stairs. What the hell? I stop peeing and dive down on the floor.

"Are you okay?" Brad calls. "Did you fall?"

"I'm fine," I say, trying to twist my flannel nightie down.

"What are you doing now?" Mrs. Keller says, appearing at the top of the stairs, frowning at me as I lie half-naked on the floor.

"Sorry," I say, "just using the facilities!"

"Well, you're too big for that! Your toilet is over here." She walks across the loft and flips a metal latch in the wood-paneled wall, revealing a small, sunny bathroom. It even has a tiny claw-foot tub. "We use the kiddie potty for potty-training toddlers," she says with significant disdain, "and I'd rather you use the bathroom, if you don't mind."

"Of course," I say and before I can add anything else to my humiliation, she stomps away. It's another hour before I can gather my wits and go downstairs, where everyone has not only finished breakfast but lunch as well and has now adjourned into the severe wood-paneled living room. I step shyly up to Brad, who hugs me hard enough that I know Mrs. Keller didn't tell him she saw my naked butt. If she had, he would be scowling at me right now, not asking me if I want to play cribbage.

"No thanks," I say, "I'd really like to just relax. Maybe read." This was my planned response to any activity I didn't want to do and I deliberately brought reading material I thought the Kellers would approve of. *Chicken Soup for the Spiritual Soul*. I didn't even bring a slutty magazine to sneak inside it. I plan to actually read this crap. I take a seat in the glassed-in porch, which is cold, but I pretend it's balmy.

I remain there for the rest of the day, rereading the same page and trying not to do anything stupid and certainly not going into the kitchen where Mrs. Keller works like a dray horse until late afternoon, when a dark-haired woman with very full lips taps me hard on the shoulder.

"You're Jennifer?" she says. "I'm Brad's sister, Sarah. Welcome to the family. Trevor! Put that down! Nana told you to leave her horse alone!" A small boy with sandy hair at the other end of the room has clamped a bronze statue of a horse between his legs, so it looks like he has a bronze horse penis. "Sorry," she says, "he's driving me nuts. Five hours in the car with him and I was ready to leave him at a gas station, you know? Mom said you got in last night. Bill had to work, he's over there." She points to a hearty-looking man lugging a suitcase and keeps chattering. "He didn't use to be so fat. He's trying Atkins, but I say it'll give him a heart attack before it takes off ten pounds. Trevor! If you don't put that down I'm going to chop off your hands! Trevor!" She marches over and yanks the horse away from him, explaining the various horrors that would befall him if he were to damage Nana's knickknacks in any way.

I stay in my chair and read until it gets too dark. I find Brad in his room, where he pounces on me. "I want you so bad," he says, getting his hands up under my skirt. We kiss until tiny Trevor appears with his finger up his nose and tells us, "Supper is dead-y."

"You mean *ready*, big guy?" Brad drops my skirt and Trevor looks at me with a perverted little grin. I give him a big smile back but he sticks his tongue out at me.

Little bastard.

We sit down for dinner under the immense, eerie deer-antler chandelier. It looks like a few generations of animals had to give their lives in order for us to have light. The family holds hands and prays. This time Daddy Ed leads us in prayer and he goes on and on forever. "Blood of the lamb" this and "spirit of Christ" that. I got thrown in there as one of the many, many people to protect, lead, and guide. "We welcome Jennifer to the family," Ed says. "No matter where she's been, no matter where her path has led her, she's here now with us and we want to thank you and to let you know, Lord, we know you've entrusted her to us and we will look after her as if she were one of our own."

I know this was all supposed to be sweet, but what's with the "wherever her path has led her" crap? He makes it sound like they took in a whore from the docks and gave her a second chance, like I've been eating out of garbage cans and sharing needles or something. Sheesh, this family has a way of cutting you down even when they're building you up.

Then we drop hands and I think now we can finally freaking eat, but no, we can't because now they sing. Yes. *Sing.* I had no idea, but I should know by now that Brad won't prepare me for anything. "Ripping the heads off kittens after dessert? Sure, we do that every Thursday! Didn't I tell you? Doesn't your family do that?"

I get a lot of those quizzical looks and "doesn't your family do that?" questions from him, like everything his family does is normal, and everyone else must be from another planet.

The Kellers sing "Cast Thine Eyes," which is apparently an old hymn everyone has heard of and everyone has memorized, except me. Mrs. Keller seems very concerned that I don't know the words, but that doesn't stop them from singing it, out loud and out proud. All forty million verses. As they bellow away, I sit with a frozen smile on my face and stare at the pine-cone centerpiece. After a hearty meal of venison shank and applesauce, the family gathers to drink warm milk and honey while playing a raucous game of Parcheesi in the living room. This goes on for nine-hundred-and-thirty-eight years.

Mrs. Keller goes to bed promptly at ten o'clock and Mr. Keller follows her about an hour after that. Poor guy, I'd give her a head start in bed, too. Anything to avoid touching her. Then Sarah and her husband put Trevor down and Brad looks at me with a mischievous grin.

"Wanna fool around?" he asks and tugs me into his room, where I nervously take off only the necessary clothing and get into his bed. "Just be quiet," he says, "so Mom doesn't hear," which isn't exactly the sexiest thing a man can say to you before he makes super-quiet, careful-not-to-squeak-the-bedsprings-because-my-mom-is-listening love to you. Having an orgasm is completely out of the question, for both of us.

Where is my well-oiled Tahitian island boy when I need him?

I'm lucky I remembered to take my tampon out. When Brad was taking his pants off I rummaged around under the blankets and pulled the sticky medium-flow tampon out and dropped it on the hardwood floor so I could throw it away later, without him noticing.

Ick.

Despite the sex being short, weird, and totally unsatisfactory, part of me liked humping Bradford in Ma Keller's house. The old bat must be sick to her stomach thinking about the two of us doing it, and thinking about her thinking about it makes me sick to mine.

Still, it's kind of hot to break such devout rules, the way certain sex fantasies are kind of hot because they're so very gross and wrong. Every once in awhile, when Brad is pumperhumping me, I think of how horrifying it would be if I had sister-wives and was just one of six women he screwed on a regular basis. I can picture myself lying in a narrow single bed wearing a high-necked plaid nightgown and clutching the Book of Mormon to my breast as I listen to my husband giving it good to my sister-wife next door.

Gross and hot.

Grot.

I sneak out of Brad's room around midnight and climb up to the kids' loft. I sleep in fits and starts and have an upsetting dream about hunting miniature deer.

It's still early when I sit bolt upright in my clown bed and smack my cranium on the sloping ceiling. "Fuck!" I say out loud. I woke up with the most terrible thought—I forgot the freaking tampon on Brad's floor. Gross. I throw on my robe and scramble down the ladder as fast as I can, nearly tripping over Boots at the bottom as she scoots past in her little wheelchair.

I tiptoe back into Brad's room. "Honey?" I whisper. He's still snoring, thank God. All I have to do is find my little damp offensive friend before anyone steps on it. I get on my hands and knees and peer under the bed. I crawl around and even turn on one of the bedside lamps, feeling blindly along the floorboards, but I can't find it anywhere. My tampon is gone.

I try to make the best of the situation. I mean, if I can't find the tampon crawling around on my hands and knees, then Brad certainly isn't going to step on it, right? Maybe that's a good thing. Maybe this is a small favor from the universe, a celestial freebie, if you will. *What the heck?* the angels said. *She's a good kid, let's help her out here and make that tampon vanish!*

"Well, this is very modern," Mrs. Keller says primly, standing in Brad's doorway. Boots rolls up behind her.

"Oh!" I say, getting up quickly. Brad mumbles something in his sleep and rolls over.

"I'd say it's a little too modern for me," Mrs. Keller says, crossing her arms.

"No, I didn't sleep here," I stammer. "I was just . . ."

"Mom?" Brad wakes up. "What are you doing?"

"Why don't you ask Jennifer? I just found her on the floor again."

Brad squints at me. I struggle for answers. "I was just . . . I forgot something, that I packed . . . before we came."

"I see," she says, and Boots whimpers.

In fact Boots keeps whimpering until we're midway through a big breakfast (creamed eggs on toast, hot apple cider) and Mrs. Keller sets down her crystal punch bowl filled with gloopy orange chiffon ambrosia. Then Boots stops whimpering and starts growling. "She's acting so oddly," Mrs. Keller says. "I hope she didn't get into the trash again."

That's when it hits me.

The forensic gears of my gerbil brain struggle to piece the facts together because as much as I would like to believe in celestial tampon fairies, that damn tampon has to be somewhere. Don't panic. Stay calm. What are the facts? What do we know? We know that Boots is acting oddly and we know that I am missing a tampon.

Boots + tampon.

Boots + tampon?

My fork freezes in midair. Oh sweet baby Jesus, I think Boots ate my tampon. While everyone at the table is talking, I look up at the sorrowful, unmoving eyes of the deer head on the wall. We lock eyes and begin a silent dialogue fit for a John Waters film.

What do I do? I ask the deer.

If you tell them, he says, *you're dead.*

If I don't tell them, the dog is dead.

Don't get hysterical.

Actually this is the perfect time to get hysterical. There's a medium-flow tampon inside the family Pomeranian.

Maybe she didn't even eat it.

Maybe she did.

If she ate it, she'll die. They'll think you're a monster.

If she didn't eat it, and I say she did, they'll think I'm an escaped mental patient.

I don't know, can a tampon kill a little dog?

You tell me. Did you ever see those Tampax commercials where a single tampon sucks up an entire juice glass of blue liquid?

No, the deer says, *I didn't.*

I look over at Boots, who's now pawing at the back door,

and picture a tampon in her belly swelling up to the size of a poodle.

I can't stand it.

I whisper to Brad that I have to talk to him and he follows me into the kitchen, where I tell him something a woman should never have to say to a man, let alone one she wants to marry. I say, "I think your mother's dog ate my tampon."

He thinks I'm being funny and then weird and then a pain in the ass. I have to repeat myself three times before he fully understands. As he grasps the complicated details of the situation—*premarital sex in religious parents' house, used tampon left on floor, crippled dog eats tampon, new girlfriend has to explain to religious parents crippled dog ate used tampon*—he begins to look pale.

"We have to tell your mother," I say.

He shakes his head no.

"Brad, we have to. It makes me look bad, not you."

He rolls his eyes.

"Okay, fine, it makes *you* look bad because you brought me to the cabin, and I'm the stupid slut who forced you to have sex in your bedroom and then flung my dirty tampon all over the place. Okay? Happy?"

Then Mrs. Keller walks into the kitchen with a stack of plates. My hands are sweating. "Mrs. Keller," I say, closing my eyes so I don't have to see her face, "there might be something wrong with Boots."

It turns out rural veterinarians don't see all that many Pomeranians. Hunting dogs and housecats, but not many "foo-foo dogs from the city." That's what the front-desk lady at the vet's called Boots. "We got a foo-foo dog from the city!" she shouts and everyone in the crowded, hot waiting room turns to stare at Boots, who stands innocently in a plastic laundry tub on Brad's lap. I sit next to Brad and Mrs. Keller sits next to me.

I have a lot of questions as I'm sitting there cramped between the Kellers, staring at the glossy tiled floor, like why is this waiting room so crowded? How could every single chair be occupied? Also, I've already done the right thing by admitting the situation to my boyfriend and his family, so why do I now have to be the one to explain to the husky front desk lady what happened?

"I'm sorry?" the front desk lady says. "You think she ate a what?"

"A *tampon*," I repeat.

"I still can't hear you," she says.

I raise my voice ever so slightly. "I think the dog ate a *tampon*." At this point the waiting room has gotten pin-drop quiet and I think I hear someone snicker. This is what I get for trying to save the dog's life.

The lady smiles. "Are you serious?"

I glare at her and count backward in my head to keep myself from lunging over the counter and strangling her. "No," I say, "I made it up. This is what I like to do on weekends." She drops her smile and writes something on the form. Then she asks me if it was new or used.

"What?"

"New or used?" she repeats, staring evenly at me. Do I detect the faintest hint of sarcasm in her voice? Is she screwing with me? I will kick her chunky front-desk ass if she's screwing with me.

"Why do you need to know that?" I ask.

"We need to know," she says.

Someone behind me coughs.

Why can't the world, just once, open up and swallow me whole?

"Fine," I say. "It was used."

I hear Mrs. Keller mumble something like, "Oh dear Lord," from her chair and that makes me think of Christopher and how he'll react when he hears this story. I realize that possibly for the rest of my life I will have to hear people tell the story of the time Jennifer nearly killed the dog with her tampon. I stare at the ceiling. I wonder if I could compose a suicide note that would convince my mother none of this was her fault.

The front desk lady leans in. "Could you repeat that?" she says. "New or used?"

Okay, now she's screwing with me.

"USED," I say at the top of my voice, so loudly people stop talking and a smattering of chuckles and snickers ripples across the room. Fine. Screw them anyway. I'm saving a dog's life. If they want to laugh then let them.

"Okay, *used*," she says tightly and writes it down. Then, in a voice that matches the one I just used in both volume and tone, she asks, "SO HOW LONG AGO DID THE DOG EAT YOUR *USED* TAMPON?"

After we finally finish the intake form, she walks over to Boots, pats her on the head, introduces herself to Brad and Mrs. Keller, and then tells us if "the obstruction" is still in the dog's stomach they can give her a simple syrup of ipecac-type medication and make her vomit it up, but if it's moved into her intestinal track, it'll require surgery.

Mrs. Keller is shocked. "Surgery? Can I go back with her? I really should go back with her." The front desk lady tells her to sit tight, Boots is in good hands. Then she picks Boots up and carries her away.

I sit there silently for the next hour and try not to let any part of my body touch Mrs. Keller, who's lecturing me on the virtues of foresight, or Brad, who's obliviously playing a stupid puzzle game on his phone.

Finally the front desk lady reappears with a much perkier-looking Boots and sets her down on the floor. That's when I realize she's trying not to laugh. I can see the faint quaking in her arm as she mirthfully says, "She was lucky. It was still in her stomach."

There! I shout in my head. *See? I saved the damn dog's life! She did eat a tampon and it would have killed her if I hadn't sacrificed my dignity and told everyone! I hope I'm going to get credit for this.* I mean, I think most people would have just acted like they had no idea what was going on. I actually did the right thing and I expect to be commended for it.

"None of us ever saw anything like it," the front desk lady says. "She barfed that tampon up so hard it shot clear across the room." Then she starts to giggle and some other idiot behind the counter joins in laughing. She wipes a tear from her eye and tells us the bill is waiting at the window.

We all drive home together in silence, Mrs. Keller at the wheel with Boots in the front seat next to her, while Brad and I sit in back. After an hour or so hovering in the cabin, Brad tells his mother we're heading back to the city early.

There are no objections.

nail him down

Valentine's Day arrives. I've been preparing all week, rehearsing self-love speeches in the mirror and taking hot baths with soothing ingredients, but no amount of imported bath oil can disguise the fact I have not one but two weddings to attend today and neither is mine.

I can accept the fact Valentine's Day is going to suck, all I'm asking the universe for is to survive it without a public humiliation or massive mental breakdown

In other words, I want this Valentine's Day to be different.

David didn't believe in Valentine's Day. He thought it was a commercial ploy to bamboozle the public not only into spending money but spending sentiment, time, and thought. "It's like you have to say, 'I love you,' even if you don't mean it," he complained. That, coincidentally, was about half an hour after he had told me he loved me. And forget candy or cards or flowers. God, no. Those were for losers.

He spent every Valentine's Day in a hotel with his buddies drinking beer and playing poker. I'm not kidding. It was a whole bunch of his artist and musician friends who never normally played poker, just this one day out of the year, to prove they were still wild and free. I of course said I had no problem with that because I wanted to be the cool girlfriend. The tough girlfriend. I laughed at all the girls who got red roses in the office.

What losers.

So now David, Mr. "I hate all establishment and commitment," is getting married and for some reason I have an irresistible urge to see the flower arrangements. Maybe because he never gave me flowers once in my life. Or maybe because I want to see just how powerful this new wife is. Did she reprogram him entirely? Did she convince him to go with white roses? Baby's breath? Black spray-painted Venus flytraps?

"I'm going to David's wedding," I tell Christopher. "It starts at noon and Hailey's is at three p.m. I can do both."

He puts a hand on his hip. "Just how many disasters do you plan on surviving in one day?" he asks. He threatens to rent an animal tranquilizer gun and shoot me. I tell him I'm going with or without him and he says, "Fine, then I'm coming with so you're accurately represented on the police report."

The night before the day of weddings from hell I can't sleep. I take three Lunestas, which should knock out a Brahman bull, but a Brahman bull is no match for a tortured woman. No, sir. I took those sleeping pills, drank half a bottle of wine, and tossed back some antihistamines for good measure, but I was still up at four in the morning, pacing the floors like a panther.

Why did David break up with me? Why wasn't I good enough? What was I missing, what could I have done? Was it how I looked? *Of course it was how I looked. It was that and how stupid you are and the fact you have no talent or charisma or luck. Plus you're terrible in bed and your thighs look like spreading bread dough.*

I watch the sun come up over the rooftops. Then I take four hours getting ready, give or take, and in the end, I look like I'm going to the funeral of a heavy metal star. Lenny would approve. I wear all black. Black dress, black heels, big black sunglasses. Christopher picks me up wearing a conspicuous shiny gray suit and a bright orange tie.

"You look like an Elton John Mini-Me!"

"I'll take that for the compliment you don't know it is," he says and links his arm in mine as he escorts me up the steps of the big stone church. We're much slower than the other guests, who stream around us like pastel ribbons, rustling past in the cold breeze.

I feel sick.

"Why are you stopping?" Christopher asks.

"I can't go in there."

"You can't?"

I shake my head no.

"No scene?" he asks. "No last-minute shenanigans or sudden global truths?"

I shake my head no again.

He sighs. "Okay, normally I'd wheedle you," he says, "but you're white. Like geisha-with-the-flu white."

"I see David's mother," I say, trembling, "over by the door. I can't let her see me."

Without another word Christopher pivots me around and we head back to the car.

That was my experience attending my ex-boyfriend's wedding. I got dressed up, wobbled up to the spectacular moment, and then fell apart like a cheap wedding cake left out in the rain.

At home, I have a few hours to rest. I kick off my heels, peel off my dress, and take a hot shower. I try to imagine myself in my special Tahitian hut with my well-oiled island man, but every time we start getting down to business, David's new bride taps me on the shoulder and says, "Oh my God, I remember you!" and my eyes fly wide open and I'm left staring at my vanilla-pudding-colored tiles.

I set my alarm clock and climb into bed. I can take a short nap and still have time to get to the church. We're all getting ready there. Hailey's hired a makeup artist. Good thing, too. I hope she knows how to make people who feel ugly inside look pretty outside.

I go to sleep.

I oversleep for Hailey's wedding.

My therapist would posit the theory that maybe I did this by accident/on purpose due to some on-the-surface/deep-down feelings of competition/jealousy/anger/rage, but how could I possibly control the fact that there was a power blip sometime during my nap, causing my alarm clock to stop functioning and flash a big, angry red 12:00? Am I that powerful? Is my jealous nature so strong that I can telekinetically shut down electricity grids?

Possibly.

I'm late. Really late. So late I don't want to figure out how late, because I'm already moving as fast as I can and if I realize that I only have fifteen minutes before the ceremony starts, I'll wrap the Scout around a tree.

No. Just breathe, relax.

I can do this.

I honk at a little old man driving down the road and roar around him. *Get out of the way, you asshole!* A terrified squirrel dashes across the road and I don't slow down. I just hold my breath and gun the engine. *Please oh please be okay, little squirrel. . . .*

My phone rings. It's Brad. He's worried, he's already at the church and where am I? I tell him I think I have the flu and I fell asleep. He would have flipped if he knew I went to David's wedding. I'm so used to lying to him it doesn't even feel like lying anymore. It feels like I'm protecting him. Protecting us. Smoothing things over, smoothing things out. This is what couples do. I think.

By the time I get to the church I am in a complete panic, sweating profusely, hair matted to the back of my head. My mother is pacing back and forth outside and I bound up the stone steps two at a time. "All right," she says, "all right, slow down. They haven't started. We have five minutes. Let's not panic, let's just get you inside so you can put on your dress."

I stop dead. "My dress?"

She closes her eyes.

"I forgot it," I whisper. "I forgot the dress."

She doesn't say anything. This frightens me more than anything and I break free of her icicle grip. "Wait here!" I say and run back toward my car. After all, I do have a dress there—sent to me with love.

By the Mormons.

Yes. The pictures will show and the stories will testify that this is how I came to wear a fundamentalist Mormon dress in my sister's wedding. It was powder blue, just like all the other dresses. The only difference was the other girls looked like sleek supermodels in their satiny kimonos and I looked like a plural wife about to go milk a cow. Some of the photographs would suggest that I was possibly the cow itself.

Brad snickered at me through the entire ceremony. I could see his shoulders shaking, even when he was supposed to be praying. Jerk.

After the ceremony everybody trooped over to the hotel, where we had to face the shrimp ordeal. The long and the short of it was the caterers forgot to order the shrimp. They realized their mistake and even called Lenny early in the morning to tell him there would be no shrimp at his wedding, to which the esteemed King of Ham apparently said, "Cool."

It was hardly the worst thing about the day, but like all frag-ile, neurotic brides Hailey had to hyperfocus on one thing and get hysterical about it, and she chose to come undone over the shrimp. "But how could Len say it was okay?" she says, face toward the ceiling, blinking hard to hold back tears. "How could my own husband tell them it was okay to forget the shrimp? Is this how the whole marriage will be? People ruining everything while he sits there and says, 'Cool'?"

"I think he realized it was a mistake," my mother says, "and chose to forgive them. That's a good quality in a husband, hon. Believe me, you, none of them are perfect."

This makes Hailey burst into tears and mascara starts run-ning down her face. Lexi hurries to retrieve the makeup artist, who's already packed up and about to get into her minivan.

"I . . . thought . . . there . . . would be . . . shrimp!" Hailey says, hyperventilating.

"Oh, you don't need shrimp," my mother says. "If no shrimp is your biggest problem in life then I say you're batting a thou-sand, kiddo."

"The wedding is ruined!" Hailey shrieks before collapsing on the bed.

"Good Christ," I mumble.

"Alrighty now," my mother says, "it's just nerves. Jennifer will go get you a shrimp tray."

What? I'll get her a what?

My mother stands up and comes over to me. "Jennifer," she says.

"No."

"Jennifer, please."

I shake my head. "Absolutely not."

"You won't be able to understand this," she says.

"You got that right."

"In fact you might never once in your life understand this, but you've got to believe me, when a bride decides something's got to be fixed, well . . ." She looks nervously over her shoulder at Hailey, who's seeping through the blotting technique. "Well, we have to fix it. She's your sister. Your only sister and she looks up to you. I'm serious! Don't roll your eyes like that, they'll stick. It's the least you can do since you showed up wearing . . . that."

"What do you want me to do, Mother?"

"The reception starts in an hour. Go to Sam's Club. Get my membership card out of my purse and go get five, no ten, shrimp party trays from the seafood counter."

"What? No."

"Your aunt Ellen has thrombosis!" she says, as though this is the ultimate reason to get shrimp.

"Sam's Club?" Hailey says, looking at us with her tear-streaked face. "Did I hear you say Sam's Club has shrimp?" She looks like someone just told her the groom disappeared, not the edible crustaceans.

"Shrimp party platters!" my mother says. "Jennifer has volunteered to go pick them up."

"She did? You did?"

"You bet she did, didn't you, Jennifer?"

Hailey jumps up from the bed, nearly knocking the makeup artist over, and in an almost never-seen move, flings her arms around me and squeezes hard. "Oh thank you, Jen! Thank you! You're the best!" I hate hate hate it when she pulls this. I can't stand it when she cries.

"I'm a makeup artist, not a miracle worker," the makeup artist says. "I need your face to fix it." Hailey goes back to the bed and I dash downstairs to find my mother's Sam's Club card.

Freaking hell.

I call Brad but he doesn't answer. He's somewhere in the lobby of the hotel with his phone off. He's probably talking to some twenty-year-old receptionist. I finally get ahold of him when I'm in the vast, baffling store. "I tried to call you before I left," I bark at him. "I had to come to Sam's Club by myself. Where were you?"

"I was right where you told me to be," he says. "At the bar watching your Uncle Eddie and making sure he only had three screwdrivers."

"Well, I could have used your help! YOU should have gone to Sam's Club. Not me!"

Brad is chuckling.

"So let me get this straight," he says. "You're in the seafood department at Sam's Club in your Mormon dress?"

"Yes! I'm in my Mormon dress. It's hysterical. People are staring at me and one little boy started crying. Plus they don't have any shrimp. None. "

"I gotta see this," he says. "Please. Take a picture of yourself and text it to me."

"Stop laughing! Hailey's going to say I ruined her wedding because I didn't get her precious shrimp party trays."

"She might say you ruined her wedding by dressing like a cult leader," he says.

"A *sister-wife*. Not a cult leader."

He sighs. "Well, great. I have an erection now."

"This is serious!" I say, storming for the exit.

"I know, I'm sorry. What can I do to help?"

"Well, you can make ten shrimp party trays magically appear!" The other line beeps in. "I have to go," I tell him. "It's the firing squad."

"Well, if your family doesn't love you anymore," he says, "you can always hop onboard mine. My parents love you."

"Sweet!" I say and hang up. Uck. That's like being loved

by Christian tarantulas. When I get back to the hotel, I almost crash into my mother, who is racing toward the banquet hall. "It's wonderful!" she says. "Brad fixed everything! Come see!" She hurries me to the reception ballroom, where the caterers are setting up big chafing dishes and waiters are placing wineglasses. The first guests are just starting to arrive from the church.

I see Brad marching toward the buffet table, followed by a string of people wearing Keller's name badges. They're all carrying trays covered with tinfoil. Twelve trays in fact, twelve trays loaded with crushed ice and fresh, succulent shrimp.

"Just called the store," Brad says. "Told the chef we had a family emergency and he called a pal at some seafood distributor."

I stare at the trays as they're set on the buffet. It truly does seem like a shrimp miracle.

"Oh, Bradford," my mother says, "I can't tell you what this means to us. This is just wonderful. You shouldn't have done it but I'm so grateful you did."

"Freshest fish in the city," he says. "I told them I wanted the best." Brad puts his arms around me and I'm very proud. Not just of him but of me for bringing him.

We kiss and he says, "You are the hottest Mormon ever."

When my sister gets to thank Brad in person she tells him he saved the day. "I usually hate Jen's boyfriends," she says, "but none of them ever brought me shrimp."

"Consider me your first call for all your seafood needs," he says. Then Hailey gives Lenny, who's standing next to her grinning, a short, sharp look like, *See, stupid? Some people know how to fix things.* My mother tells Brad once again he's a godsend and my father thumps him on the back. We join the happy guests as they eat cake, dance late, and comment on how amazing the shrimp is. Brad is perfect. He eats the chicken Kiev and says it isn't dry at all. He drinks the cheap white wine and comments on how good the wines from Minnesota are getting. He even dances the Funky Chicken.

Then, at the end of the evening, everybody's outside on the sidewalk where a white stretch limousine festooned with powder blue streamers is pulling away with Hailey and her new husband, driving them to the airport where they'll fly off to their Hawaiian honeymoon. Everyone crowds together on the sidewalk waving. It's still cold out, and you can see everyone's breath as they yell good-bye.

"Marry me," Brad whispers, putting his arms around me.

"What?"

"Marry me!" he says loudly.

"Why?" I realize it's not the appropriate response, so I add, "Really?"

"Yes!" he says.

One of my cousins slaps me on the arm. "Did he just propose to you? Did he? Oh my God, this guy just proposed to Jennifer! This guy just proposed to Jennifer!" I see my mother's face peering through the crowd at me, questioning curiously and smiling, my father at her arm. My whole family is here, everyone turning and looking as rumor spreads through the crowd. I'm smiling too—I think—a frozen smile that almost hurts as I greet everyone's expectant faces.

There's a big solid, silent moment. Heavy.

I can't stand it.

"Yes!" I say and everyone cheers.

I think it's just nerves or the excitement that makes me feel queasy a few minutes later. Like someone punched me and knocked the breath out of me. I have to go inside to be alone for a breather, while Brad receives handshakes, back slaps, and hearty congratulations outside.

Suddenly I'm somebody. At work I never saw so many flower arrangements on anybody's desk. Roses, carnations, even a small juniper in a red foil bucket that says To NEW BEGINNINGS! All these gifts and congratulation cards pile in along with personal notes from people telling me *how happy* they are for me and Brad.

These are all the very same people who have scowled at me in the past or gossiped about me behind my back or been mean right to my face. *Good Luck! Best Wishes! Bon Voyage! Sucker Punch!* It's unbelievable. Now that I'm "official" it's like they're all scared for their jobs. Like I have any control over that. The cafeteria lady even gives me a free lunch. "Well, you're going to be Mrs. Keller now," she says with a toothy grin.

In cosmetics Brianna looks positively stunned. "I can't believe it," she says. I don't even have the heart to be mean to her or rub it in. I might be offended if I didn't know exactly where she was coming from. I've been that girl.

I am that girl.

Christopher is furious. We have a very awkward lunch.

"Just like that?" he demands. "Brad just proposes in the street?"

"Yeah," I say. "I guess he was swept away by the ceremony and my family and everything."

"Swept away by your family? *Your* family?"

"I guess I just manifested it." I grin. "When you expect positive things, then positive things happen!"

"Oh, knock it off," he says.

"It's true."

"Go manifest your mouth shut," he says and crosses his arms. He looks at my hands. "So he just proposed without a ring?"

"He's giving me his grandmother's ring." I try to keep my voice buoyant and bright, like a red beach ball being tossed around on a stormy sea.

"Are you pregnant?"

"No. God! No!"

"Then why is he proposing so soon after meeting you? It's only been a month and a half!"

"He loves me!" I say, my voice shrill. "We're meant to be together! These things happen sometimes! Sometimes you just know!"

"Poppycock!" he says.

"Poppycock? No one says poppycock."

"Poppycock," he repeats warningly.

"Whatever. Fine. Poppycock. Try to be happy for me. Just because it's a whirlwind romance doesn't mean it isn't real."

"Honey, nobody with a trust fund has a whirlwind romance. Doesn't happen."

"What are you saying?"

Christopher just gets up grumbling and leaves the table.

I distinctly hear him say "poppycock" again.

The only person who doesn't machine-gun me down with questions is Ted. He's silent. He doesn't ask me how Brad proposed or when's the big day, he just carries on as if nothing had happened. I guess that's fine. I mean, he doesn't have to make a big deal about my wedding. It's just a little weird to have everyone talking about it everywhere we go and he just pretends like it isn't happening.

"Jen, you sweetheart!" one of the PR girls squeals when she sees Ted and me walking down the hall. She rushes up and hugs me so hard one of her earrings catches in my hair. "I just heard Brad proposed to you! The girls and I want to take you out to celebrate! Party hearty with the bride!"

"Oh my God, that would be so awesome," I say deadpan, trying to get a smirk out of Ted.

"How about tonight?" she asks. "It's Blender Madness at the Anchor!"

"You know, I actually have to have my corns shaved down tonight. They're really thick. I'll probably be bloody and hobbling by cocktail hour, but send up a cheer for me!"

"I will!" she says with a weird face, like she's trying to smile while a cockroach is crawling up her leg. I look at Ted to see if he's smiling, but nothing.

I go to the Skyway to get a Cinnabon and on the way my phone rings. It's my mother, who tells me Lenny and Hailey came back from their honeymoon to bad news. Apparently Lenny's factory announced cutbacks and some other guy on the floor got promoted. Lenny lost his job. "That's how it goes with ham," she says. "Cutthroat all the way."

She tells me she tried to cheer Hailey up by telling her I got engaged to Brad Keller, but this didn't cheer my sister up as much as she'd thought it would. "I just don't know what they're going to do," she says. "They can't live here. Did you ever see their bathroom after Lenny takes a shower?" I tell her I'm very sorry for them and I promise to call and see if I can help.

And I will, right after I get me a Cinnabon.

I make my way over to the counter, order the usual, and I'm about to pay when I spy Brad and Ed coming down the hall with a couple of the other executives. I panic. I don't want them to see me here. This is not what the future wife of the president would be doing. She would be tending prize roses or polishing silver or attending a Chinese art forum at the museum. She would *not* be ordering a dinner-plate-size cinnamon roll slathered in icing, which she plans to wolf down in the emergency stairwell.

I look around wildly, but there's absolutely nowhere to go. They are almost at the counter, any miracle that's going to happen has to happen now, so I bolt through the little swinging door (meant only for employees) and crouch down next to the oven.

The counter girl watches me as I sit between the hot aluminum oven and the industrial waste can. "I said you could have more icing," she says and snaps her gum.

"My fiancé!" I say, "in the gray suit!"

"Big guy?"

"Yes! Did he see me?"

She doesn't say anything for a few seconds. "How ya doin?" She nods to somebody walking past. My heart is hammering in my chest. What's wrong with me? Why would I leap behind the Cinnabon counter? Is this what adults do? Is this a mature, normal thing to do?

"What's happening?" I hiss.

"Just wait," she says quietly. "Be cool. He just walked by." *Wow.*

The Cinnabon girl just became my hero. No, she was always my hero. I have to think of what the next status upgrade is. "Is he gone?" I ask. "My knees are starting to hurt."

"Pull the bucket out. Under the sink. I sit on it and read when it's slow."

I pull a red overturned bucket out from under the sink and there's a thick, dog-eared romance novel on it called *Hot Eternal Love*. There's an unmistakable smudge of icing at the corner. "No comments on the book," she says.

I nod. "No comments," I say, "but from my experience you get hot or you get eternal or you get love, but never all three together."

"That's a comment," she says.

"Sorry." I sit on my bucket and stare at the terra-cotta tiles on the floor, which are remarkably clean.

"Okay," she says, "he's gone. He's around the corner."

I stand up and brush off my skirt. "Thanks."

She holds the swinging door open for me and I step out into the corridor, people rushing past without so much as a glance. I try to dust the cinnamon sugar off my skirt and then I reach for my Cinnabon, which has been waiting on the counter this whole time. The counter girl stops me. "Let me get you a fresh one," she says. "These are warm."

She drops a big, fresh cinnamon roll in a box with a pair of stainless steel tongs and then uses a little white paddle to smear extra glops of icing on it. She pushes the box across the counter at me. "No charge," she says.

"No, really, I insist. Let me pay you. That was totally cool. I just didn't want, I mean, thank you for, you know. Thanks."

"No problem," she says. "Take it. You won't be back for a while."

"I won't?"

"Nope. After a ducking they stay away for a while."

"A ducking?"

She snaps her gum. "Takes time. There's the shame. Then guilt. Then you'll swear to never come back, and then you will."

I blink.

"You're not the first one to duck behind the counter," she says.

"I'm not?"

"We have duckings here on a semiregular basis. People don't want their co-workers to see them eating a Cinnabon, or their bosses or their Weight Watchers sponsors or whatever." She shrugs. "Lots of people have Cinnabon shame."

"Gosh, Satan," I say, "you're completely awesome."

"No problem."

"Can I ask you something? The icing. Is there, I mean, is there like a pharmaceutical-grade painkiller in it or something?"

She looks at the cash register. "There's a Cinnabon recovery program available but I'm not really supposed to talk about it."

I stuff a ten-dollar bill into the tip can on the counter. I tell her I don't want the Cinnabon, but then as I'm walking away I stop, spin on my heel, and dash back, where she's already holding the box out for me in anticipation of my return.

"Drink lots of water," she calls as I hurry away. "Helps when you're coming down."

"I actually hid behind a fast-food counter," I tell Christopher on the phone. "I was like Anne Frank hiding from the Nazis." I stretch out in the tub with two limp cucumber circles over my eyes.

"Poor lamb," he says and then, "Jeremy! Stop it!'

The hammering in the background stops.

"God, he's driving me crazy with that light fixture," Christopher complains. "We haven't had a light in the bedroom for two weeks because Restoration Hardware got the order wrong. The one they sent was perfectly fine, but Mr. Meticulous had to send it back."

I sink lower in the water. "How could they keep quiet for so long in that attic?" I wonder. "I was sitting on that bucket for like five minutes and I was ready to run out screaming."

"You have to admit, lighting in the forties was beautiful," he sighs. "All that milk glass and alabaster. Even the streetlamps were still gas. Imagine walking down the street by candlelight! They really knew a thing or two about indirect lighting. I'm sorry, can you excuse me a second? JEREMY! I am going to come in there and smash that chandelier into pieces with a hammer!"

Jeremy stops hammering again and he says something muffled to Christopher.

"Say hello to Jen," Christopher tells him. "She thinks Brad is a Nazi."

"I don't think he's a Nazi!" I say. "I love Brad!"

"Well, you said you were like Anne Frank hiding from the Nazis," Christopher says. "Who were the Nazis?"

"I don't know, Brad was walking with his . . . I mean, I didn't want it to look like . . ."

"Here's Jeremy!"

"Jen?"

"Jeremy?"

"Honey, don't listen to Chrissy. He has kitty litter in his vagina today."

Christopher shouts at him and then they must tussle with the phone because I hear scuffling and the line goes dead.

I hang up and sink down under the water so the cucumber slices float up to the surface of the water. Nice and quiet. Just me and the sea.

And Brad . . . the Nazi?

Mrs. Keller invites my family to the house for brunch, and after the grand tour, she ushers us into the grand dining room. I stand beside my family in my fresh kelly green empire-waist dress, my hair pulled back in a preppy black headband, trying to look every bit like Grace Kelly. I doubt there's even a fleeting resemblance.

"Those are eggless crullers," Mrs. Keller says, pointing to the crispy fried brittle things on the sideboard, "and that is quince custard."

Hailey's nose wrinkles. "It's orange gloop!" she whispers.

"Shut up," I warn her.

"Over here we have pumpkin biscuits," Mrs. Keller continues, "blood sausage, spinach soufflé, creamed beef on toast, Philadelphia scrapple, and chicken livers with orange sauce."

"What's a scrapple?" Hailey whispers. "Didn't we play scrapple at Aunt Joan's house?"

"Shut up! Eat it and like it."

"No way. I'm not freaking eating it. I'll tell you what, Lenny won't either."

But just then Lenny leans behind Mrs. Keller and helps himself to a string bean right from the casserole dish. "Just like my grandma made 'em," he says, "with almond slivers!"

"Yes, Leonard," Mrs. Keller says, "you help yourself. I love string beans with almond slivers too." What, is she in love with Lenny? "And for dessert there's raisin-spice cake," she says, "and of course steamed chocolate sponge pudding."

"Steamed sponge?" Hailey says. "What the freak?"

"Look," I tell her as everyone shuffles toward the buffet, "just take a little of everything or she'll notice." Hailey shakes her head. "No way," she says. "I'm not freaking eating food they ate in ye olden days." She even goes up to Mrs. Keller, probably to ask her for Froot Loops, but at the last minute she thinks better of it and goes to the buffet, where she plops a spoonful of spinach soufflé on her plate.

I sit at the table directly across from Brad, which is where I always sit. It's where I've always been told to sit. I looked it up in a Miss Manners book and it does say couples shouldn't be seated next to each other, but I think Mrs. Keller just likes to see us apart.

After the coffee is poured and we say grace, my mom asks Mrs. Keller what she thinks about "these kids" getting married.

"We think it's the most wonderful thing in the world!" Mrs. Keller says, clasping her hands together. "The moment I met your darling Jennifer, I thought to myself she's just the kind of girl I hoped Bradford would marry. More cream?"

"And we love your Bradford," my mother says.

Mom did pretty good for the brunch, I have to say. She looks good in her new dress. I went over there yesterday to see what everyone was planning to wear, and thank God, because Hailey shrugged and said, "Jeans and a T-shirt?" and my mother said she hadn't thought about it. I yelled at them and said they couldn't go over to the Kellers' house looking like hillbillies; this was important to me. My mother promised they would look decent, and basically they do, although my dad didn't wear a tie and Hailey put a banana clip in her hair. She did pull Lenny together, though, who's wearing a seersucker jacket and a yellow tie. Mrs. Keller said he looked dashing.

"These two spend so much time together," Mrs. Keller sighs, looking dreamily at her son. "Young love!"

"That's true." My mother nods. "We haven't seen much of Jennifer since she met your Bradford, have we, sweetie pie?"

I shake my head no and watch Hailey pushing her eggs around her plate. Then Brad tells them all I'm moving into his house a week before the wedding and that pretty much stops the conversation cold.

"Before the wedding?" Mrs. Keller says, her forkful of blood sausage frozen in midair. "How odd."

"Lenny and me moved in together way before the wedding," Hailey says.

"Leonard and *I*, dear," Mrs. Keller corrects.

"Yes," my mother says, "Leonard and I."

"Yeah, but we was doin' it before we got married," Lenny says. "I don't think Ma Keller here would like that either."

I'm smiling so hard at Lenny right now I think the veins in my temple might pop and shoot the table with arterial spray.

"That's right, Leonard," Mrs. Keller says, "you are absolutely correct."

Leonard laughs and wipes his mouth with the back of his hand. "My ma thought she was loose, too!" Hailey smacks him. "What?" he says, rubbing his arm. "She did!"

Ed clears his throat. "So you're in the insurance business," he asks my dad.

My dad finishes chewing and takes a sip of black coffee before he says, "You bet."

"Local group then?" Mr. Keller asks.

My dad nods. "Yep. State Farm. Thirty years and no retirement in sight."

We all laugh awkwardly.

"Well, we ought to get you into the office," Ed says. "We need a good insurance man."

"Really?" my mother says. "That would be wonderful!"

My dad frowns. "We don't handle—" but Ed puts his hand up. "We'll figure all that out. You're family now!"

"Well, that's very generous," my mother says, "isn't it, dear? Dear? You have a little gravy on your chin. There." My dad grumbles something about next week being tight and saws into his creamed beef. I don't think he likes the Kellers.

"Lenny lost his job," Hailey pipes up.

"Is that so?" Mr. Keller says, and the two of them talk shop until Ed decides Lenny would make a perfect loading-dock supervisor and tells him to come in on Monday. "Family has to stick together!" Ed says, and I know it's terribly nice of him, but for some reason I feel like ripping the tablecloth from the table and breaking all the china on the floor.

After we eat, there's coffee in the living room and my mother and Mrs. Keller tidy up in the kitchen. I clear plates, and so only catch bits of their conversation. "I just think she's an amazing girl," I hear Mrs. Keller tell my mother. "We're so lucky to have her join the family." She sounds so sincere, so real, that I almost think maybe her stern thing is all an act. Maybe she actually really likes me, and this is like prewedding hazing. I mean, certainly a lot of women must have wanted to marry Brad. I bet she has to weed them out and make sure they're good enough for him. I'd do the same thing.

"We're going to see the wedding planner next week," Mrs. Keller says. "Isn't that right, Jennifer?"

"I can't wait, Mrs. Keller," I say.

She smiles at me. "Oh, call me Mother Keller now or just Mother. That is, if your mother doesn't mind!" The two of them laugh lightly.

I grimace. "All right, Mother . . . Keller," I say. "Thank you for the delicious brunch."

"You're welcome, dear! I'm so glad you liked it. I was afraid your stomach was upset. You didn't touch your scrapple."

I've never had so many new things at one time. New clothes, new shoes, new everything. I've never held onto someone's credit card for them or carried their country-club membership card in my purse. I've never dated anyone who changed the way other people look at me, at least not in a good way. My family and friends and even co-workers. People at work who never made eye contact with me before suddenly know my name.

Not to mention HOW amazing and good it felt to finally pay off my Mr. Jennings bill.

"Mr. Jennings!" I say when he tracks me down. "How good of you to call."

"Miss Johnson?" he says, doubtfully.

"I've been looking forward to talking to you again!"

"I left a few messages," he says. "I already extended your account twice and I'm afraid it's going to collection today."

"No need for that, Mr. Jennings." I take out Brad's platinum card. "Let's just pay this account in full, shall we?"

"This is Jennifer Johnson, right?"

"Soon to be Jennifer Keller," I say. "I got engaged."

"That's great, Miss Johnson," he says.

I give him Brad's account number and listen to tinny Muzak while he processes my bill.

"Okay, you're all set, Miss Johnson."

"It's been really nice getting to know you, Mr. Jennings," I say. "I wish you well."

"Good luck, Miss Johnson. I'm glad you didn't end up with that guy who made you wait around in a bar. I'm glad everything worked out."

"Well . . . thank you," I say and hang up. No reason to tell him the guy who made me wait around in a bar is now my fiancé. It's the last time we'll ever speak so why bother explaining that a man who pays off your credit cards can make you wait as long as he wants to?

Brad didn't actually pay off my credit cards, the Kellers did, but Brad asked them to. I'd feel weird about it if I didn't hate the credit-card companies so much. I did the math once and if I paid the minimum monthly balance on a five-thousand-dollar debt until it was totally gone, I would end up paying them something like thirty thousand dollars. So did I feel bad knowing the Kellers paid my credit cards off?

Hell no.

Not that everything's perfect between Brad and me. We fight. Everyone fights, but it seems like anything can get us going. I tried to bring some things over from my apartment to brighten up his house, but he was like, "What the hell is this?" He was holding a vintage starburst clock. It's actually one of the most expensive things I own and I thought it might work with his décor, but he made it immediately clear that his mother doesn't like clutter.

"She doesn't like your weird crap," he says and we had a huge fight. I told him he couldn't change who I was and his mother shouldn't have anything to do with how we decorate the house, but in the end, even after he relented and admitted I was right, I brought the starburst clock back to my apartment. He didn't ask me to, I did it on my own and I can't say exactly why. It just didn't look right in his house.

Plus, what's wrong with trying something new? Maybe I'd be happier in a cleaner, calmer environment. Maybe all these toys represented a part of my life that was ending and maybe that was a good thing.

I get jealous. I'm always wondering who's calling him and who he's texting. I'm never sure if he's sure about me. I read this *Vogue* article about a fashion designer who got cancer and her husband, who was also a fashion designer, made a whole collection of cancer-inspired clothes for her. All these headscarves and gauzy red chiffon. It got me wondering if Brad would do that for me.

"Would you still love me if I had cancer?" I ask him at the breakfast table.

"If you had what?"

"Cancer."

"Do you?" he asks, putting his spoon down. "Are you telling me you have cancer?"

"No," I say, irritated. "Hypothetical cancer."

"Hypothetical?"

"Just answer! Would you still love me if I had cancer?"

"What kind?"

"What do you mean, what kind?"

He thinks about it for a minute.

"Why are you thinking about it?"

"I'd still love you," he says.

"Oh well, thanks. Be sure to put that on the card."

"Jesus, Jen."

"Would you love me if I had my legs cut off?"

"What?"

"My legs, zip! Gone."

"How would your legs get cut off?"

"I don't know, a car accident, a hot air balloon disaster, who knows?"

"You're crazy."

"Picture it. I'm in a wheelchair, still getting used to my titanium legs and you have to help me to the toilet and into the bathtub and you'd probably have to help me put the fake legs onto my stumps every morning . . ."

"Will you stop it?"

"I want to know what you'd do. I have a right to know."

"Why? Why do you think up all this crap?"

"Because if something horrible happens to me, you have to be prepared to take care of me." He just looks at me and shakes his head. I can't believe how he's acting. He should kiss me on the forehead right now and tell me of course he'd take care of me. If I was talking to Christopher and I asked him if he'd take care of me he'd say, "Oh, sweetie! Of course! I'd buy you windup toys and tie a ribbon around your head!" He'd give me a big hug. He wouldn't sit there like an unplugged appliance and pause and wonder and think about it. He wouldn't care if my legs were cut off or my vagina didn't work; he would be there for me no matter what.

"What if my vagina just permanently closed?"

He makes a face.

"You don't love me," I say, "not really."

Silence.

"You don't! What if I had surgery, and they accidentally permanently sewed up my vagina. Would you stay with me then?"

"Does that mean we could do anal?"

"No, we can't do anal! I just had a traumatic surgery and am lying there processing my new life as a vaginaless woman, and you want to do anal? How many times have I told you I don't want to do anal, ever? I mean ever, Brad. Get it through your head. And that is not going to change because I have a run-in with a tractor. Boy howdy, you can bet that rule will be as intact as ever."

"But if you use the right lube and the guy goes slow . . ."

"No! God! I told you it feels disgusting and plus now I know you wouldn't stay with me if I had my vagina sewed up." I can feel hot tears welling in my eyes. I do not want to cry, so I blink several times and tilt my head back, trying not to.

"Oh, come on," he says, "don't do that."

"You don't love me." I cover my face with my hands and burst into tears. I expect him to comfort me, or put his arms around me, but he doesn't. He just sits there and stares. I keep crying. After a while I start sniffling and can only manage a few small crocodile tears. Still he doesn't move to help me. I can't believe this. How can a guy just sit there and do nothing when I'm weeping in front of him? Is he some sort of psychopathic monster? One of those narcissists who had an emotionally manipulative mother?

What am I saying? Of course he did.

I turn and look at him with my red eyes and mascara-streaked face. Can't he see I'm in pain? Can't he see I need tenderness right now? But no, he's happy as a lark. In fact he tells me he has to go into work tomorrow, which is a Saturday. So not only is this fat bastard going to leave me if I have cancer; he's going to ditch me on a Saturday and I'm not even sick yet.

I throw myself into work. I show up early and I stay late. I volunteer for shit jobs nobody wants just to buy a few more hours at the office every day. My motives are to maintain mental health and keep out of Mrs. Keller's hair and off Brad's bad side, just until the wedding's over, but other people in the office think otherwise.

Ashley is really starting to fray at the edges.

"Are you trying to make me look bad?" she says, holding up the sheet of brainstorming ideas I gave her. "Because I know a thing or two about making people look bad, and I don't think you want to go there with me."

I tell her I was just goofing around and jotted down some ideas. "It's no big deal," I say. "Throw them out if you want to. I was just trying to help."

She stares at me as if trying to decipher my maniacal strategy and storms off. This won't be the end of it. Ted tries to cheer me up, and it's too bad I can't open up to him because Ted probably has it the worst. He has to put up with me the most. When you do the actual math, I spend more waking hours with him than anyone else. At least he's joking around with me again. A little. We just stay away from certain topics.

We have to put the finishing touches on our print ad for the HOUSEBOUND sale, Keller's annual housewares sale, where we try to unload out-of-date vacuum cleaners, microwaves, electric hair removal systems, and daiquiri blenders. Keller's doesn't have that big of a housewares section; the whole department takes up just half the basement, so we don't have that many sales and we pretty much suck at marketing them. Plus, we're two weeks behind on ad copy, mostly because my phone won't stop ringing. I can't get any real work done while people are calling me to double-check toothpick counts.

Ted sits next to me at my desk with the HOUSEBOUND files open and my phone rings.

"Jen? It's Sarah. Listen. I got Trevor fitted for his pantaloons, but he's so busy down there always pulling on his thing, I'm thinking we should go one size bigger. Then I can stuff something in there so he can't get at it and he won't walk down the aisle like a monkey tugging on his thing. I don't know what I'll stuff down there, maybe like a baseball glove or stuffed animals or something. Trevor! Leave that dog alone! Trevor!"

I shut my eyes. "Pantaloons?"

"I gotta go," she says. "Now he's tugging on the dog's thing."

"Sarah, what pantaloons?"

"Nana made him ring bearer," she says. "Trevor! Get off of him! Good cripes. I gotta go. Bye."

I hang up and cover my face.

"You really don't have to work on the copy," Ted says. "You know, if you're busy or whatever."

"No," I say, "I want to. It's like we're in the home stretch here."

"Then you're free," he says.

"Yeah, then I'm free. Really, really super-freaking free."

"Want to talk about it?"

"No."

Ted hands me the Keller's ads set to run in Saturday's paper. The first ad is promoting our TYKE-TASTIC! section, furniture and room accents for toddlers. Little race-car beds and canopied princess chaise lounges, that kind of thing. This particular ad features a little blond girl in overalls sitting with her teddy bear on a miniature leopard-skin couch.

"Why would we sell a miniature leopard-skin couch?"

"Dunno," he says.

"I mean, why would a little kid need a leopard-skin any-thing? What kind of copy are we supposed to write? Looks like it's time for baby's first porn shoot? Tricks really are for kids?" I bat the paper away so he hands me the next one, which has a picture of a comely woman whose ethnicity is completely up for grabs. She has cinnamon-colored skin and light hazel eyes. Her hair is neither blond nor brown, but a silky butterscotch that shines as she laughs and holds the handle of a Devex five-series vacuum cleaner. The copy beneath her airbrushed smile is in bold white quotes. It says: "I need a vacuum cleaner that's as strong as I am!" I look at Ted and hand it back. "That's what we're going with?"

"Ashley wrote it."

"But what does that even mean? A woman should compare herself to an appliance? Her vacuum cleaner has to take as much shit as she does? I don't believe it. That's like saying this woman wants a vacuum cleaner that will suck up all the crap in the world and hold on to it just like she does! Like consuming other people's garbage is her job!"

Tears begin to brim. Shit. I hate crying in the office

"Okay." Ted frowns. "Are we still talking about the copy?"

"Yes, we're talking about the copy! I want to know why all men assume women are supposed to take their shit and their mother's shit!"

"Um, okay," Ted says, "I think I'll mosey along now. I'd love to stay for the 'I hate men' speech, but I need to catch this online seminar on keeping your bitch in line."

"I don't hate men! Not real men."

"No," Ted says, backing away, his eyes wide open, "no, please, not the 'real man' speech."

"I will not be denied my real man speech," I tell him, "because real men aren't afraid to say 'I love you.' They respect women and they go down on their girlfriends after they get blowjobs."

"Hey," Ted says, "I always go down on girls. That's just like company policy with me."

"A real man is emotionally generous."

"And financially generous," Ted adds.

"Yes. And they do dishes and they like their mother and they have raw pirate sex with you."

"Have you actually met one of these freaks?" he asks. "Because I think maybe—maybe you had a seizure while you were watching the Lifetime channel again."

Normally I'd be joking right along with him, but today I can't. I don't know why I'm acting like this. Why everything is sounding alarms in my head and I feel like I can't breathe. I feel hot tears ready to escape. So I burst into the bathroom, where I try to sob silently into a wad of toilet paper, which disintegrates into bits in my hands. I guess what I really need is to find a toilet paper that's as strong as I am.

Mrs. Keller sets up my first appointment with the wedding planner. "You'll have no interference from me!" she says, smiling tightly. "I trust Mrs. Straubel completely. I know you'll be fine. You tell her what you want, and we'll tweak it all later. I gave Brad my solemn oath I wouldn't monopolize your big day!"

Notice she didn't say she trusted me completely.

I go to the wedding planner's shop, which is in a depressing strip mall in Rosedale. As I push open the glass door a little brass bell rings, and the smell of spiced oranges hangs thick against a wall of framed photographs showing happily married couples.

So many happy couples, it seems impossible anyone would ever be alone. Some are kissing, some are gazing intently at each other, and some are waving as they sprint down the chapel steps while being pelted with rice.

"Right there!" a woman in back says. "Have a seat and help yourself to a cup of tea!"

I obediently sit down on the prickly wicker couch and try to pour myself some tea, but I knock the cup over and send it sailing onto the floor. A stocky gray-haired lady comes barreling out of a back room a few minutes later, her solid body neatly packed into a heavy blue wool suit, her thick legs opaque in ivory stockings, and her formidable feet anchored by black orthopedics. She reminds me of senior-citizen centers and denture commercials and diabetes medical home delivery services. Functional, practical, and creepy. She moves pretty fast for a bigger woman and she seems very harried and annoyed as she plops down in the big wicker chair beside me.

"I'm Mrs. Straubel," she says, offering me a terse handshake. She grimaces/smiles at me and there's a tiny bit of spinach in her teeth. Why does Mrs. Keller, who could use anyone, use her? Then I spy the Lutheran cross on the wall. That's why.

Mrs. Straubel speaks Jesus fish.

"My apologies again!" she says, frumping and fah-lumping around in her seat, trying to get comfortable. "I was on the phone with *Bridezillas*. Can you believe that? That television show about the wacko brides? They called me and asked if I had any clients who were, you know"—she rolls her eyes around clockwise in her head—"cuckoo! I told them even if I did I wouldn't be telling them that over the phone. That's not information you hand out. Sure, I've seen plenty of breakdowns and even some breakups, but that's not the kind of thing most people want filmed." She gives me a wink. "Gee, sweetie," she says, "you want some water?"

I say no thank you.

"Honey, I've done a million and ten weddings," she says. "Don't you worry. I've seen it all. Fire, floods, tornados, food poisoning, grooms that cork off in the middle of the service, jilted lovers who try to break up the ceremony, the works. Don't you worry, you leave the worrying to me. That's my job. Your day will be perfect."

I feel somehow she might be filming this.

"We handle everything down to the last detail," she says. "Now, what theme were you thinking of?"

"I don't want anything fancy," I say. "I wrote that on my form. I just want it simple."

"You know, Mrs. Keller loves themes," she says. "Biblical themes. We did Sarah's wedding and they went with a Jonah and the whale theme."

"I don't really want a theme."

"It was so cute. They had aqua bridesmaid dresses and pink coral centerpieces. Mrs. Keller loved it. I think she still has a piece of coral on her mantel."

I don't know what to say. I don't want to be difficult and I know Mrs. Keller has a very particular way of doing things, but I tell Mrs. Straubel I'd like something more refined. "Well," she says, taking the pen out of her hair and snapping open her FranklinCovey day planner. Of course. "It's your day, and we'll do it any way you like. Let's just look at your intake form." When she says intake form, I'm hit with the image of a long line of women in white wedding dresses queuing up to go to jail. Bride jail, where they recite vows and string pearls all day.

"Well, this is cute," she says. "You wrote 'fun' here. See that? We can do a lot with that."

"I meant, like, not too serious."

"You bet. Now let me ask you something, Jennifer, and this is important. Would you say you have a fun relationship? A relationship where you like to have fun? Now be honest, there's no right way or wrong way to have a relationship."

"Well, you haven't seen some of my relationships!" I laugh until I catch her stony face. "No, um, sure we do. Brad and I are very fun!" My cheeks feel like hot plates set on low.

"*Very* fun!" Mrs. Straubel says, as though I've finally answered a question correctly, and she writes something on the form. What could she possibly be writing? *Get whoopee cushions?*

"And, Jennifer," she says, "would you say the two of you have modern personalities?"

I have no idea what she means. "Well, we're not old-fashioned," I say.

"Good." She checks something off her list. "Modern. Good. We're almost done here, hang in there, kiddo, because I know the wedding planning process is an ordeal. Believe me, I completely understand. It's exhausting and frightening and you have no idea what's going to happen next, right?"

I stare blankly.

"Okay," she says and shifts in her chair. "God, my sciatica is killing me. Ever have sciatica? You're probably too young. Just you wait, it's like someone's carving at the back of your leg with a meat cleaver. Strikes out of the blue. Sitting in this chair feels like I'm locked in one of those Viking iron maidens!"

Now why would she say Viking? Does she know I'm Danish? Is she messing with me?

"I had a bride who got sciatica the actual day of her wedding." Mrs. Straubel sighs. "What a tragedy. She had to say her vows sitting in a chair with her husband squatting next to her. Not a pretty sight. No one should have to squat at their wedding." She takes a big breath and blows the thin gray bangs off her forehead. "All right, back to the salt mines, where were we?"

I can hear the fan in the back hall running. I finally say, "We were at fun."

"Right! Fun. Okay, based on your answers, Jennifer, I'd like you to look at these." She pulls out a heavy white photo album and hands it over. "Now look at page fifteen there. You'll see something I think might fit very nicely."

She shows me a picture of the manger scene from the Bible. Baby Jesus is in his little hay manger and his plaster parents are watching over him while the three wise men look on. Also, there's a camel. "I don't think I get it," I say, hoping she won't be offended.

"Your wedding theme could be Mary and Joseph," Mrs. Straubel says, "the most popular couple in the Bible!"

"Popular?"

"Well, they gave birth to Christ, didn't they? It would be so cute. We could put little haystacks on the tables with incense and myrrh, only not real incense. Mrs. Keller has allergies."

I shift around in my chair.

"I don't know," I say, "I still don't think I get it."

I wonder if sciatica is viral, because I feel like I'm catching it. I feel like someone's hacking at me with a meat cleaver, only it isn't my legs, it's all over.

"Now you have to trust me," Mrs. Straubel says. "I know what your mother-in-law likes."

"Wow. Mother-in-law. No one's called her that before."

"Well, you better get used to it," she says grimly.

I nod. I'll never get used to it. It's too scary, too menacing. Too overpowering. If Mrs. Keller becomes my mother-in-law,

I don't know what will become of me. Who will I be then? Girl servant? Tyrant-in-training? I feel like my clothing is shrinking and cutting off circulation to my wrists, neck, and ankles. I can't breathe. My momentary show of irritation has dissipated and now I am dry and wind-worn, ready to be blown away by the slightest breeze.

"You better take all the help you can get," Mrs. Straubel warns me, "because that lady—and I'm not talking out of school here because Mrs. Keller has said this to me out loud herself—but that lady is picky and when she's not happy, nobody's happy."

My heart is beating in rapid, short bursts, like it's out of breath. It's so quiet in here, interrogation-room quiet. The perfect intake facility for bride jail. I look at her notepad. "Mrs. Keller told you what she wanted for my wedding theme, didn't she?"

Mrs. Straubel shrugs. "She might have mentioned it, we talk all the time. It might have come up. Let's just say you're lucky I know what she wants. You're going to have your hands full with other things, like making your new husband happy. He's Mr. Picky himself," she says, "but I'm sure you already know that."

All I know is that I want to get out of this place so bad I could dive through the plate-glass window.

"You do what you want," Mrs. Straubel says. "All I'm saying is she's a picky lady and she's got good taste, plus she's footing the bill, so maybe her ideas are all right to consider."

There's the back-hall fan again and another wave of spiced orange smell. I feel hot and queasy. "So, she likes themes?" I finally say. I sound like a small mouse peeping out of a hole in the wall.

Mrs. Straubel nods and smiles.

"You leave it to me," she says. "You'll be glad you did. Everything will be perfect."

I leave the wedding planner's shop and walk across to the

mall, where Mrs. Keller will meet me for lunch. That's when I can tell her my wedding has a theme. Mary and Joseph, the most popular couple in the Bible.

"You can't say you were bullied into it," Brad says, exasperated. "Mother said she wasn't even in the room." I bite my lip and hold the phone slightly away from my ear. We've been talking so long my cell phone is blister-hot, like it's getting angry, too. I don't want to sound whiny, but things have gotten so far out of hand, my stomach is in a constant state of torment. I'm nauseous or have diarrhea or am constipated all the time. Not that I would ever mention any of those words to Brad.

"It wasn't your mother," I say. "It's the wedding planner. She talked me into things I don't want."

"So change them back," he says.

"I can't! Things have already been ordered. You can't just change stuff up."

"So you want a different wedding planner? Is that it?"

"No! Mrs. Straubel's done all the family weddings. I don't want to rock the boat."

"Well, rock it or don't," he says. "I have a meeting."

"Fine," I snap, "I'll let the Grace Church Lutheran choir sing 'In His Hands' at our wedding. It'll kill me, but I'll do it. For you."

"That's my girl," he says and hangs up.

Unbelievable.

I sag into my desk chair. A Lutheran choir. That's only the latest horrible thing they've done to my elegant, simple wedding. They've also increased the guest list to three hundred, made the color scheme baby blue "with silverish accents," and forced me to have Sarah as my maid of honor. I say they "forced" me, but I couldn't prove it in a court of law. Somehow all these decisions are "mine," even though I didn't make any of them. Mrs. Keller uses Mrs. Straubel who uses her skittish staff to inform me what my decision should be. If for some reason I want something different, it becomes impossible or improbable or financially absurd.

When I said I wanted white linen tablecloths, I was told it would be astronomically expensive, while the colonial-blue skirting, which looked like the exact color of Mary's robe, was available for a song. When I asked for the irresistible fifty-dollar 1940s vintage wedding cake topper I saw on eBay, it was mysteriously purchased by a bidder named "QueenAnne," who paid five hundred dollars for it, and a new cake topper showed up from Williams-Sonoma the next day. A set of sterling silver doves.

This is how it goes until my dream wedding no longer bears even the slightest resemblance to my actual dream. At some point I sort of give in, like how castaways eventually accept their situations. After a certain amount of time you have to stop scanning the horizon with hope and just go build a palm-frond shelter. Do you prefer a palm-frond shelter to the comfort of your own bed? You do not. Did you hope your boat was going to sink and that you'd be stuck on a hostile island with a blue and silver color scheme? You had no idea it was even possible. Yet here you are, stranded, and at some point you just have to go lie down in the freaking palm fronds.

"You have to be reasonable," my mother says. "They're paying for everything. So what if she chooses a few things?"

I can't believe her. "A few things? She chose my wedding dress and she chose the *underpants* I'm supposed to wear underneath my wedding dress. They're like these creepy lace shorts, because she says the other kinds bunch up."

"Well, she makes a good point," my mother says. "You don't want a bunching issue."

A bunching issue?

They're all against me now. Even my own family. Hailey has been delighting in torturing me with after-you-get-married facts. "After you get married he won't hide his farting anymore," she says. "And after you get married he stops buying you presents."

Ha. Well maybe *her* husband stopped buying her presents.

I have no doubt that presents won't be a problem. Brad LOVES spending money and ever since we got engaged, he seems to have a lot more of it. He buys me a big, black Mercedes-Benz SUV. It just shows up in the driveway with a sticker still in the window and a tiny red bow on the hood, the kind you'd put on a regular present. "I wanted to get one of those really big red bows," he says, "but nobody knew where to get one."

"Wow," I say, arms crossed and staring. "It's really . . . big."

"It's a GLK with a four-cylinder compressor motor," he says. "Do you like it?"

"I don't think I've ever driven a car that big before. I don't know if I know how."

"It's got four-wheel drive for the winter," he says. "Mom told me if we ever had . . . you know, if there are ever kids around, you'd need something safer to drive."

I stare at him. "Your mother told you to buy this for me?"

"No!" he says. "It was my idea. I just asked her what kind would be good for a woman. It's for putting up with me and my family and all the other stuff," he says. "I know you're stressed out." He taps the hood. "I made sure it had seat warmers."

I don't know what to say. On the one hand, a man just bought me a Mercedes-Benz. That should make me happy. I should be grateful. On the other hand, it's an SUV, a soccer mom car for when I start popping out babies. Plus, it was hand-selected by his mother, which makes me livid. I decide to remain neutral.

"Thank you," I say, not uncrossing my arms. "It's very thoughtful."

"You don't like it?"

"No. I mean, yes. Of course I do. Where's my car?"

He looks confused.

"My other car," I say. "My 1985 safety-orange Scout? The car I saved up for and bought by myself. The one that I love?"

He blinks. "Oh, I traded it in."

"You . . . traded it in? What do you mean, you traded it in? It's gone?"

He looks at me like I'm crazy.

"Did you get the little angel wings pin out of the dashboard?" I ask him. "The one my mother gave me? Where are all the maps that were in the glove box? What about the hand-embroidered map of Mexico pillow in the backseat?"

I don't wait for him to answer; I just run in the house and call the dealership. I want my Scout back. This must be some sort of theft, but what would I tell the police? My fiancé traded in my used car and bought me a brand-new Mercedes, so please arrest him?

Just breathe, relax.

It's going to be okay.

I talk to the sales manager and the assistant sales manager at the car dealership, asking them if they know the whereabouts of my 1985 safety-orange Scout. They're confused at first and want to speak to Brad, but I start yelling like an enraged teenager, demanding to know where they get off selling my property without my consent, and if I can't locate my truck, maybe my fleet of lawyers or the Minneapolis police or the guys I'm going to hire to break their legs can, until they apologize profusely. They admit my truck was pretty unique, not many of them like that around, and it was only on the lot for a few hours before it sold. The guy who bought it is going to repaint it and trick out the wheels.

The Scout is gone.

My apartment is cluttered with packing boxes and various piles of crap. One pile, the biggest one, is all the crap left that's being thrown out. The second pile is all stuff I don't need but don't want to throw away yet. The last pile is smallish, it fits on the kitchen table; it's the stuff I'm bringing to Brad's house. I'm breaking my lease early so I can move in with him full time, not that it wasn't full time already. My apartment has become a larger version of a storage space, housing the clothing and belongings I don't really use.

Blooper is still on the kitchen counter.

I knew it would be a big job, getting rid of all my stuff, but I didn't know it would be an astronomical, mind-numbing, soul-killing job. The first thing I did was pack up the really precious things and try to give them to friends and family. Even if I can't display my treasures in my own home, maybe people close to me can.

"What is it?" Christopher asks, making a face at the box.

"It's the aluminum Christmas tree!" I say. "Very retro. Very kitsch."

"That's so sweet!" he says, handing the box back to me.

"What's wrong?"

"Don't want it."

"Christopher, you loved this tree."

"No, I didn't. It was a pity compliment."

I try to give my dolls to Hailey, citing the idea her unborn children might like them. She also turns her nose up at me. "Those are all used! I bet there's lice in them or bedbugs or whatever you had in that creepy place of yours!"

I wise up on the third try and leave a box of precious treasures in my parents' garage without telling them, which I'm later told went out to the curb with the rest of the recycling. Everything was tossed except the carefully boxed dollhouse and Tinkertoy family. Mom considers those family heirlooms, so they were safe. (When I packed the Tinkers up I told them this would be like a calming holiday for them, not a punishment, but they didn't look convinced.) She grudgingly lugged them all up to the attic and let me know, once again, she wasn't going to live forever, and I'd better find a better way to store all my crap. "You're moving into that big house!" she complains. "Why not put it there?"

"It's complicated," I tell her, "and crowded."

I cart the leftover "possibly valuable doodads" over to a little second hand shop and try to sell them to the guy in an argyle sweater vest behind the counter. I thought I could save the money I got for hocking my life's work for a rainy day, or maybe spend it on wine.

"I can't give you anything for these," the guy says.

"Nothing?"

He shrugs. "They're all used or damaged or heavily . . . played with."

"But they're perfectly good toys. This one came straight from Japan."

"Ship 'em back," he says. "Have them pay you in yen."

I box all the toys up and give them to Salvation Army. What a waste. Thousands of dollars of cheap plastic crap and it all ends up in a junk shop.

I've also been on my cell phone with Mrs. Straubel for the last half hour, going over details and waiting for her to finish hacking up phlegm. I just told her Christopher and his boyfriend were doing my hair and makeup and she says, "Honey, we can't have a couple of those wandering around the house, your father-in law will have business partners there."

"A couple of what?"

"You know. *Queers*."

I don't know what to say to this. People are usually so good at hiding their horribleness.

"Mrs. Straubel," I say, "I'm sorry but I have to go. We can finish up later." I hang up the phone because Lana, my downstairs neighbor, is coming up the stairs. I ask her if she wants some tea and she says no thanks, she really has to run. I go pick up Mrs. Biggles from her favorite spot on the couch and snuggle her in my arms. "So you'll take good care of her?"

"Of course," Lana says.

"And you already know about her allergies?"

"Yep. No lactose, no wheat."

"I can't stand doing this, it's just Brad's deathly allergic to cats."

"I know," she says, "you told me."

"Okay then," I say and kiss Mrs. Biggles on the head. She feels so light in my arms, like she almost isn't there. "You already have her pillow and her catnip toy?"

"And her ear drops and her flea collar," Lana says. "I'm so sorry to rush, but I have a job interview. You can come visit us any time you want."

"That'd be nice," I say, handing my cat over to the girl from downstairs. "I'll do that." Lana takes the cat and gives me a small smile that doesn't really communicate anything. Then she leaves. With my cat. They're gone. Mrs. Biggles is gone.

I go from staring out the window to hyperventilating in record time.

"You had to do it," Ted says on the phone. "Please don't cry."

"I'm a bad . . . bad . . . bad mother."

"You're a good mother. You found Mrs. Biggles a good home."

"Lana is nice, ri . . . ri . . . right?" I try to catch my breath. "You've been bowling with her."

"She's very nice," Ted says. "Great overall game scores. I'll visit Mrs. Biggles, too. She'll still be in your life, it'll just be different. The same, but different."

I thank him and say he should charge me for all these talks; he's helped more than my therapist has. I tell him I feel better, but I don't. We get off the phone and I watch television until late at night. I don't answer any of Brad's calls.

Eventually, around two in the morning, I load up my car. It's a total of two boxes. The rest of the things in my apartment will be cleaned out by the maid service Mrs. Keller hired. The walls look stained and dirty, like this was a tenement, not a young, vibrant working girl's oasis. I grab my purse and sassy working-girl figurine, who I seat-belt in on the front seat next to me. She's coming with me. I pull out of the driveway, forcibly refusing to think *for the last time*, and I see Lana's curtains briefly swish aside. There's Mrs. Biggles, sitting in the window. I stare at her little outline as I drive away, until my tears blur the picture.

Be strong, be sensible, be smart.

Don't look back.

My porcelain doll and I drive to Brad's house on the back roads, since I've been drinking enough for the both of us. I get to his house and everything is quiet. Extremely quiet. Central-air-and-controlled-humidity quiet. Mechanical-blinds-and-heated-floor quiet. Like a pristine, sterile vault where women with soul seem loud. I tuck my sassy working girl in a high up cabinet in the kitchen. One Brad never opens.

• • •

They throw me a farewell party at work. I've always thought that the office farewell party was more of a group spanking machine than anything else. Sort of a last chance for employees to politely insult you or take a swing at your future plans. Why else do it? Because everyone really wants one more piece of sheet cake? Because the person departing forgot to get the phone number of the few people in the office they actually like? No, I think of a farewell party as your final glass-chewing assignment.

"I really expected them to make you a junior VP or something," Big Trish says, chomping down on a bite of strawberry cake. "I mean, with you marrying into the family and everything, it's kind of weird they didn't. Are you going to be like what now? A housewife?" I watch her lips smack together. Who orders a strawberry cake? A person who hates whomever that cake is for, that's who. I know Big Trish ordered this cake. I think I once told her I hated strawberry ice cream.

"She gets to live the life of leisure now," Ted says, arms crossed, legs crossed, leaning against the refrigerator and beneath the GOOD-BYE AND GOOD LUCK! banner, the one we use for every farewell party, which has come loose at one end and sags down so it reads, GOOD-BYE AND GOOD . . . I resist the temptation to stand on a chair and pick the sagging end up to see if it possibly reads GOOD-BYE AND GOOD RIDDANCE!

"Just don't stay out of the work force for too long," Ashley says as she saunters through the door and pauses briefly over the hacked-up cake. "Once you're out, it's never quite so easy to get back in, is it?"

Great.

Why did she come? This is proof they're trying to be sadomasochistic. Ashley would never voluntarily show up somewhere unless there was something in it for her. She pours herself a cup of coffee. "So what are your big plans?" she asks, looking smug.

What I really want to say to her and Big Trish is, "Well, I'll be rich now, so I won't be doing anything that doesn't amuse me and I've always wanted to explore Fabergé egg collecting," but I can't because Ted's right there and I don't want to say anything that would hurt him.

Plus, if I said that, I'm afraid they might hear the hesitation in my voice. They might see the worry in my eyes, because even though people think marrying into a rich family would solve all your problems and give you the fabulous life you've always wanted, ever since I became part of the Keller clan, I've never had to do so many unamusing things in my life. Last week I had to go with the family to Trevor's play and sit through a three-hour rendition of *Pinocchio*. I'm sorry, but having to watch a children's play if you don't have a child actually in the play should be classified as cruel and unusual punishment. Then we all had to go to Circus Tubs, where Trevor thought it was funny when the guy in the panda suit bopped me on the head with his big foam bamboo shoot, so the family cheered the panda on and the panda bopped me fifty times at least.

"It's for the family," Brad says whenever we have to do something inane, spine-numbingly boring, or creepily religious. Brunches, birthdays, barbecues, card nights—I've never known a family who gets together so often. It's unnatural. I have been to twenty church services or more since we started dating, more than in the past ten years combined. I've spent enough time with the family's favorite pastor, Pastor Mike, to observe he is very gay. Brad thinks this is ridiculous, he's known Pastor Mike since he was five, and all that hugging and back rubbing, that's just good-natured kindness. "Ha," I tell him. "Boy, did he see you coming."

I don't want Ashley or anyone suspecting that I'm not in heaven, because I am in heaven—I mean, it's not exactly heaven, but it's not far from it. Every relationship takes work and no couple is perfect. So what if Brad has lost his temper a few times and actually embarrassed and/or scared me? People get angry. I get angry. Hell, I launched a CD across the room at Brad like a flying circular saw and it cracked in half when it hit the wall. So I can't be marching around telling him to stop screaming at the waiters and hiding cookies from me when we all have flaws.

Maybe that's why I want a huge piece of this horrible strawberry cake. I haven't had anything sweet in so long. I went on this diet and I've been really watching what I eat, and Brad out of love and concern is equally particular about what I eat. It's not that he thinks I'm fat. God no. He tells me I'm beautiful all the time, but he also knows I am trying to lose weight, by my own choice, and that things like cookies and cake are too much of a temptation. He knows I make every effort to reduce calorie intake and that I am in fact getting better about splurging, which is why I will not be having any cake today!

Thank you, Big Trish, for ordering a cake I hate!

The PR girls stop in and kiss me good-bye. They all chipped in and got me a farewell coffee mug that says GOODBYE GIRL! I thank them and tell them I'll treasure it. Then I put it by the sink, where I'll leave it when I go. Christopher manages to break away from his visual display duties and brings me a farewell cappuccino. I tell him nothing will change, we'll be buddies like we always were and he says sure and I say sure and we both look down at our feet.

After the party's over and everyone wanders back to their various work stations, I clear out my desk, take what's left of the things in my cubicle, and stuff them in a cardboard box. I can't even bear to look at the photograph of Mrs. Biggles, whose picture I find in a bottom drawer. "Can I have it?" Ted asks.

"You want a photograph of my cat?"

"Yeah."

"Why?"

"I don't know," he says, "at least it's something."

I give him the photograph and my map of the world and my dictionary/thesaurus set. "Brad has a way nicer set at his house," I say, and then I wish I hadn't.

My cubicle looks so strange with everything gone, like it did the first day I started working at Keller's. I was so young then, and it wasn't that long ago. I thought this place was just a lily pad, a jumping-off spot to the next big thing. I was going to be a novelist, a travel writer, a big-time ad agency executive. Now it looks like the next big thing is never working again, which doesn't fill me with the kind of happiness I'd expected. I've gotten so negative in my thinking lately. I haven't listened to Dr. Gupta in forever.

I sit at my desk and go through my computer files one last time to see if I forgot anything. It's nerve-wracking to leave a computer behind, you have to delete every personal e-mail, document, and computer game you downloaded. I started doing entire system scans for the words "fuck," "shit," "asswipe," "bitch," "miserable," and "kill." I found quite a bit of sensitive stuff that way. Ted helped me do a system reinstall, which he says will reset everything to the way it was when it was brand new. Still, I sort through my old e-mails one more time, forwarding anything I want to keep to my personal account, looking for strays I didn't catch before. I see an e-mail from Exploding Hearts, saying it's been awhile since I checked my account and they miss me. I'd completely forgotten about my profile; I guess now it's time to finally cancel this stupid account forever.

I'm surprised to see an e-mail from AndyMN. Three e-mails from him actually. In the first one he apologizes for taking so long to contact me. He had some weird reaction to the food on our date, which is why he was acting kind of funny. Then he couldn't find my number. His second e-mail is glum. He says he understands he blew it, he had his chance with me and circumstances conspired to make him muck it up. He says he's sorry, because he thought I had the most beautiful face he'd ever seen. The third e-mail just says good-bye and good luck and if I ever want to cross paths with him again, e-mail him at his Yahoo account. He wishes me a grand life.

A grand life.

I don't e-mail him back. At first I think I might. I even jot a few sentences down, but everything sounds stupid and fake, which it is. I close my account. It's forever and for permanent, like everything seems to be these days. Then I put my coat on and get ready to go. I tell Ted I'll call him tomorrow night so we can plan when we're having dinner together and he nods. I hug him. When I'm about to let go, he hugs a little harder.

I take a last walk through the Skyway, reminding myself I can always come back; it's not like the Skyway is going to disappear if I don't work at Keller's anymore. I buy a Cinnabon for old times' sake and the Cinnabon girl says she wants to cry, I was her favorite customer.

"You're the best," I tell her.

"I know," she says sadly, "I know."

I stop into Frontier Travel, where Susan tells me to hang on while she finishes a phone call. "I've been waiting for you to come by," she says, shuffling through some papers on her crowded desk, "just in case you never found that millionaire. I asked my boss in New York if he needed any regional Midwest writers and he said if I found someone here I liked, I could try them out on something small, like this right here."

She hands me a fax. On it is a writing assignment from the

Frontier Travel headquarters in New York. "It's just a short piece about classic diners," she says. "You'd have to drive up the North Shore and have a slice of pie or something in each one, then write up a blurb about each place. Frontier's trying to put this Americana tour together, since everyone's afraid to be an American traveling overseas these days."

I frown and hand the fax back. "I did find one."

"Pardon?"

"A millionaire husband. I mean, I'm getting married. In a few weeks."

"Oh," she says, and looks at the fax in her hand. "Well, couldn't you write the story anyway? It's travel writing. What you always wanted to do."

I stare at the floor.

"I know it isn't much," she says, "but my boss is great and I know he'd give you bigger stories, like there's this tour we're putting together in France—"

"Sorry!" I say loudly. I feel like I'm walking around a big, dark hole, but I don't know what the hole is. I just know I don't want to tumble into it. "That's so nice that you asked," I say, "really, but with everything so busy and everything, I just, you know, I can't."

"Okay. Well, if you change your mind, let me know, I guess."

"I will!" I say, backing into the safety of the Skyway.

"And congratulations," she says. "Best of luck in your new life."

"Thanks," I say and then I hurry away.

I take the Keller's chandelier-lit customer elevators up to the eighth floor because, after all, I'm not an employee now; I'm just a customer. I lock myself in a bathroom stall and then I dig out that delicious, disgusting Cinnabon and cram it into my mouth, gluey icing smearing on my face and my fingers, cinnamon chunks crumbling down my shirt and bouncing onto the tiled floor. I tear off the crusty outer folds and rip at the hot, moist inner cinnamon heart, which gives itself up like a porn star, unfolding, yielding, and giving me every horrible thing I want. This is me sitting in a public bathroom eating a Cinnabon.

Just for old time's sake.

Christopher and Jeremy give me a "mental health day" for my wedding present and it includes a spa massage, hydrotherapy session, craniosacral skull realignment, an hour in a flotation sensory-deprivation tank, and a meditation class. I know they mean well and by the looks on their faces, it is a gift they'd love to receive. I'm learning that's the big problem with gifts, wedding or otherwise. People give you what they themselves would love to get. It would actually work really well if people bought each other gifts and then traded back. I guarantee you, everyone would be happy.

Christopher and Jeremy, for instance, would be pleased as gay penguins to be locked inside a plastic porta-potty filled with warm water, floating there endlessly, not knowing if anyone was ever going to let them out, if it meant they would look rejuvenated afterward. Not me, thank you. I'll do the massage and the craniosacral whatever, because I think that's just a fancy word for head rub, and I'll even do the meditation class, but nothing will get me to set foot inside a sensory deprivation tank. "I'm claustrophobic," I tell them.

"Since when?" Christopher demands.

"Since I thought about someone snapping me inside a large liquid-filled Tupperware storage tub."

"Let her do what she wants to," Jeremy says, defending me. "It's a gift, not a set of marching orders." Thank God for

Jeremy. Thank God for both of them, really, because the day does turn out to be fantastic. I get kneaded, exfoliated, and realigned. I have so many calming treatments that my feelings can bubble to the surface, and by the time I go to the Zen Center on Lake Calhoun, which exudes peace, tranquility, and calm, I'm ready to burst into tears. A girl with green eyes greets me at the door. "Welcome to the Zen Center," she says. "Namaste."

"Namma-stay to you, too," I say having no idea what it means but trying to brush away the prickly sensation that if Mrs. Keller knew I was here, she'd inform Brad I'd joined a cult.

"First time?" she asks, smiling.

I nod.

"Well, we ask that you take off your shoes here and put them toe-first into the cubbyholes over there. Then please go to the main hall, where you can collect your meditation mat and pillow. Then you can go to the sacred center, and we do ask that you bow toward Buddha before you enter, and find yourself a comfortable place on the floor. After the meditation hour please refrain from speaking and take your mat and meditation pillow back to the hall."

"Wow," I say, "complicated."

She smiles, not unkindly.

I follow her directions to the best of my abilities. I take my shoes off, get my mat and pillow, and go to the sacred center, but I'm halfway across the room of people sitting perfectly still and not speaking before I realize I didn't bow before entering. I don't know how seriously they take that, so I backtrack, bow, and reenter. I'm already a nervous wreck.

I sit down and the Zen teacher rings a gong. He tells us to sit cross-legged on our mats, hold our palms loosely in our laps, close our eyes, and push away all thoughts. He says our minds should be clear and pure, like a cold mountain brook flowing over the world without resistance.

What unfolds before me is an unstoppable spool of horrible memories and vivid daymares. I remember every ex-boyfriend I ever had, every bad date, every mean thing anyone ever said to me. I remember fuck-ups at work I'd forgotten about, horrible fights with my mother and sister, and the haunting memory of a pet gerbil named Dice who died because I forgot to give it water. "Just follow your breath," the instructor says. "Breathe deep."

I open one eye to see if anyone else might also be having a panic attack, but no, they all seem blissful and serene. I would be blissful and serene, too, if I didn't have to spend all my time keeping Mrs. Keller from sneaking liver onto my wedding menu. I could sit here like a zombie smiling at nothing if my whole world wasn't going to hell in a Jesus-fish handbasket.

"Clear your mind!" the teacher says. "Focus on your breath. All your thoughts can be put on a shelf for now. You'll get back to them later. Just breathe in and imagine you are filling yourself with clear blue water with each breath." *Okay, then we would be drowning*, I think, but immediately I put that thought up on the shelf, although that shelf is getting crowded and things are starting to fall off. It's hard to clear your mind when it unspools like synaptic copper wire, which tangles and chokes you.

The more I try not to think of things, the more I think of them. Each thought sparks and fires, igniting the next and then the next, and they all crowd around with grenades and guns in a cranial coup d'état. My memories are out to get me. After the meditation, the girl with green eyes comes up to me and asks me how I liked it. "Fantastic," I say, "really soothing. Really, um . . ." I'm fighting back tears and that's just stupid. I'm at a Zen center for freak's sake.

"Are you okay?" she asks.

"Life gets so stressful," I say, my voice getting so high-pitched that probably only dolphins can hear it. "Sometimes I just want to end it all, you know? Just not wake up?" I look around. I sound a little hysterical.

She smiles. "Life has a way of continuing," she says.

"Plus, killing yourself is not as easy as it sounds," I chirp, forcing myself to pull it together. "I've researched it. You have to really, really plan it out. My old roommate's cousin jumped off a building because he hated his life and he even wrote I HATE MY LIFE on a piece of paper and safety-pinned it to his sweater before he jumped. Turned out he didn't kill himself; he just paralyzed himself from the neck down. Can you imagine? How much does he hate his life now, right?"

The soothing girl tips her head the way the RCA dog does when he's listening to a gramophone. I'm so far removed from her groovy vibe, she's probably not even sure if I'm speaking English. I'm mortified and so I go out into the mediation garden and sit on a stone bench while I wait for Christopher to pick me up.

I watch a little pebble fountain, which bubbles like a brook. A cheeky little sparrow hops down and starts to peck at the paved walkway. Poor guy. I know these little guys stay in Minnesota through winter, but how? He could fit in the palm of my hand and his heart must be no bigger than an almond. How could he live through a blizzard?

I check my pockets to see if I have anything to feed it, like maybe I've stashed a whole-grain muffin in the lining of my coat. I even consider walking to the corner store, but I know Christopher will be here any minute. Poor little bird. What does it eat? It looks hungry. The sparrow finds a cigarette butt that has rolled to the edge of the path and starts pecking at it. It must look like bread. What's a cigarette butt doing in a Zen garden? The sight of this little sparrow with his almond-size heart pecking at someone else's careless trash is too much. I think of Mrs. Biggles and I start weeping.

"I don't think this counts as meditating," Christopher says, suddenly coming down the garden path. He sits next to me and tucks an arm around my shoulder. "Although Buddha did say to live is to suffer, or something like that, so you've got that part right."

"I can't cry right now. We've got professional photographs tomorrow." I dab at my eyes and we sit there for a minute, the fountain bubbling, the bird back in his tree. "I don't want to get married," I say. It just pops out like a beach ball that's been held under water. I expect Christopher to look shocked or worried or even angry, but he just tilts his head against mine.

"I know," he says.

"You do?"

"I've known since he asked you. No happy bride gets a subscription to *Good Housekeeping* the week she gets engaged."

"They have helpful hints," I sniff.

"I know. You just don't seem happy."

"What will make me happy?"

He sighs, starts to say something, and then stops. "Shit. I got nothing. Can we just get some whiskey or ice cream?"

"No aphorisms? Not one?"

" 'When it rains it pours'?"

"No good."

" 'Life is not about waiting for the storm to end, it's about learning to dance in the rain'?"

"Just shut up, and let's get ice cream. I want rocky road."

"That's funny!" he says, coming along behind me. "Get it? Rocky road!"

"At least life can't get any worse," I say. What an idiot I am.

It's three in the morning two days before the wedding and I'm on the phone, pacing back and forth across the kitchen floor. I can't believe what I'm hearing.

"What do you mean, the police station?" I ask. "Was he arrested?"

I'm told no, Brad wasn't arrested. Not even formally charged. He's just being held along with all of his other friends who threw him the bachelor party. It's Brad's lawyer on the phone, a myopic nasal drip who makes sure he says absolutely nothing every time he speaks. He tells me Brad will be released shortly and he'll make sure he gets home safely. Brad can explain the rest.

I'm panicked; I call Christopher. No answer. I don't know what to do. I don't want to call my mother or Hailey. I can't think of anyone else I can call at three in the morning, so I call Ted. He's groggy and a little out of it when he answers the phone, so it takes a few times of me repeating myself before he starts to catch on.

"Brad had a bachelor party?" he says. "Why didn't I get invited?"

"He got taken to jail, but they won't tell me what for."

I hear a deep sigh as he readjusts the blankets or something. I never thought of Ted in bed before. "Well, it probably has something to do with girls," he says. "That's what usually does it."

"Girls?"

He clears his throat. "Prostitutes."

"Oh my God."

"Don't panic, I'm just telling you I've had a few buddies who wound up in trouble at their bachelor parties and it's either too much booze or a hooker."

"Oh, please let it be booze!" I pace up and down the kitchen floor. He tells me everything is going to be all right, and I always believe Ted when he says that. "God, I'm sorry," I say. "This is so awful of me to call you. I just didn't know who else I could tell. You know you're invited to the wedding, right? You were always invited, I just thought you wouldn't want to come."

"I am coming," he says. "I'm Christopher's date."

"You are?"

"Yep. He said it'd be good for me and his boyfriend can't go."

The other line beeps in and Ted says to call him back if I need anything, including a ride downtown to pick Brad up. I tell him it's okay, I think it's covered, and plus, Brad would never do that for him. "I know," Ted says. "I wouldn't do it for Brad either, but I'd do it for you."

On the other line is Brad. I'm hysterical. I'm crying. I start shouting at him I'm so frightened and out of my mind, so he hangs up on me.

He calls back a minute later. "Are you calm now?" he snaps. He's been drinking. I can hear it in his voice.

"What happened?" I ask, trying to keep all hysteria, worry, anger, disgust, judgment, and despair out of my voice.

"It was just some mix-up," he says, "no big deal. I'll be home in twenty minutes. I think this cabdriver can find it. Can you find it, buddy? Yeah, he says he can find it."

I sit at the dining room table for what seems like an hour, staring at the napkin holder. It is the same napkin holder Mrs. Keller has in her house.

Nickel-plated doves.

This sensation in my stomach, this gnawing pit, is getting wider and wider until I feel like I'm being swallowed whole. I can't do it. I can't marry this man. I know I thought it was everything I wanted, but it isn't everything I wanted.

Then the back door swings wide open and there's Brad with his red parka askew and his hair messed up. He's grinning.

"Had a little trouble," he says.

"What happened?"

"Oh, just trouble," he slurs, waving his hand, "the guys got dancers and they . . ."

He stops talking and stands there staring at the floor.

"They what?"

"Then the police showed up." He stumbles. I lunge to catch him before he grabs the counter and steadies himself. My heart is rapid-fire pummeling in my rib cage. I can hardly breathe. "Did you do something with one of the dancers?"

He starts to say something, raises his hand, and then pitches forward, cracking his head on the edge of the barstool and passing out on the floor.

I rush to undo his shirt and put my ear on his chest. He's breathing, thank God. That's when I see something red below his navel. It's like clown paint. Big, red, oily greasepaint. I undo his pants. It's lipstick, smeared down to his abdomen. I fish his flaccid penis out, like a little, sticky hairless mouse in my hand. The base of it is ringed with red lipstick.

He groans and I rush to the phone and call the big house. I don't know what else to do. If I call an ambulance, they'll see the lights anyway. We are fish and this is our bowl. Maybe I've already died. It feels like I have and I've been reincarnated as Ryan Seacrest, the doomed goldfish on the top of the microwave.

Ed is the first on the scene. He's wearing quintessential old-man striped pajamas with leather slippers. "All right," he says, slinging an arm underneath Brad and hoisting him up. He walks/drags him to the bathroom and turns on the shower. Then Mrs. Keller arrives, her hair in a gauzy netted thing, her lavender bathrobe cinched shut.

She goes into the bathroom, too.

I collapse at the kitchen table and put my head down on my arms and weep. I can hear them in the bathroom, the happy family.

"There, there," Mrs. Keller says to me, returning from the bathroom. "Ed will take care of everything. You'll see. Let me make you some tea." She goes to the stove and puts the kettle on. Then she roots around my cabinets searching for tea. In a million and one years I would never touch anything in her kitchen without being asked, but she looks ready to prepare Thanksgiving dinner in mine. She clucks her tongue when she comes across the kangaroo salt shaker in the cupboard. "Honestly, Jennifer," she says, "you have to give up these toys. I hope you're not planning on cluttering up his beautiful house with these . . . things." She puts the salt shaker on the counter like it's a vile thing that might scurry away.

"I think you should worry about Brad's toys," I say, my voice shaking.

"Boys will be boys," she sighs. "You can't expect too much from them."

"Didn't you see?" I ask her angrily. "Didn't you see his . . ."

She holds up a hand to stop me. "I saw."

"How could he do that?" I start to cry again. The fact that her son is comatose in the bathroom with hooker lipstick on his cock seems to be wildly unimportant.

"Now, Jennifer," she says. "Jen. You have to look on the bright side."

"What is that?"

"You're marrying a powerful man," she says. "He's not powerful now, but one day he will be, and he'll also inherit a great deal of money." The kettle starts to whistle and she turns the flame off.

I sniff. "I don't care about money."

She smiles and dunks an Earl Grey teabag in the cup. I wonder where my smiley face cup went. "You say that now," she says, "but as you get older and your looks fade and your opportunities dwindle, security will become very important to you. More important than, say, situations like this."

"What are you saying?"

"I'm saying that with the privileges that go with being safe come some responsibilities and some sacrifices." She sets down a cup of tea in front of me.

I stare at the small wisp of steam coming off my hot cup of tea.

"Sacrifices?" I repeat.

"Yes. But there are perks for making sacrifices. Lots of perks. For instance, Mr. Keller has an apartment downtown. He uses this apartment for certain meetings he can't have anywhere else. I accept this fact and he in turn accepts that I buy myself a new car every year, among other things."

I'm staring at her, trying to comprehend what she's saying, because I think it's possibly the most disgusting thing I've ever heard.

I am in a cuckoo clock.

Ed comes out of the bathroom. "Alrighty then!" he says. "Coffee on?"

"Tea," Mrs. Keller says.

"Well, I guess anything hot'll do." I get the strange sensation they've done this all before. I turn to look at Ed, who's always been good to me, always been the relative voice of reason, and I'm praying he'll say something that makes sense. Instead he shrugs. "Got to admit he's doing better than before Hazelden."

My eyes widen. "Hazelden?"

"He was in rehab," Mrs. Keller says and sips her tea. "Didn't he tell you?"

Her face seems warped and waxlike. Someone has to wake me up from this nightmare.

"Alcohol in general," she says, "vodka in particular."

Ed shakes his head in disgust. "I told him he had to come home and beat it. I told him it was a lousy beverage, for crying out loud! A beverage! Like milk!"

"Ed was traveling while Bradford was incapacitated," she says. "I don't think he ever fully understood the program."

"Some program," he says. "All that twelve-step hooey."

"The twelve steps work for him," Mrs. Keller says, and a photographic montage of all the drinks Brad and I have had together starts firing off in my mind.

"Oh baloney," Ed says. "We admitted we had become powerless to milk and milk had taken control of our lives. *Blah, blah, blah.* And those damn tokens! Should I give you a prize for every month you don't drink milk? Hell, I should get a thousand prize thingies! I haven't had milk in years!"

"He's lactose-intolerant," Mrs. Keller says, "but really, Ed, I can't say I appreciate the swearing."

"Ah, nuts," he says and stands up. "I'll go check on him."

My mind is unpinning, it's hard to breathe, I feel like I'm wading into very dark water.

"You're upset," Mrs. Keller says. "Drink some tea."

I take a sip, because, why not. I'll try anything to make

this roaring in my ears go away. Brad was in rehab? At Hazelden? That's like a hard-core treatment center somewhere in Minnesota. I think the king of Dubai went there to beat heroin.

"I've got to get out of here," I say and stand up.

"Now, Jennifer, don't rush. We're all here to support you, dear, and besides, where do you have to go?" She smiles at me pleasantly.

I sit back down.

"I have places to go," I say, "plenty of places. My mother's, my sister's, my friends'."

"Yes, yes," she says, "of course anyone would be happy to have you stay with them for a few days, maybe even a few weeks, but think about it, Jennifer, what about after that? When your anger is gone and your friends are tired of you sleeping on their couch? You have to think about the future. Your friends aren't going to financially support you and neither is your family. Not for forever. Plus, haven't they sort of, oh how do I say it, put in their time already?"

That hurt. Possibly because it's true.

"My point," she says, "is that even though Bradford isn't perfect, he's willing to support you for the rest of your life, and your children, too. Not just support them, but give them a life you never could give them on your own. Private schools, Ivy League colleges, medical care. Whatever they need they'll have. And think about your family," she says. "Your father signed a large contract with Keller's, and young Leonard has become the loading-dock foreman."

"Yes," I say miserably, "I know."

I picture my ratty old apartment, my dirty grout.

It's true, I never want to go back there. Never.

"We went to great expense to get Bradford to come home.

We told him we were going to stop supporting him if he didn't come home, go to treatment, start working, and raise a family."

"Start a family?"

"Oh, yes," she says. "Getting married was part of the deal. We converted this house just so he could raise children. Added on the third bedroom. We told him we would cut him off completely unless he would abide by our rules. We even gave him a deadline."

"A deadline?"

"Yes. Be sober and engaged by Valentine's Day this year or else he was on his own. Cut off completely. No more help, no more money, no more bailing him out. We were so worried he wouldn't find a girl in time, but then he took an interest in you, which made Ed terribly happy, as you can imagine, what with you looking like Ada and everything." She pronounces *Ada* with a sharp *a*, as though she was trying to spit something out of her mouth. "He was always in love with Ada," she says. "If it were legal, he would have married her."

I cover my face with my hands. I can't believe any of this.

"You'll understand better when you have children. There gets to be a point when you can't stand the constant worrying and you have to do something drastic. We had to do something drastic with Bradford because he was running around hurting himself. You were the answer to our prayers. Still, I guess we answered some of your prayers too."

I'm trying to hang on to reality right now, because I feel like I'm hallucinating. My name is Jennifer Johnson. I work at . . . I don't know where I work anymore. I don't know where I live anymore. I was having a wedding and now my fiancé turns out to be an alcoholic sex addict with religious-zealot parents who are telling me it's all okay.

Mrs. Keller reaches over and puts her thin clawlike hand on top of mine. I stare at the large emerald ring perched on her manicured finger.

"We don't want you running around hurting yourself, either," she says. "Brad will make this up to you. I promise he will. Just think about your wedding and how happy your family will be. Not just now, but in the future. Just stand back, breathe deep, and look at the possibilities. One little incident like this can't undo a lifetime of opportunity."

Ed comes out of the bathroom with his arm around Brad, who's mumbling something incoherent. I've never seen him so completely knocked out before. I've seen him drink, slur his speech, and not be able to drive, but this is something else. He looks like he's having a diabetic reaction or something.

"He's all cleaned up," Ed says heartily, "just needs to sleep."

They manage to get Brad to the couch and lay him down. Mrs. Keller takes off his shoes and gets a blanket to tuck him in, like a little boy. After he's all arranged they head for the door and tell me to call them in the morning. Mrs. Keller says Brad probably won't remember much of this tomorrow, he usually never does. As she leaves she blows Bradford an air kiss.

"Nighty-night, Prince Charming," she says.

I leave the house early the next morning. I don't want to see Brad. I get into my stupid mammoth Mercedes and go to Macy's and pick up the wedding participant thank-you gifts, little engraved silver letter openers we're giving the caterer, the photographer, the florist, all the people we're already paying to work at our wedding. Mrs. Straubel says we're expected to give them gifts. Unbelievable. Where's my gift for showing up at the wedding?

For wearing in a hot, itchy dress I didn't choose and enduring a church service while standing up? Shouldn't I get something? Like maybe a silver-plated gun so I can shoot myself in the head?

As I'm pulling out of the parking ramp, I accidentally cut off a girl in a rusty old station wagon. I didn't even see her; this car has so many blind spots I might as well be driving a shipping container down the street.

Luckily she slams on her brakes just in time and avoids crunching into me. "Fuck you, rich bitch!" she yells as I roar past.

I look at her in the rearview mirror and catch sight of myself in my dark oversize Prada sunglasses and trim pastel jacket. I realize what it must look like. It must look like a wealthy, bossy, self-important woman just cut her off.

Ha. If she only knew!

I want to tell her, "It's all borrowed, sweetie, it's all an expensive loan," but I smile at myself instead. I just got called a rich bitch, and a part of me liked it.

At home Brad is sleepily coming down the stairs as I struggle through the door, dropping shopping bags on the kitchen floor.

"Hey," he says.

"Hey," I say.

He rubs his head and asks if there's any coffee. "Killer headache," he says. "The guys really made me hit it hard."

I stand there staring at him and I can tell by his casual posture and unquestioning expression that he has blacked out last night. At least a major portion of it.

So this is it.

This is when I decide whether to let him have it or to pretend everything is okay. Do I read him the riot act and storm out? Break off the engagement? Call all my friends and family and tell them the wedding is off? End everything? No more wedding, no more marriage, no more rich bitch? Or do I make him coffee?

These choices we make, they seem so small—they're made in a split second and yet they can have a ripple effect for years.

The doorbell rings.

Brad wanders off with an open robe to answer it. I'm left in the kitchen by myself with my very important thoughts, surrounded by a paper garden of shopping bags.

"Jen?" Brad shouts. "It's for you!"

It's the travel agency's messenger service dropping off our plane tickets and hotel confirmation for the Virgin Islands. That's where we're going on our honeymoon. Our hotel suite has its own pool and mini-waterfall.

I sign the slip and take the package.

I'm about to say something when the phone rings. Brad says he's going to take a shower.

He leaves and I answer the phone, because what else am I going to do?

There are perks for keeping quiet. My reward for overlooking Hookergate is a pearl necklace, a yellow Chanel suit, and my own membership at the Country Club. Mrs. Keller sends it all over with a note congratulating me on my upcoming nuptials, which is a word I despise. It reminds me of rupture and nipple. There's also something sinister and sexual about it, like coitus, which makes me wonder if Ma Keller is hoping for a quick grandchild. My mind flashes to that scene in *Rosemary's Baby* when everyone is standing around Mia Farrow copulating with the devil, all anticipating the birth of a new demon seed.

Which makes me think of Trevor.

• • •

I don't even want to go to my own bachelorette party. We're having high tea at the Grosvenor Mansion. After Brad's big night out with the boys I did consider scratching all my plans and hiring male strippers, but the truth is, I don't want male strippers. I want high tea. I want everyone to wear lovely hats and sit still.

"Are you sure you want me to come?" Christopher says. "I know the Kellers aren't exactly queer-friendly. It's okay if you want me to skip it. I know the head waiter there, I'll just call and tell him to stir Mrs. Keller's Darjeeling with his Earl Grey."

"Mother Tarantula won't be there," I say. "You're coming. You have to come. This is my bachelorette party and you're the best girlfriend I have."

It kills me not to tell Christopher about Brad and the lipstick, but I can't. It's too horrible. He'd probably tie me up in Fendi scarves and ship me to Reykjavik in order to stop me from getting married, and despite everything I don't want to be stopped. I've worked too hard, put too much time in, and invited too many guests to back out. It's vanity that has the real teeth here. Common sense and self-preservation are defenseless against vanity.

My vanity, anyway.

My vanity turns out to be uglier and stronger than I ever imagined.

So, Christopher comes to the Grosvenor Mansion, along with my sister and all my other bridesmaids. All five of them.

We arrive at the big fake stone castle and walk past the manicured English garden and row of British flags. "Welcome to Ye Olde Grosvenor Mansion," the host says. "Your journey across the pond begins here." We're shown to our light, airy table, which is covered with white linens and silver. I'm briefly pleased until someone throws a pink plastic dildo on the table.

"For your honeymoon!" someone shouts. "Hope you don't need it!"

The waiter, who had come up to the table to take our order, sees the dildo, turns on his heel, and walks away.

I'm mortified.

"Give me that!" I snatch it up and hurl the disgusting thing under the table. "Didn't I say no gifts?"

"We all brought gifts," one of the girls whines. "It's tradition."

"Fine," I say, "but nothing disgusting! We're having high tea, for freak's sake!"

"Okay, open this one," somebody says and passes over a shiny pink metallic bag. I don't know what's in it, but I already hate the wrapping.

I try to smile as I dig in the pink tissue paper, and I pull out a big, hairy latex vagina, which starts vibrating in my hand.

"It's for Brad, for when you're tired!"

Everyone breaks apart laughing until I throw it back in the bag as hard as I can and it stops moving. "Listen," I hiss, "you can all drop to the lowest common denominator if you want, but you're not dragging me with you."

Silence. Everyone just sort of looks at each other. The waiter comes back and I tell him we want the Queen Elizabeth high tea all around and then I give him Mrs. Keller's credit card. When he leaves the table is silent. Everyone looks nervous and worried. That's fine by me. I'm starting to get the hang of Mrs. Keller's intimidation deal. It's better to have people scared of you and quiet than acting like monkeys and ruining everything.

The waiter brings out a large silver cart and starts serving us tea. Little white pots and three-tier trays of tiny tea sandwiches and itty-bitty desserts. I just love it.

"These are the cucumber sandwiches," our waiter says, "and these are watercress. The egg salad and chopped ham sandwiches are on the second tier, and you'll find fruit tarts and éclairs on the last."

When he's gone Hailey picks up a triangular sandwich and says, "What's a watercress? This is like the weird stuff Mrs. Keller eats. You're turning into her!"

"Hailey's Swedish," I say. "She's adopted."

"Well, I'm glad I'm not Danish," she says. "I wouldn't want my country of origin to be named after a breakfast pastry."

She's really tap-dancing on my last nerve.

"My biological family is from the upper province of Kierkegaard," Hailey says.

"Oh, nobody knows where you're from," I snap. "They probably found you wedged inside a shrimp party tray at Sam's Club!"

"Jen!" Christopher says. "That's mean!"

"I actually prefer Jennifer," I say. "Could you call me Jennifer?"

Christopher looks completely confused, like he doesn't know if I'm being horrible-ironic or just horrible-horrible.

I know I'm being horrible-horrible.

I excuse myself and go to the ladies' room, where I run my wrists under cold water. I wonder if the queen of England has to put up with this.

When I come out of the bathroom, I run right into Ted.

He's standing there in the hallway under a pair of antique lacrosse sticks. His face is unusually pale. "Hey, gorgeous," he says nervously.

"Hey, what are you doing here? I'm having my bachelorette party."

"I know, Christopher told me. Nice place."

"What's going on?"

"Look," he says, tugging me down the hall, "I know this isn't the best timing, but I have to tell you something. I've wanted to tell you for, well, for years now, but I've been scared. Terrified actually."

He grabs my hands.

"What are you doing?"

"Just listen," he says. "This isn't easy for me, but now I'm out of time."

"Ted, quit it. This is weird."

"You can't marry Brad," he says.

"I can't?"

"No, because he doesn't know you, not really. I know you and I know the real stuff, the good stuff. I know you swear like a merchant marine at old ladies when you drive and that no matter what you order at a restaurant you'll end up eating my food. I know you'll knock over any glass of liquid left on your desk for more than an hour and you'd give up your health insurance to keep the Lifetime channel on."

"That only happened once," I say.

"I know you hate lingerie, you sleep in old boxers and wife-beater T-shirts. I know you never, and I mean never, have cash. You only use plastic. If you park at a meter you have to borrow quarters from people walking by. I know you routinely forget where your car keys are, but you can remember what I said at a company picnic five years ago."

"You told me not to eat any more cake."

"I know you think you're fat, but you're not, you're gorgeous. The most gorgeous woman I've ever seen and you're perfect just the way you are. You're kind and generous and you're strong. You won't watch documentaries about endangered animals because they make you cry. I don't have a lot of money, but you'd be happy with me. You would. I know all the things about you Brad doesn't and I love you for them. He's a pudgy douchebag mama's boy. Plus, I have Mrs. Biggles."

"What?"

"Lana got that job. She couldn't keep her. She felt terrible. She called me the next morning and I went over to get her."

"Mrs. *Biggles*? Why didn't you tell me?"

"Because it would have made you feel awful," he says, "because you couldn't do anything about it anyway. But you can do something now, Jen. Come with me. You don't love Brad, you just love the security you think he can give you, but he can't give you any security because he doesn't even know who you are. I know who you are, and I love you. You'll be miserable being Mrs. Brad Keller and you know it. You'll have to be domestic and cook and clean and you hate cooking. You're dangerous when you deep-fry things."

I can't believe I'm hearing this. My bachelorette party is in the next room. I'm getting married tomorrow. Ted smiles. He looks just like a little boy confessing some terrible thing he did, but maybe it really isn't terrible at all.

Maybe it's wonderful.

"I love you," he says. "I've always loved you and I think you love me. Do you?"

I look deeply into his eyes. "Yes," I say and smile, but he isn't smiling back. Why isn't he smiling back? Didn't I just say "yes" out loud and in a clear voice? Did I do it wrong?

Pastor Mike clears his throat. "I think we're looking for an 'I do,'" he says.

Brad rolls his eyes.

"Oh, I do!"

"Then by the power vested in me," the minister says, and I can't hear the rest because the sound drains out of the room and the color too, like one of those old TV sets where the image gets smaller and smaller until it's just a blue dot, a star in another light system far, far away. I'm dizzy. The pastor is mumbling slow speed and I am moving through taffy or tar or thick vanilla pudding. My arms are concrete and my lips can't move. A hot, heavy ring is wedged onto my finger and my heart slows down, beating more and more heavily until I wonder if it will just stop altogether.

Then the scene comes racing at me full tilt and all the sound in the room, which had been drained and pale before, rushes in with vivid clarity. People clapping, bells ringing, Brad laughing. I take a sharp, hard breath, like I just came up for air after a deep dive. "What's going on now?" Brad whispers. These were his first wedded words to me.

What's going on now?

I catch myself as I stumble after him and we rush down the aisle, the applause clapping in our ears, and we tumble breathless into a waiting limousine, where Brad starts complaining about something, and the whole world outside seems like one big blurry mistake.

At the reception I run for the bathroom with three bridesmaids trailing behind me. They cluck and fret as I lock myself inside the small peach airless space, where I stand with my back to the door, my fingers on the silver lock, staring at myself in the mirror.

Shellacked hair, severe jaw, tight mouth.

I'm looking at Mrs. Keller.

I am Mrs. Keller.

A rapid knocking on the door. My heart racing. "One minute!" I cry out, and actually look around the room for an escape window, but there are no windows, only the door, which I eventually open. I let myself be led to the reception tent where the band starts up.

I smile.

Here comes the bride.

It's funny because I'll remember the whole event—my wedding, that is—the same way hostages and victims of violent crime do. In scattered snapshots, incongruent and without explanation. A piece here and a chunk there.

I'll remember someone shouting, "Here they come!" as we swept down the church steps and how the light sprinkling of rain felt like heaven. I'll remember Lenny dancing by himself and my mother kissing Abbygael, who wore a purple wizard's hat. I'll remember meeting Brad's ex-girlfriend, Hannah, who was inexplicably invited to the wedding.

I'll remember Hailey laughing like a horse and wishing I could stop her.

I'll remember the small violet flowers floating in silver bowls on every table and the hot, scratchy blanket of beard stubble that grazed my cheeks all night. I'll remember my mother telling me how beautiful I am and Ted giving me a kiss. God, I love Ted. I really, really love Ted. He looks good in a suit even though he isn't smiling. Dashing even.

I never saw him in a suit before.

I will not be able to remember my father. Not at any point. He was there, I know, as the photos will show, but I did not see him. Not once. I also won't remember Christopher very clearly or that he held my hair back in the bathroom, where apparently I was sick.

It's a dream wedding! Not my dream, but somebody's. I

know because I'm told how lucky I am all day and night by countless happy, smiling, reassuring people. The gifts table drifts past me at some point, white cards perching like moths on a mountain of satin bows and white paper. Toasters and china and stemware. So fragile! Things that can break and chip and shatter.

It's all here. Everything I ever wanted.

Brad and I even have thrones at the reception table. They're spray-painted and covered with gold glitter, which will rub off on my dress. There's a banner over them that says, THE LUCKIEST COUPLE IN THE WORLD! There are also crowns on the table and brass scepters with little Jesus fish on them. As God is my witness I'm going to find out who makes those little Jesus fish and I'm going to stop them.

Brad appears and offers me his hand for our first dance together. Everyone applauds. He smiles and I recognize him, maybe for the first time.

He's the doofy parking lot guy in the red parka.

It comes crashing down on me like Kennebunkport cobblestone. I let Ted go and I married Brad, who thinks I actually like wearing thongs to bed. Why would I marry Baby Huey? He farts while downloading porn. He wears printed T-shirts under dress shirts and thinks no one notices. He occasionally hires hookers. He sold my Scout and made me give my cat away.

This is who I married.

This is Prince Charming.

This is the fairy tale rewritten in the real world.

People are cheering and clinking their champagne glasses with forks. Why are these lunatics always clapping at everything? Who gave them forks? Cameras explode in silver spiderwebs across the room and the music swells. I'm smiling so hard it hurts.

"Let's roll," Brad says, and I distinctly suppress the urge to scream as I take his hand and step forward.

Just breathe. Relax.

I can do this.

acknowledgments

Thanks to the eternal patience and steady editing of Jeanette Perez. This book would not exist without her. Also thanks to Carrie Kania for her endless vision and Christmas Kringles, to Jen Hart for crucial input and boundless energy, and to Alison Callahan who is/will be/can't-not-be terribly missed. Many thanks to my elegant agent, Elizabeth Sheinkman, and the fearless Felicity Blunt, along with all the good eggs at the London offices of Curtis Brown.

Thanks to Billy Collins for writing me little poems, to MPR and Ira Glass for supporting me, to Pete Turchi and the Warren Wilson MFA program for teaching me, and especially to Mac, as always, for changing everything. Breadloaf 2000 kittens, you are always with me. You know who you are.

Marcy Russ edited, Harry Drabnik found blue sea glass, Jason Shapiro sang heavy metal, Thompat Beene lurked mysteriously, Lance Reynalds kept the faith, Chris Romeo gave me wheels, Jodi Ohlsen-Read checked in, Rick Bursky inspired, Adam 2B called from distant lands, R. D. Zimmerman advised, Geoff Herbach commiserated, Carrie Andersen read everything, Joel Switzer delivered gold, My Lee Xiong brought good spirits, Andrew Peterson, Bart Regehr, David

Sunderland, and Tim Peterson are the best bees a girl could ask for.

Many thanks to my family, especially my very funny mother, as well as Colin and Jenna, who watched Walter during the roughest patches. So, too, James Larkin must be commended, a fine man who has a tougher constitution now, and a new and abiding appreciation for my Lunesta prescription. I couldn't have done it without you.

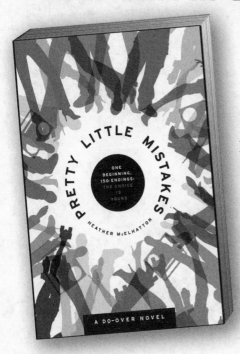